MODERN HUMANITIES RESEARCH ASSOCIATION

CRITICAL TEXTS

VOLUME 21

Editor
MALCOLM COOK
(*French*)

*HISTOIRE DE LA DUCHESSE DE C****

by

Stéphanie de Genlis

Introduction, notes, and English translation

by Mary S. Trouille

HISTOIRE DE LA DUCHESSE DE C***

by

Stéphanie de Genlis

Edited by

Mary S. Trouille

MODERN HUMANITIES RESEARCH ASSOCIATION
2010

Published by

The Modern Humanities Research Association,
1 Carlton House Terrace
London SW1Y 5AF

First published 2010

ISBN 978 0 947623 95 1

ISSN 1746-1642

Copies may be ordered from www.criticaltexts.mhra.org.uk

TABLE OF CONTENTS

LIST OF ILLUSTRATIONS

Cover: Copper engraving by Luigi Schiavonetti drawn from an oil painting titled *The Duchess of C. Coming out of the Cavern* by John Francis Rigaud. (Courtesy of the British Museum)

ACKNOWLEDGMENTS

When I first began research on Genlis for a chapter of my doctoral dissertation some 25 years ago, most of her works were out of print and were little known even among specialists in eighteenth-century studies. The publication of Gabriel de Broglie's 1985 biography renewed interest in her life and works, and over the past thirty years, much scholarly work has been devoted to her writings. Yet the texts themselves still are not as widely available as they deserve to be, particularly among readers in the English-speaking world.

The idea for a critical edition and modern translation of the *Duchesse de C**** first came to me a decade ago when I taught this text for the first time in a graduate course on marriage and domestic violence in eighteenth-century France. Because both the novel and novella were out of print, we had to use photocopies taken from the Bibliothèque nationale's microfilmed copy of the 1782 edition of the novel. Given the novella's intrinsic value and appeal from both a literary and socio-historical perspective, I felt that a critical edition of the French text and modern English translation should be made available at an affordable price to a broader audience of students and scholars.

This project would not have been possible without the encouragement of Malcolm Cook, who directs the editorial board of the MIIRA's Critical Texts Series. I also wish to thank Illinois State University for a summer research grant that enabled me to work at the Bibliothèque nationale in Paris to complete the ancillary materials and to establish an authoritative edition of the French text. I am also very grateful to the Women's Caucus of the American Society for Eighteenth-Century Studies for the Editing and Translation Fellowship that covered the cost of the illustrations. In addition, I wish to express my sincere thanks to the staffs at the Newberry Library, Chawton House Library, Northwestern University Library, British Museum, and Bibliothèque Nationale for their research assistance and for their help in finding illustrations for this edition. Special thanks go out to Sylvie Romanowski for her comments on early drafts of the introductory materials, to Jonathan Druker for his help with the Italian texts, and to Gillian Dow for invaluable information she provided regarding Genlis's account of the duchess's story. Above all, I wish to thank Courtney Quaintance for her generous help in identifying the Duchess of Girifalco, for tracking down information about her, and for her translations of the Italian texts into English.

INTRODUCTION

It is hardly a coincidence that fictional tales of sequestered wives and spousal abuse abound in the late eighteenth and early nineteenth centuries at a time when the laws and customs concerning marriage and parental authority had become the subject of intense debate. In the sinister family dwellings of Gothic romance, women writers expressed their sense of imprisonment within traditional family and legal structures. One of the earliest and most popular of these female Gothic tales was Stéphanie de Genlis's *Histoire de la duchesse de C****, a 20,000-word novella that first appeared in 1782 as an embedded narrative in her best-selling novel *Adèle et Théodore*. It tells the story of an Italian duchess secretly imprisoned by her husband for nine years in a dungeon under his palace after he drugs her, simulates her death, and buries a waxen figure in her place. After intercepting her letters to a friend, he had suspected her—unjustly—of adultery with a man she refuses to name, but who is in fact the duke's own nephew Belmire, with whom she had fallen in love before her marriage. The duke gives her the choice either to name her supposed lover or to be imprisoned for the rest of her life. Fearing that her husband will have Belmire killed, she sacrifices herself to protect him, even though it means she will be separated, perhaps forever, from her parents and infant daughter.

Genlis's novella is based on the experiences of Olimpia Barberini Colonna (1731-1800), daughter of Giulio Cesare Colonna di Sciarra, Prince of Carbognano (1708-1787), and Cornelia Constanza Barberini, Princess of Palestrina (1716-1797). In 1747, at the age of sixteen, Olimpia was married to Gennaro Caracciolo, Duke of Girifalco (1720-1766). Genlis gives the duke's name as 'Cerifalco,' a mispelling of 'Girifalco,' the name of his duchy centered in a town of that name in the province of Catanzaro, in the region of Calabria in southern Italy.

The Duchess of Girifalco's story was widely known in eighteenth-century Italy and was chronicled by several nineteenth-century Italian historians. The most accurate of these accounts appears to be that of Antonio Coppi in his history of the Colonna family, *Memorie colonnesi*, published in 1855:

Among the daughters of Prince Giulio Cesare [Colonna] and Cornelia Barberini was Olimpia, born on the first of November in 1731. In 1748, she was married to Gennaro Caracciolo, the Duke of Girifalco.

The duke lived in a castle in southern Calabria. Mistreating his wife, he kept her under lock and key and let her speak with no one but her confessor. With the help of this man, the unhappy princess informed her father of all that had happened, and he went immediately to Naples, where he obtained permission to free her and take her with him to Rome. There, she retired to the Teresian Monastery, known as the convent of the Barberini nuns, where she died in 1800.

Later, it was said that this powerful nobleman, on the basis of mere suspicions, had his wife locked up in one of the dungeons of the castle and that he kept her there for several years, announcing to the public that she was dead and even commemorating her death with solemn funeral rites. Supposedly, her moans were eventually heard by two Capuchin monks passing by the castle one night, and she was freed by the governor of the province.[1]

A longer, more romanticized version of the duchess's story was published in 1838 by Pompeo Litta in the second tome of his thirteen-volume *Famiglie celebri italiane.*[2] He claims that after Olimpia was rescued by her father and went to live in the convent, she never spoke a word to anyone about what had happened to her, nor did she allow others to speak of it in her presence. (See Appendix G for the original Italian texts and English translations of Coppi and Litta's accounts, along with a third account by Alessandro Ademollo.)

In a footnote that appears in *Adèle et Théodore* at the beginning of the duchess's tale, Genlis explains that the story is based on the experiences of the Italian Duchess, whom she met in Rome in 1776 during a trip to Italy with the Duchess of Chartres and her entourage.[3] In the 'Editor's Preface' to a separate edition of the duchess's story published in 1783, Genlis again insists that the main elements of the story are true: 'The *Story of the Duchess of*

C*** [...] is no doubt most unusual, and yet it is essentially true, except for a few changes that enhance its appeal.'[4] Recalling her meeting with the duchess in her memoirs, Genlis explains that the story of her imprisonment was related to her not by the prisoner herself, but by her father. Given the date of their meeting and details provided by the duchess's biographers, the events on which the story is based appear to have taken place in the 1740s and 1750s.[5]

Later in her memoirs, Genlis recalls how she recounted the duchess's story at a dinner party:

> Seated between witty M. de Champfort and M. de Rulhières, I told them the Duchess of Cerifalco's story and added that it would make a fine novel. They replied that tales of women imprisoned in dungeons could be found in a thousand works of fiction, and that this story, unusual as it was, would make a very ordinary novel. I insisted that the subject could be made fresh and original by describing, step by step, the ideas and feelings one might experience in the course of nine years spent in a dungeon. They claimed that it was impossible to imagine oneself in a situation of that kind.[6]

After the publication of *Adèle et Théodore* in 1782, M. de Rulhières congratulated Genlis on the tremendous success of her novel and particularly on that of the duchess's tale. He found this episode so vivid that he was convinced that Genlis herself must have lived through a similar experience. Although never imprisoned like the Duchess of Girifalco, Genlis had as a child often dreamed of persecution and dramatic reversals of fortune, as she explains in her memoirs: 'I envisioned a destiny for myself that I filled not only with remarkable events, but also with reversals of fortune and persecutions. I liked to think that I would have the strength to withstand such misfortunes. A thousand times, I imagined myself an outlaw, falsely accused, wandering in exile, and forced into hiding [...].'[7] The vividness of Genlis's depiction of the duchess's ordeal may well have come from her ability to identify so intensely with victims of injustice and persecution. It is ironic that Genlis would later be forced to flee France during the Terror, falsely accused of plotting against the Jacobin government, forced into hiding and exile, just as she had once imagined.

Fig. 1: Portrait of Genlis by Louis-Léopold Boilly (1761-1845), lithography by Thierry frères. (Bibliothèque nationale de France - BnF)

The novel was praised by critics and public alike and quickly became a bestseller. In a review of *Adèle et Théodore* in the *Correspondance littéraire*, Melchior Grimm wrote: 'Of all Mme de Genlis's writings, this is the one that has created the greatest sensation and the one read with the most enthusiasm.'[8] The duchess's tale was singled out for special praise; it became so popular that Genlis published it in a separate edition in 1783 under the title *Histoire intéressante de madame la duchesse de C****, with a new preface explaining why she felt a separate edition was needed:

> The duchess's story charmed all the readers of *Adèle et Théodore*. However, some found it out of place in a novel intended for young readers and for those whose affectionate concern for young people had not been dissipated by frivolity and vice. In their view, the story's highly dramatic style and tone seemed to disrupt the novel's harmony, and this is why we chose to publish it in a separate edition.[9]

As Genlis's fame as a writer and educator spread, both the novella and the novel from which it was drawn were reprinted numerous times and published in translation in England where they enjoyed considerable success as well.[10] The novella is thought to have inspired the plot of the Gothic novel *A Sicilian Romance* published in 1790 by British novelist Ann Radcliffe.[11] In 1791, an opera loosely based on Genlis's tale of the duchess written by Dalayrac and Marsollier was performed for the first time at the Théâtre de l'Opéra-Comique-Feydeau in Paris.[12] Titled *Camille, ou Le Souterrain,* Marsollier's libretto is far inferior to Genlis's story in style, character portrayal, and plot construction. Despite these weaknesses, it was translated into Italian and served as the basis for Ferdinando Paër's opera *Camilla, ossia Il sotteraneo*, which premiered at the Vienna Kärntnertortheater in 1799. The French opera was staged a number of times in the decades following, including a performance in 1841 by the Théâtre de l'Opéra-Comique-Favart in Paris.[13] The Bibliothèque nationale's catalogue lists eight texts published by seven different publishers in the first half of the nineteenth century under the same title as the French opera. Unlike Marsollier's libretto, these editions present the same version of the duchess's story as Genlis's *Duchesse de C****, but without attribution to Genlis or any other author. It may be that these publishers borrowed Marsollier's title in order to capitalize on the popularity of Genlis's story, but without having to acknowledge her authorship, perhaps to avoid having to pay royalties. Whatever the reasons for this subterfuge, these multiple editions of Genlis's tale attest to its enduring appeal to the public's imagination.

The main narrative of *Adèle et Théodore* concerns the Baron and Baroness d'Almane, who withdraw from Parisian society to devote themselves to the education of their children, Adèle and Théodore, aged five and six. Seven years later, they take their children to Italy, where they become friends with the Duchess of C***. The duchess is very taken with Adèle's intelligence and talents, but concerned by the twelve-year-old's romantic tendencies, she gives her mother a written account of her experiences to warn young Adèle and her brother of the dangers of romantic passion.

Both the main plot (the education of Adèle and Théodore by their parents) and the embedded narrative (the duchess's story) concern parent-child relationships. The d'Almanes's happy household and close relationship with their children form a striking contrast to the young princess's lack of communication with her parents, her miserably unhappy marriage, and her nine-year separation from her daughter. Her father imposes a loveless marriage on her, but without knowing she had engaged her heart elsewhere and without realizing that the husband he chose for her was cruel and vindictive. Despite her marked aversion for the duke, the heroine finds it impossible to confide her feelings to her mother, so ashamed is she for engaging her heart without her parents' knowledge. She sacrifices her happiness to please her parents, but also to make up for her imprudent behavior. Thus, while the narrative frame concerning the d'Almanes shows an idealized picture of marriage and family life, the duchess's embedded narrative shows the dark side of marital and parent-child relationships.

Genlis suggests that a key didactic aim of the duchess's story is to illustrate the responsibility of parents for the happiness of their children's marriage. Like her fictional alter-ego Mme d'Almane, Genlis attaches greater importance to a couple's compatibility than to considerations of wealth and rank, which nevertheless still enter into the decision. Adèle's parents carefully choose her spouse several years in advance in order to monitor his behavior and to give the couple time to become acquainted. In contrast, the duchess's father chooses a husband for her based solely on his wealth and high social position, as if they (along with his physical attractiveness) will make her happy. Moreover, he agrees to the duke's marriage proposal without even consulting his daughter and insists that she marry him within a month.

Genlis clearly sends a mixed message regarding parent-child relations. While the duchess's story implicitly criticizes parents who place social and economic considerations above their children's marital happiness, the explicit lessons she presents are aimed instead primarily at their children. Most prominent among these is the lesson of filial obedience—particularly the need for a girl to confide in her mother and to seek her guidance.[14] Of equal importance is the lesson of self-control: the dangers both of romantic passion and jealousy and the need to free oneself from the shackles of desire and excessive sensibility. These warnings tie in with one of the key lessons of the main narrative of *Adèle et Théodore*: that romantic love is fleeting and therefore provides a poor foundation for marriage. Instead of idealizing romantic passion like so many writers of the period, Genlis seeks to illustrate its dangerous consequences.

A third lesson of the duchess's story is the importance of religion as a source of strength and consolation. In recalling her captivity, the duchess focuses on the spiritual growth and wisdom she acquires. She is able to overcome the gloom and loneliness of her prison through her faith, which she expresses through the composition and singing of hymns and through prayers for those she loves. The horrors of imprisonment gradually give way to an inner journey of self-discovery and spiritual growth.

Genlis's *Histoire de la duchesse de C**** is a complex blend of the sentimental and Gothic genres. Exposing the tensions and imbalances underlying the family structures often idealized in sentimental novels, Gothic fiction literalizes Freud's notion of the 'uncanny'—of the utterly familiar as strange. This notion of the defamiliarized familiar applies well to what Michele Massé refers to as 'marital Gothic'—tales in which the husband, under the sway of jealousy or avarice, suddenly turns into a monster, his home into a prison, and the couple's marriage into a waking nightmare.[15] However, in Genlis's tale, the wife's eyes are opened to her husband's evil nature *before* her marriage, although she does not feel the full force of that evil until he takes her to his country estate to imprison her. The sight of the forbidding castle and the jangling of the drawbridge chains, combined with her husband's sinister behavior, provoke in her a deep sense of foreboding. Much Gothic terror focuses on anxiety about boundaries—those separating the protagonist from the outside world and those separating the protagonist from sinister persons or forces lurking within. The sound of chains rattling or of a door grating on its hinges is used in Gothic romances, as in horror movies today, to express the anxiety associated with thresholds. The duchess again experiences this 'terror of the threshold' when her husband takes her through a secret passage into the dungeon under his castle. For several months, her sanity hangs in the balance. But thanks to the renewal of her religious faith, she is able to triumph over the darkness and solitude of her prison. In this way, what began as a Gothic romance and tale of horror ends as a moral tale of renunciation, self-discovery, and spiritual growth.

After her conversion experience, the duchess's only painful moments are during the summer months, knowing that her mother and daughter are visiting at the same castle where she is being held captive. She is painfully aware of the irony underlying the fact that her mother sought solace there with her persecutor at the foot of an empty tomb. The theme of live burial is common in Gothic tales, as is the figure of the 'dead' mother secretly imprisoned in or near the family's home. Some critics have suggested that live burial symbolizes the repression of the sequestered woman's sexual desires, especially since it is sexual activity—real or suspected—that her captivity is often designed to punish. This analysis applies well to the duchess. After being imprisoned for alleged sexual transgressions, she represses and sublimates her love and desire for Belmire through religious fervor and, after her release, through devotion to her daughter and charity toward the poor. Above all, live burial is a metaphor for the prison of forced marriage to a husband one does not love or even like. The live burial of the heroine mirrors the structure of the Gothic text, which typically involves embedded narratives—as is the case with the duchess's captivity narrative, triply embedded in Genlis's novel.

Like many Gothic tales, the duchess's story is dominated by the image of the castle—a place of sequestration and persecution subject to the absolute will of the castle's lord and master. In marital Gothic tales such as this, the old adage 'a man's home is his castle' takes on a new, sinister meaning. With its vast chambers and labyrinthine passages, the castle symbolizes the husband's absolute authority over his wife and child, as well as his ancestral power and prestige. In Genlis's tale, however, the castle has only negative connotations for the heroine, since her husband presents it from the start as a place of punishment where his sullied honor will be avenged and protected.

The castle embodies the law of the father (the absolute authority of fathers, husbands, masters, and kings), just as the dungeon symbolizes all that law represses (disobedient children, unruly wives, insubordinate servants, rebellious subjects). Yet, while affirming the power of patriarchy and the status quo, the Gothic also reveals the cracks in the castle walls and the prisoners languishing in the dungeon—the repressed who threaten to return and to topple the weakened structure from within.

Paradoxically, after simulating his wife's death, the duke presents the castle to others as a monument to her memory—complete with a magnificent (but empty) tomb—and claims that he cannot bear to leave this place so filled with memories of her. His claim of attachment to the castle is ironic in that it is of an entirely *negative* nature: he is as much a prisoner of the castle as his wife—chained to it by his desire for revenge, as well as by fear of her death and fear of discovery.

In an effort to discover the identity of his wife's lover, the duke subjects her to a summary trial in which he confronts her with evidence of her alleged adultery and then orders her to defend herself against his accusations. During this interrogation, the duke makes frequent use of judicial terms, as if to legitimize his role as judge. As is often the case in Gothic tales, the trial serves not as a means for the accused to defend herself, but rather as a means of interrogation and as a way for the accuser to justify the punishment he has decided upon in advance. And, like other Gothic villains who conduct such trials, the duke functions as judge, jury, and executioner, seemingly beyond the reach of the law.

A key issue in Genlis's tale is the question of the duchess's innocence or guilt. In a footnote placed at the beginning of the duchess's first-person narration, Genlis declares: 'The basic facts of this story are entirely true [...]. The only fictional parts of the story concern the love plot and the characters of the lover and the female friend.' Elsewhere in her account, Genlis insists more explicitly that the duchess was innocent of adultery. And in her memoir, she maintains that the duchess 'never knew, nor could any one ever discover, why her barbarous spouse shut her up in the dungeon.'[16] However, in 1786, in a letter to a friend, Anna Seward reveals that the duchess was rumored to have had a lover—a rumor related to her by her brother-in-law, who was living in Italy when the duchess was liberated from captivity:

> When, in 1764, Mr. Porter came over from Italy to marry my lovely sister, he told us that singular and almost incredible circumstance of a woman of fashion in that country having then been just discovered and rescued from a nine years' confinement in a subterraneous dungeon [...]. But he did not, like Madam Genlis, represent her as innocent, though, with great horror and compassion, he instanced that dire revenge as a consequence of Italian jealousy, which had not reconciled itself to the *cicisbeo* privileges.[17]

In eighteenth- and nineteenth-century Italy, a *cicisbeo* was the publicly acknowledged gallant (and often lover) of a married woman, who accompanied her to social events, church, and other gatherings and who had privileged access to her. This arrangement, called the *cicisbeatura* or *cicisbeismo*, was widely practiced, especially among the nobility of Genoa, Nice, Venice, Florence and Rome. Typically, husbands tolerated or even welcomed the arrangement.[18] This clearly was not the case, however, with the Duke of Girifalco, whose jealousy and desire for revenge had such disastrous consequences. Rumors of a love affair circulated widely in eighteenth-century Italy and are echoed in nineteenth-century chronicles concerning the duchess. For example, in his *Famiglie celebri italiane,* Pompeo Litta writes:

> She was caught by her husband with a young man kneeling at her feet who fled at the moment when the duke entered the room, and then she was locked in one of the underground dungeons of the Castle of Girifalco. Olimpia was constant in her refusal to disclose the name of the young man, who might have been massacred by her brutal husband [...].[19]

Other chroniclers, such as Coppi and Ademollo, maintain that the duke imprisoned his wife 'on the basis of mere suspicions' and suggest that the rumors of an adulterous affair circulating after her rescue were based on malevolent speculation rather than on actual fact.[20]

Genlis was certainly aware of these rumors concerning the Duchess of Girifalco, but she insisted on her innocence, no doubt out of respect and friendship for her and her family. Moreover, portraying the duchess as an adulteress in the novel would have undermined the moral lessons she wished to convey to her readers.

* * *

Genlis's subtle analysis of the power relations between husband and wife and of their characters shows keen psychological insight and constitutes the most compelling aspect of the duchess's story. Although she draws heavily from Gothic conventions in her portrayal of the duke, she is careful not to portray him as an inhuman monster. Despite his cruelty to his wife, he is intensely human and displays certain redeeming qualities, particularly love for his daughter. For all his faults, the duke arouses our pity because of his passionate love for his wife at the beginning of their marriage. The ferocity of his jealousy and of his desire for revenge reflects the force of his passion. He is as much a victim of their unhappy marriage as his wife. He imprisons her not only to punish her for her presumed infidelity, but also out of rage and frustration for his own failure to win her heart and to control her desire. Before carrying out each step in his plan of vengeance, he hesitates and falters momentarily—moments of hesitation and doubt as he confronts the enormity of the irrevocable punishment he is about to inflict on this woman he once loved so passionately. The entreaties he addresses to her—to take pity on herself in order to escape the punishment he has prepared for her—may be addressed as much to himself; they seem to reflect an inner struggle with his conscience. The empty tomb he erects for his wife is a monument to a failed and empty marriage, as well as a focus for his anguish and remorse.

Stephanie Felicité DUCREST
ci-devant Cʳˢˢᵉ de Genlis
de S.A.S. Monsgʳ.

Marquife de SILLERY
Gouvernante des Enfans
Le Duc d'Orleans.

Fig. 2: Portrait of Genlis by Jacques-Louis Copia (1764-1799) drawn from a portrait by Miris. Below the portrait appears a poem by Billardon de Sauvigny that reads: 'Vertus, graces, talents, esprit juste, enchanteur,/ Elle a tout ce qu'il faut pour embellir la vie./C'est le charme des yeux, de l'oreille, du cœur./Et le désespoir de l'envie' [Virtues, grace, talents, a mind both sound and enchanting,/She possesses everything needed to make life beautiful./She charms the eyes, the ears, the heart./ And is envied by all.] (BnF)

Genlis's portrayal of the duchess, like that of the duke, draws heavily on Gothic conventions; yet her analysis of the tensions and contradictions in the heroine's character is equally subtle and complex. From her first meeting with Belmire, she is torn between an irresistible attraction to him and a deep sense of guilt. Rather than taking an active role in the unfolding of events, she sees herself as a passive spectator. When the young count asks for permission to seek her hand in marriage, she is unable to utter a single word and responds only with tears. Her muteness reflects an inability to comes to terms with her desire and to exert a will of her own. This is only the first of several instances in the duchess's story of what Eve Sedgwick refers to as 'the barrier of unspeakableness' that typically blocks the Gothic heroine from taking an active role in the events that shape her life.[21] At every turning point in the story, this same barrier of silence prevents the duchess from expressing her true feelings and desires.

Paradoxically, it is only after her imprisonment frees her from social constraints that the duchess is finally able to speak the truth and to express the hatred and scorn she feels toward her husband. When he later offers to make her captivity more comfortable, providing she reveal the name of her presumed lover, she dares to express her love for this other man openly for the first time. And when the duke criticizes her lack of shame in expressing this adulterous passion and her desire to die—both sins in the eyes of the Church—not only does she declare herself free from her husband, but she holds him responsible for her intended suicide and threatens him with divine retribution for his cruel injustice toward her. She emerges from her habitual masochistic stance to take a kind of pleasure in seeing the terror and remorse she has provoked in her husband. This scene constitutes a major turning point in the story and marks the heroine's transformation from victim to subject, from defendant to accuser and judge.

The power relations between the duke and his captive thus become curiously reversed. The husband becomes imprisoned by his role as jailer, a slave to his desire for revenge. Unwilling to take others into his confidence, he is unable to leave the castle for more than a few days at a time because he must provide food and water for his prisoner. The duchess finds it paradoxical that the chains of hatred could thus become heavier and more binding than the bonds of love. Equally paradoxical is the power that her powerlessness gives her over her husband—the threat of her own death, as well as the threat of divine punishment. However, hearing that her parents are well and are caring for her daughter, she resolves to live to pray for their happiness in the hope of one day being reunited with them. The renewal of her religious faith enables her not only to renounce her passion for Belmire, but also to forgive her husband and to feel deep pity for him. In contrast, the duke's life becomes utterly poisoned by his jealousy, by his desire for revenge, and later by doubts and remorse for his actions, particularly in light of his wife's fortitude and repeated claims of innocence. Yet caught in a trap of his own making, he cannot free his wife without exposing his own crimes. The stronger she becomes, the weaker he grows until he falls into a mysterious illness that eventually kills him.

Despite her moral victory over her husband, the duchess remains entirely dependent on him for her survival. She finds herself in the paradoxical situation of praying for the health of her jailor. When he falls ill and is unable to bring food to her, she nearly dies of starvation. When she is finally freed, her joy is clouded by compassion for her husband who had just died and by remorse for the misery she caused him. To the very end, her feelings toward him remain deeply ambivalent—a complex mixture of aversion and pity, anger and forgiveness.

As is often the case in Gothic romance, the duchess's tale ends in an idyllic pastoral setting that seems to efface her Gothic experience. After her release, the duchess devotes herself to her daughter's education and then, five years later, after her daughter's wedding, she withdraws to a simple, solitary life in the country devoted to helping the poor.

* * *

We have already touched on various aspects of the duchess's character that mark her as a typical Gothic heroine: her sense of guilt despite her innocence, her repression and sublimation of desire, her self-imposed silence and self-sacrifice, her passivity and status as a victim, and her experience of the sublime as a psychological escape from captivity. What distinguishes Genlis's story among other Gothic tales is the acuity of her psychological analyses. Of particular interest is the fine line Genlis draws between masochism and altruism, between the status of victim and that of subject. Recognizing that she is in large part responsible for her unhappy fate, the heroine finds a certain masochistic pleasure in her self-sacrifice and feelings of remorse. To protect the man she loves, the duchess endures nine years of imprisonment and separation from her family. Yet her captivity allows her to escape from an unhappy marriage and to grow spiritually in a way she might not have otherwise. Paradoxically, it is her imprisonment that gives her the freedom to move from the position of victim to that of subject.

Equally perceptive is Genlis's exploration of the fine line between self-sacrifice and a desire to control others. On the surface, the heroine's renunciation of marriage to Belmire and substitution of her daughter as his wife may seem like an act of self-sacrifice motivated by altruism or perhaps by feelings of guilt. But at a deeper level, it may be seen as an act of passive aggression against Belmire (to control him without having to give up her autonomy), against her daughter (whom she may see as a rival for his affections), and against her dead husband (by marrying his only child to his rival). One could argue that the duchess imposes an arranged marriage on her daughter to satisfy her own needs, much as her parents had done to her.

The duchess presents her decision not to remarry as an affirmation of her freedom from the chains of passion. Yet what she sees as a victory over her passions may in fact be an unhealthy repression of her sexual desires.[22] By making Belmire her son, she puts the barrier of incest between them and, in a sense, desexualizes him. Like the Princesse de Clèves, heroine of Mme de Lafayette's seventeenth-century novel, the duchess declines the marriage proposal of the man she once had loved—and perhaps loves still—out of a sense of responsibility and guilt for what resulted from that passion, but also from a desire to escape from the emotional suffering that a renewal of passion might bring. Yet by rejecting the marriage plot, Genlis avoids what some critics consider the deepest contradiction of the female Gothic[23] in the Anglo-American tradition: that the heroine's impulse toward transcendence is almost always translated into an impulse toward marriage, itself the very source of suffering that escape is supposed to alleviate.[24] Unlike her counterparts in the British Gothic, the duchess refuses to re-enter a marriage economy in which her identity might again be limited to serving as a mirror for the self-representations of father and husband.

Although the duchess finds a certain serenity and transcendence in her pious, solitary life devoted to helping the poor, she continues to suffer from the effects of her long imprisonment. She is plagued by physical weakness and ill-health, melancholy, disorientation and difficulty concentrating, by an intense fear of darkness and solitude, and by a general lethargy reflected in the slowness of her speech and movements. Much like the *male* protagonists of the Anglo-American Gothic, the duchess emerges from her experience with lowered expectations, permanently marked by what she has suffered.

Despite her criticisms of patriarchal family structures, Genlis was hardly a revolutionary in the social reforms she proposed. The ideals and models she advocated—of enlightened mother-educator, maternal nursing, closer parent-child relations, improved female education, and companionate marriage—were in no way incompatible with the subordinate status of eighteenth-century women. Yet through the ambivalence and discontinuities in the heroine's feelings toward her parents and husband, Genlis conveyed a veiled protest against the abuses of parental and marital authority. For readers today, the devices she used to veil or mute these protests are as interesting as the critiques themselves. We have seen how Genlis muted her criticism of parental and marital tyranny by stressing the need for forbearance, obedience, and forgiveness. Another device was to set the duchess's story in Italy, often represented as a land of violent passions and extreme behavior in the popular imagination of her contemporaries. By setting her story outside France, Genlis was able to criticize French social institutions and practices more freely than she might have otherwise.

The popularity of Gothic romance reached its peak at a time when women's role in society had become a matter of intense debate. However, with some notable exceptions such as Mary Wollstonecraft, the majority of women Gothicists—including Genlis—paid lip service to traditional views on women through their adherence to the rules of female decorum, both in the way they wrote and the way they portrayed their heroines. Yet, at the same time, they expressed subtle challenges to this conservative gender ideology in their work by exposing the injustices and dark side of the social order. The Gothic genre allowed women authors to express their frustration and sense of vulnerability in the face of repressive social institutions and practices. By portraying extreme cases of violence and the resistance—and ultimate vindication—of the victims, these texts present both a call for reform and hope for the future.

Fig. 3: Portrait of Mme de Genlis at eighty. 1830 line engraving by Jules Porreau drawn from an 1826 portrait by Mme Chéradame, née Bertaud (1793-1829). National Portrait Gallery, London. (BnF)

Stéphanie-Félicité Du Crest de Genlis was born near Autun in Burgundy in 1746. The son of an old aristocratic family that had recently married into merchant money, Genlis's father lost his estate while she was still a child, and she spent her adolescence in embarrassing poverty. In her *Mémoires*, she recalls the humiliation of having to display her talents as actress and harpist in the salons of wealthy relations in order to provide room and board for herself and her mother and later to attract a suitable husband. Since she had no dowry, her beauty, charm, and talents were her only assets in a highly competitive marriage market. Marriage at seventeen to the future Count of Genlis made her position more secure and led to her entry into the royal court as *dame d'honneur* to the young Duchess of Chartres in 1772. That same year, she began the affair with the Duke of Chartres, the future Philippe-Egalité, that sealed her fortunes—socially, politically, and professionally. Her sharp intelligence and insistence earned her the job of governess to his daughters and eventually as *gouverneur* (head tutor) to his sons, including the future king Louis-Philippe. She thus became the first woman in France—or any other country—to direct the education of royal princes. From this prestigious position, she published a popular series of stories and plays for children and the best-selling pedagogical novel *Adèle et Théodore* (1782) that earned her an international reputation as an educator. This professional activity had a determining influence on her vocation as a writer; for, like *Adèle et Théodore*, many of her early works were of a pedagogical nature: theater pieces and didactic tales designed to amuse and instruct her pupils, a variety of textbooks, and treatises on education outlining her theories and methods.

Forced to flee France during the Terror and to support herself through her writing, Genlis expanded her literary career and was much praised for the historical novels she published following her return to France, particularly for *Mademoiselle de Clermont* (1802) and *La Duchesse de La Vallière* (1804). At the time of her death in 1830 at the age 84, she had published over 140 volumes[25] in a wide variety of genres—pedagogical works, novels, plays, satirical pieces, literary criticism, and a 10-volume set of memoirs—and lived to see her pupil Louis-Philippe become king of France. Yet despite the celebrity she achieved in her lifetime, Genlis was largely forgotten until the mid-1980s when Gabriel de Broglie's monumental biography renewed interest in her life and works. Over the past twenty-five years, much scholarly work has been devoted to her writings, but the texts themselves still are not as widely available as they deserve. It is my hope that this edition of the *Histoire de la duchesse de C**** will enable scholars and students alike to become better acquainted with this major figure among eighteenth-century French women writers.

[1] Antonio Coppi, *Memorie colonnesi* (Rome, 1855), p. 405-6. Translation by Courtney Quaintance. See Appendix G for the original Italian text.

[2] Pompeo Litta, *Famiglie celebri italiane*, 13 vols (Milan: P. E. Giusti, 1819-1852), II (1838), folio 20 verso. The complete text of Litta's account is presented in Appendix G, along with an English translation.

[3] Stéphanie-Félicité Du Crest de Genlis, *Adèle et Théodore, ou Lettres sur l'éducation,* 2nd edn, 3 vols (Paris: Michel Lambert & F. J. Baudouin, 1782), II, p. 329, n. 1. In an article about a gallery in the Palazzo Barberini containing portraits of the family, art historian Maria Giulia Barberini quotes a letter written by Cornelia Costanza Barberini describing a violent lightening storm in 1776, during which the Duchess of Girifalco was present in the palace. She identifies the duchess as Olimpia, Cornelia's daughter born in 1731 and married in 1748 to Gennaro Caracciolo, Duke of Girifalco. [See Barberini, 'La galleria dei ritratti nel mezzanino di palazzo Barberini. Una strategia di famiglia,' in *I Barberini e la cultura europea del seicento*, ed. Lorenza Mochi Onori et al. (Rome, 2007), pp. 605-18 (605 and 617, n. 4).] Interestingly, 1776 was the same year that Genlis spent time in Rome and dined regularly with duchess's parents at their home, where she met the duchess.

[4] '*L'Histoire de la duchesse de C**** [...] est singulière sans doute, et cependant le fond en est vrai, à quelques changements près, qui en augmentent l'intérêt.' Genlis, *Histoire intéressante de madame la duchesse de C**** (Lausanne: H. and L. Vincent, 1783), pp. iv-v.

[5] For a chronology of key dates in the Duchess of Girifalco's life story, see Appendix A.

[6] Genlis, *Mémoires inédits de Madame la comtesse de Genlis, sur le dix-huitième siècle et la révolution française, depuis 1756 jusqu'à nos jours,* 10 vols (Paris: Lavocat, 1825), III, p. 177. The complete French text of this passage is presented in Appendix C, along with the English translation.

[7] 'Je me composais une destinée; non seulement je la remplissais d'événements singuliers, mais j'y plaçais des renversements de fortune, des persécutions; j'aimais à me figurer que j'aurais la force d'y résister. Je me suis supposée mille fois proscrite, calomniée, errante, forcée de me cacher [...].' Genlis, *Mémoires,* 10 vols (Paris, 1825), I, p. 39.

[8] 'De tous les écrits de Mme de Genlis, c'est celui qui a fait la plus grande sensation et qui a été lu avec le plus d'avidité.' Frédéric Melchior Grimm, *Correspondance littéraire, philosophique et critique,* 16 vols (Paris: Garnier, 1877-1882), ed. Tourneux, XIII, p. 394.

[9] The complete French text of Genlis's preface to the novella is presented in Appendix B, along with the English translation.

[10] World Cat lists 112 different editions of Genlis's novel in six languages besides French (English, Spanish, Italian, Dutch, Polish, and Russian), as well as 59 separate editions of the duchess's story under various titles in English and in French. Twenty-nine French editions of the novel were published between 1782 and 1810 alone.

[11] On the parallels between Genlis's *Duchesse de C**** and Radcliffe's *Sicilian Romance*, see Judith Clark Schaneman, 'Rewriting *Adèle et Théodore*: Intertextual Connections between Madame de Genlis and Ann Radcliffe,' *Comparative Literature Studies* 38, 1 (2001), 31-45.

[12] Nicolas Dalayrac and Benoît-Joseph Marsollier, *Camille, ou Le Souterrain, comédie en 3 actes, en prose, mêlée de musique* (Paris: Brunet, 1791), libretto by Marsollier and music by Dalayrac. The text is available in electronic form on the BNF's website Gallica. For a discussion of Marsollier's opera and Paër's Italian translation of his libretto, see Stephen Meyer, 'Terror and Transcendence in the Operatic Prison, 1790-1815,' *Journal of the American Musicological Society,* 55, 3 (Autumn, 2002): 477-523 (504-5 and note 40). Another play loosely based on Genlis's tale of the duchess is Ann Taggart's *Constantia: A Tragedy, in Five Acts* (London: M.A. Nattali, 1824).

[13] For a review of this performance, see F. Stieger's article in the *Revue et gazette musicale de Paris,* 8, 45 (8 August 1841): 370-71.

[14] Joan Hinde Stewart notes that 'despite having grown up with an irresponsible mother and a fiscally incompetent father, Genlis the educator never stopped insisting that children owe their parents blind obedience.' *Gynographs: French Novels by Women of the Late Eighteenth Century* (Lincoln: University of Nebraska Press, 1993), p. 232, n. 4.

[15] Michelle Massé, *In the Name of Love: Women, Masochism, and the Gothic* (Ithaca, NY: Cornell University Press, 1992), p. 7.

[16] Genlis, *Mémoires* (1825), III, p. 48. See Appendix C for the complete French text of this passage and the accompanying English translation.

[17] Anna Seward, letter of 9 August 1786 to Mrs Stokes, in *Letters of Anna Seward written between the years 1784 and 1807*, 6 vols (Edinburgh: Archibald Constable, 1811), I, p. 399. I wish to thank Gillian Dow for bringing this letter to my attention and for other invaluable information she gave me regarding Genlis's account of the duchess's story.

[18] See Appendix F for further discussion of the role of the *cicisbeo* in eighteenth-century Italy.

[19] Litta, *Famiglie celebri italiane*, II, folio 20 verso.

[20] Coppi, *Memorie colonnesi*, pp. 405-6 (406); and Alessandro Ademollo, *Il Matrimonio di suor Maria Pulcheria al secolo Livia Cesarini. Memorie particolari riguardanti le famiglie Colonna, Orsini, Altieri, Cesarini, Sforza, e Sforza-Cesarini nei secoli decimosettimo et decimottavo* (Rome: A. Sommaruga, 1883), p. 163, n. 20. See Appendix G for the complete Italian texts and English translations of these accounts.

[21] Eve Kosofsky Sedgwick, *The Coherence of Gothic Conventions* (New York: Arno Press, 1980), p. 17.

[22] Suellen Diaconoff interprets this aspect of Genlis's novella quite differently. She sees the duchess's refusal of Belmire's marriage proposal not as a repression of her amorous and sexual desires, but as a healthy victory over these passions. Drawing a parallel between the Duchess of C*** and Louise de la Vallière (heroine of Genlis's historical novel *La Duchesse de la Vallière*), Diaconoff argues that their lives embody 'the quality of dramatic, personal decision-making that moves them beyond romantic passion into role models of female self-realization' and that through their stories, Genlis offers the woman reader 'an alternative vision of herself as a rational, ethical, and moral individual capable of making difficult decisions.' See 'The Romance as Transformative Reading: Félicité de Genlis,' in *Through the Reading Glass: Women, Books, and Sex in the French Enlightenment* (Albany: State University of New York Press, 2005), pp. 77-100 (98).

[23] Ellen Moers first used the term 'female Gothic' in 1963 to refer *any* Gothic fiction by women and maintained that the Gothic simply 'has to do with fear.' See *Literary Women* (Garden City, NY: Doubleday, 1963; repr. 1976), p. 138. I agree with Anne Williams that these definitions are inadequate and prefer the one she has proposed: 'a [Gothic] narrative organized around the female perspective which necessarily views the male as 'other.'' See *Art of Darkness: A Poetics of Gothic* (Chicago: University of Chicago Press, 1995), p. 141. Presumably, Williams means the reverse by the term 'male Gothic': a narrative organized around the male perspective that views the *female* as 'other.' Contrary to Moers's claim, the female Gothic (like the male Gothic) can be written by authors of either sex.

[24] For feminist critiques of the marriage plot in the Anglo-American female Gothic, see Eugenia C. DeLamotte, *Perils of the Night: A Feminist Study of the Nineteenth-Century Gothic* (Oxford University Press, 1990), pp. 185-87; and Williams, *Art of Darkness*, pp. 103-4.

[25] The exact number of Genlis's publications is difficult to determine. There are 550 entries under her name in the Bibliothèque Nationale's catalogue. Although many of these listings are for different editions of the same texts, this still gives a sense of her prodigious output.

ABOUT THE TEXT AND TRANSLATION

The text for this edition and translation of the *Histoire de la duchesse de C**** is taken from volume 2 of the second edition of Genlis's novel *Adèle et Théodore, ou Lettres sur l'éducation* published in Paris in 1782 by Michel Lambert & F. J. Baudouin, who also published the original edition earlier that same year. This second edition, reviewed and corrected by Genlis, bears the inscription: 'seconde édition, revue, corrigée & augmentée.' The *Histoire de la duchesse de C**** is found in volume 2 of this edition, pp. 274-373. This version of the duchess's story is almost identical in content to that published by Genlis in a separate edition the following year under the title *Histoire intéressante de madame la duchesse de C**** (Lausanne: H. and L. Vincent, 1783). The key difference between the two versions is that the novel presents Genlis's commentary on the significance of the duchess's story (expressed through the voice of the Baronne d'Almane, her fictional alter ego), as well as a broader narrative framework for the embedded tale (the d'Almane's trip to Albenga where they become acquainted with Mme de C***). For this reason, the decision was made to publish the version presented in the novel.

Genlis's preface to the separate 1783 edition of the duchess's story provides further commentary on the story's significance and has been reprinted in Appendix B, along with the English translation. Subsequent references to the duchess's story in *Adèle et Théodore* are presented in Appendix D, also followed by a translation of these passages into English.

Genlis's novel was tremendously popular and underwent frequent reprintings well into the nineteenth century. Despite various editorial changes discussed below, the versions of the duchess's story published in subsequent editions of *Adèle et Théodore* are the same in substance as the second 1782 edition, with one important exception. In the second edition (as in the first), the first footnote appearing in the duchess's story reads as follows:

Le fond de cette histoire est parfaitement vrai: les neuf ans de capitivité dans un souterrain où le jour ne pénétra jamais, la supposition de la mort de la duchesse, la manière dont cette dernière vécut et dont elle fut nourrie, sa délivrance; tous ces détails sont exactement vrais. Il n'y a d'invention dans cette histoire que l'amour et les personnages de l'amant de de l'amie. L'auteur, en 17**, a vu à Rome madame la duchesse de C*** et tous les jours dînait avec le père de cette personne intéressante.[1]

[The basic facts of this story are entirely true: the nine years of captivity in a dungeon impenetrable to the light of day, the duchess's presumed death, the way she lived and was fed, and her rescue; all these details are completely accurate. The only fictional parts of the story concern the love plot and the characters of the lover and the female friend. In 17**, the author saw the Duchess of C*** in Rome and dined every day with this intriguing woman's father.]

In contrast, in the fourth edition published in 1804 by Maradan in Paris, we find a much shorter version of this footnote:

Le fond de cette histoire est parfaitement vrai. L'auteur, en 1776, a vu à Rome madame la duchesse de Cerifalco, et tous les jours dînait avec le prince de Palestrine, père de cette personne intéressante.[2]

[The basic facts of this story are entirely true. In 1776, the author saw the Duchess of Cerifalco in Rome and dined every day with the Prince of Palestrina, this intriguing woman's father.]

In this fourth 'revised, corrected, and augmented' edition, Genlis chose to identify the duchess and her father by name and to specify the year she made their acquaintance in Rome—information she had concealed in the 1782 edition. Yet in the 1804 edition, she also chose to omit the enumeration of factual details taken from real life, as well as the claim that the love plot and the characters of the lover and the female friend were purely fictional.

One can only speculate why Genlis made these changes. Since the Duchess of Girfalco died in 1800, her father in 1787, and her mother in 1797,[3] Genlis may have felt more at liberty to identify them by name in the editions of the novel and novella published after Olimpia's death. But because she and her parents were still alive when the story was first published in 1782, Genlis may have wished to protect the family's reputation by insisting that the love plot was of her own invention. The fact that this implausible claim is *not* made in the 1804 edition suggests that the duke's jealousy may indeed have been caused by his wife's attraction to another man and that she was therefore partly responsible for the failure of her marriage. This is, after all, a key point that Genlis stresses in drawing the moral of the duchess's story: the dangers of romantic passion and the disastrous consequences of failing to confide in her mother. The duchess was in fact rumored to have been involved with another man, as correspondences of the period and nineteenth-century biographers suggest. (See the Introduction and Appendices E and G regarding the duchess's rumored affair.) The decision was therefore made to present both versions of this footnote in this edition. Although somewhat contradictory, together they provide a better understanding of the text and offer insight into the challenges of literary interpretation.

In addition to this substantive change, Genlis also made a number of editorial changes in the 1804 edition. She divided many of the longer paragraphs into shorter ones, changed the passé composé past tense to the more formal passé simple, and changed non-proper nouns (such as *Heroïne* and *Lettre*) to lower case throughout. She also modernized some spellings (changing *vûe* to *vue, asyle* to *asile,* and *&* to *et*). Finally, she corrected a few grammatical errors (for example, changing *après m'avoir entrevû to après m'avoir entrevue*). These changes have all been incorporated into the 1782 edition used as the basis for this edition.

To make the French text (as well as the translation) more readable for a modern audience, several additional changes have been made. In all editions of the duchess's story, Genlis makes frequent, even excessive use of ellipses, as was sometimes the practice in eighteenth-century novels. Because they tend to distract from the story rather than to enhance it, the ellipses have been removed, except in a few cases where they serve a clear stylistic purpose, such as creating suspense or reflecting confusion or hesitation on the part of the characters. In the late eighteenth century, quotation marks were still a relatively new form of punctuation that Genlis uses at times, but not consistently. For this edition, following modern usage, all dialogue has been set in quotation marks, with paragraph breaks added each time there is a change in speaker. (However, I have retained Genlis's use of italics to indicate quotes within a quote.) Overly long paragraphs still appearing in the 1804 edition have been divided into shorter ones where paragraph breaks are warranted. Similarly, overly long sentences connected by commas, colons, or semi-colons have, in many cases, been divided into shorter sentences. Finally, all spellings have been modernized. The most frequently encountered differences involved changing imperfect endings (from *-ois, -oit,* and *-oient* to *ais, -ait,* and *-aient*) and plural adjectival forms (from *-ans* and *-ens* to *-ants* and *-ents*) and removing hyphens where they no longer occur in modern usage (such as in *aussitôt* and *non seulement*).

A thornier issue facing the translator of Genlis's text is her inconsistent use of tenses, particularly in certain key passages. In such cases, the decision was made to use one tense consistently, whichever seemed to fit the context better, in order to create a smoother flow and greater stylistic unity. For example, the passages describing the duchess's discovery by Belmire and her subsequent rescue by her father both shift from past to present tense and then back to past tense. In these two passages, the decision was made to use present tense throughout in order to heighten the feeling of immediacy and suspense that Genlis no doubt sought to generate.

A final issue involved the spelling of the duchess's name. In the original 1782 edition of *Adèle et Théodore*, Genlis referred to her as 'la Duchesse de C.....' with the word *duchesse* capitalized and capital C (for Cerifalco) followed by an ellipsis consisting of four or five periods in some passages or by three asterisks in others. We find the same inconsistencies in the 1804 edition of the novel, although both *duc* and *duchesse* are generally spelled with a lower case *d*, in keeping with modern French practice. In the separate edition of the novel first published in 1783, Genlis used asterisks (C***) both in the title and in the text itself for the duchess's last name. We find similar variations in the spellings adopted in the various English translations of the novel and novella; some translators used a single period (C.), others a series of hyphens instead of periods or asterisks in the duchess's name, as in the title of Maria Stanley's translation: *The Duchess of C----*. For the present edition, the decision was made to follow the spelling in the novella's title as it appears in the catalogue of the Bibliothèque Nationale: *Histoire intéressante de madame la duchesse de C****. In the translation, in keeping with modern English practice, duke and duchess (and other titles of nobility) are set lower case when used alone, but capitalized when used with their last name. In the French text, titles of nobility are set lower case throughout, whether used alone or with their last name, in keeping with modern French usage.

* * *

Almost immediately after their publication, both *Adèle et Théodore* and the *Histoire intéressante de la duchesse de C**** were translated into English, as well as into five other European languages (Spanish, Italian, Dutch, Polish, and Russian). Published under the title *Adelaide and Theodore,* the 1783 translation of Genlis's novel was hugely popular in late eighteenth-century Britain, where it was read as a system of education by authors such as Catherine Macaulay, Mary Wollstonecraft, Maria Edgeworth, and Clara Reeve. We even find reference to Genlis's novel at the end of Jane Austen's *Emma*. A number of British women, including Maria Edgeworth, took advantage of the short-lived Treaty of Amiens of 1802 to visit the famous French educator in her apartments in the Arsenal.[4] The novel's popularity and influence in England was due in large part to the heated debates on both sides of the Channel concerning female education and to Genlis's challenge to Rousseau's paternalistic views on this subject expounded in *Emile*.[5]

The 1783 translation of Genlis's novel underwent numerous reprintings and reworkings in the decades following.[6] A number of these English editions are available as electronic texts through various university libraries in Thomson Gale's Eighteenth-century Collections online series. However, one needs to be physically present in the subscribing libraries in order to access these electronic resources. Gillian Dow recently published an excellent critical edition of the 1783 translation of the novel with Pickering and Chatto in the Chawton House library series.

There were also several translations of the separate 1783 edition of the duchess's story, published under various titles. These include *Moral Tale. The Dutchess of C----* (Manchester: G. Nicholson, 1798), *The Dutchess of C----. Moral tale* (Manchester: G. Nicholson, 1800), *The True and Affecting History of the Duchess of C---* (London: S. Bailey, 1800), and *The Inhuman Husband; or The Narrative of the Duchess of C—* (1830). The duchess's story was also published in serialized form in several British magazines under various titles including 'The History of the Dutchess of C---. Written by Herself,' in *Universal* (July-September 1785); 'Female Fortitude, or the History of the Duchess of C----, Written by Herself,' in *Lady's* (Jan-July, 1786); and 'Memoirs of the Dutchess of C-----,' in *New Magazine of Choice Pieces* II, 17 (1810).

The chief drawback to all the existing translations of the duchess's story (most of which date back to the late eighteenth or early nineteenth century) is that the English often appears stilted and old-fashioned to the modern reader. The full title of Maria Stanley's translation published in 1820 illustrates this point:

> The affecting history of the Duchess of C----: who was confined nine years in a horrid dungeon under ground, where light never entered: a straw bed being her only resting-place, and bread and water her only support, conveyed by means of a turning-box by her inhuman husband: whom she saw but once during her long imprisonment, though suffering by hunger, thirst, and cold, the most severe hardships: but fortunately she was at last discovered and released by her parents.

The 1783 translation published by Bathurst in London and reprinted in the 2007 Pickering and Chatto edition is similarly stilted, as the following passage illustrates:

> I have it at last—I am possessed of this history, so desired, so interesting, so extraordinary!—This precious manuscript, written by the very hand of the Duchesse de C.! I am trusted with it for four-and-twenty hours; and am permitted to translate and take a copy of it!—I have read it—and I shall not, without inexpressible regret, leave the heroine of such a history—This woman, as virtuous and interesting as she is unfortunate—Oh! what a destiny is hers![7]

Even in its own day, the 1783 translation was met with criticism from some reviewers, particularly from one in the *British Magazine and Review*, who encouraged 'a lady of the first literary talents' (probably Maria Edgeworth) to complete and publish her own translation:

> Should that lady renew her intention, the present performance, we apprehend, would be but little read. To say the truth, this translation is so indifferently executed, being in many places egregiously ungrammatical, and generally very inelegant, that if even the lady in question should not be induced to take up her pen, we hope, at least, some person of respectable talents may be prevailed on to render the excellent Letters of Madame la Comtesse de Genlis worthy of the attention of the English nation.[8]

Given these drawbacks, we felt that a modern translation should be made available to students and scholars in an affordable edition with modernized spellings, translator's notes, and ancillary materials we have provided. In both the introduction and the translation, we have sought to draw attention to the complex gender issues raised by the text, while remaining true to the story's social and historical context.

The different translations of Genlis's novella are nearly identical to the version of the duchess's story presented in the various translations of her novel, with one important exception. An additional paragraph is found at the end of the translation of Genlis's novella published in 1798 by George Nicholson in Manchester, England, under the title *Moral tale. The Dutchess of C—:*

> How unfortunate has been this amiable, this virtuous, this touching woman! How severe her sufferings! Ah, may we guard our hearts against the fatal impressions of love! May a passion never be known that can produce such misery and guilt! And let us not fail to deduce from the narrative of the Duchess of C*** two important truths: the first, that indulgence of the passions may plunge us into the deepest abyss of human woe; and the second, that there is no calamity that religion cannot help us bear.

This passage does not appear in the original French text of the novella published in 1783 (under the title *Histoire intéressante de madame la duchesse de C****), nor is it found at the end of the duchess's narrative in *Adèle et Théodore*. It appears to have been drawn from a passage in *Adèle et Théodore* preceding the duchess's story in which she speaks privately with Mme d'Almane. After expressing her concern about Adèle's excessive sensibility, she agrees to let the baroness copy her story so that her daughter could read it and profit from the lessons it teaches:

> 'Ah! Madame, mettez tous vos soins à garantir son cœur des funestes impressions de l'amour; qu'elle ne connaisse jamais cette passion fatale qui peut produire tant de malheurs et tant de crimes! [...]. J'ai désiré laisser à mes petites filles, encore dans la plus tendre enfance, un détail qui peut leur être utile un jour— une leçon frappante qui leur apprendra deux importantes vérités: la première, que les passions peuvent nous précipiter dans le plus profond abîme des misères humaines; et la seconde, qu'il n'est point de maux que la religion ne puisse faire supporter.'

> ['Oh, Madame, you must do all you can to protect her heart from the deadly impressions of love! May she never know that fatal passion that can cause such unhappiness and so many crimes! [...] I wished to leave for my granddaughters, who are still very young, an account that may be useful for them some day—a striking lesson that will teach them two important truths: the first, that passions can plunge us into the deepest abyss of human miseries; and the second, that there are no misfortunes, no suffering so great that religion cannot help us bear.']

It may be that the translator chose to add this paragraph to the end of the novella in order to enhance its didactic impact, in keeping with the moralistic framework of the duchess's narrative in the novel.

NOTES

[1] Genlis, *Adèle et Théodore, ou Lettres sur l'éducation,* 2nd edn, 3 vols (Paris: Michel Lambert & F. J. Baudouin), II, p. 329, n. 1.

[2] Genlis, *Adèle et Théodore, ou Lettres sur l'éducation,* 4th edn, 4 vols (Paris: Maradan, 1804), III, p. 96, n. 1.

[3] For this and other information concerning Olimpia's parents, see Caroline Castiglione, *Patrons and Adversaries: Nobles and Villagers in Italian Politics, 1640-1760* (Oxford & New York: Oxford University Press, 2005), pp. 108 and 181. See in particular the family tree on p. 181 that gives birth and death dates for Olimpia and her parents. Also see George L. Williams, *Papal Genealogy: The Families and Descendants of the Popes* (Jefferson, NC: McFarland, 1998), pp. 128 and 213.

[4] Maria Edgeworth met with Genlis during her stay in Paris in the winter of 1802-1803. Her admiration for Genlis is demonstrated by the fact that she began a translation of *Adèle et Théodore* in 1782 soon after it was published and even considered publishing a full translation. But after completing the first volume, she abandoned the project when a rival translation appeared in 1783. For details of Edgeworth's work on Genlis, see Marilyn Butler, *Maria Edgeworth: A Literary Biography* (Oxford: Clarendon Press, 1997), pp. 7-9. Also see Stuart Gillespie and David Hopkins, eds., *The Oxford History of Literary Translation in English,* 5 vols (Oxford; New York: Oxford University Press, 2005-2008), III, p. 357.

[5] Genlis's challenge to Rousseau's views on female education is made most explicitly in her preface to the second edition of her novel. In the novel itself, she proposes what was no doubt the most comprehensive, ambitious plan of studies for women in eighteenth-century France—a plan she had tested and perfected with her own daughters and pupils over a twenty-year period. Regarding Genlis's critique of Rousseau, see Mary Trouille, 'The Influence of Class and Politics on Women's Response to Rousseau: Stéphanie de Genlis and Olympe de Gouges,' in *Sexual Politics in the Enlightenment: Women Writers Read Rousseau* (Albany: State University of New York Press, 1997), pp. 237–91 (243-52).

[6] Regarding the English translations of *Adèle et Théodore* published in the 1780s, see Gillian Dow, ''The Good sense of British readers has encouraged the translation of the whole': Les traductions anglaises des œuvres de Mme de Genlis dans les années 1780,' in *La Traduction des*

genres non romanesques au XVIIIe *siècle,* ed. Annie Cointre and Annie Rivara (Metz: Centre d'études de la traduction, 2003), pp. 285-97.

[7] The identity of the author(s) of the 1783 translation of Genlis's novel has become a matter of debate among scholars. The translation was long attributed to Thomas Holcroft, who is known to have translated other works by Genlis. [See, for example, Grace A. Oliver, *A Study of Maria Edgeworth* (Boston: A. Williams, 1882), p. 81; and Augustus J. C. Hare, ed., *The Life and Letters of Maria Edgeworth,* 2 vols (Whitefish, MT: Kessinger Publishing, 2004; reprint of 1894 edn), I, p. 17.] However, in her critical edition of the 1783 translation of Genlis's novel, Gillian Dow maintains that it was the work of two or more women, based on the preface to the second edition of the translation published in 1784 that identifies them as 'some Ladies, who through misfortunes [...] are reduced from ease and opulence to the necessity of applying, to the support of life, those accomplishments which were given to them in their youth for the amusement and embellishment of it' ('Note on the Text,' p. xxvi). Dow speculates that several women may have collaborated on the 1783 translation based on discrepancies in spelling among the three volumes, the prefatory note from the 1784 edition cited above, and a dedicatory note that appears at the beginning of a 1791 reprint of the translation: 'To the Reverend Christopher Hunter from the editors and translators, Mrs. Watson and her daughters.' However, given the popularity of *Adèle et Théodore* in Britain and Holcroft's involvement in other translations of Genlis's works, he may very well have published a rival translation of her novel during this same period.

[8] *British Magazine and Review,* 3 (October, 1783), 293-95. Cited by Gillian Dow, 'Les traductions anglaises des œuvres de Mme de Genlis dans les années 1780,' p. 292.

HISTOIRE DE LA DUCHESSE DE C***

DE

STÉPHANIE DE GENLIS

HISTOIRE DE LA DUCHESSE DE C***

Du journal de la baronne

D'Albenga, ce mardi.

Enfin mon journal devient intéressant, et sûrement, ma chère amie, tout ce que je pourrai vous mander de Venise et de Rome ne vous causera pas autant de plaisir que la relation que je vais vous faire. Je ne veux point vous prévenir, afin qu'en lisant ce journal vous ayiez une partie de la surprise que j'ai éprouvée moi-même.

Le chemin de Saint-Maurice à Albenga[1] est rempli de passages très effrayants. Mais cette route offre des points de vue admirables, entre autres celui qu'on trouve au haut de la montagne qui domine la ville de Languella. La descente de cette montagne est très escarpée et fort dangereuse. Nous l'avons descendue à pied, et nous pouvons même dire à pieds nus; car les rochers que nous gravissons depuis trois jours ont tellement usé et percé nos souliers, que les semelles en sont presque entièrement emportées; et ne prévoyant pas que nous dussions autant marcher, nous n'avons pas eu la précaution d'en prendre plusieurs paires. A dix heures du matin, nous faisons arrêter nos porteurs sur le sommet d'une montagne de laquelle nous découvrons la ville d'Albenga,[2] au milieu d'une plaine délicieuse, ce qui est une singularité très remarquable sur cette côte, toutes les autres villes étant situées sur des rochers.

Nous descendons la montagne, et nous nous trouvons dans une plaine immense et fertile, entourée de rochers et de montagnes majestueuses, dont quelques-unes sont couvertes de glaces. L'aridité des rochers, l'aspect imposant des montagnes, forment un contraste singulier avec la beauté riante et la fertilité de la plaine. Les prés y sont émaillés de pensées et de lys; le laurier-rose y croît sans culture; et on y voit tous les champs entourés de longs berceaux de vigne. A travers ces charmantes galeries à jour, on découvre la verdure, les fleurs et les fruits renfermés dans l'enceinte de ces légers treillages, dont toutes les arcades sont ornées de guirlandes de pampres élégantes et flexibles, et que le moindre vent fait mouvoir. Il semble, dans ce délicieux séjour, que la terre y soit cultivée, non pour les besoins de l'homme, mais seulement pour ses plaisirs. Tous les objets qu'on y rencontre sont agréables. C'est là, ma chère amie, que vous verriez de véritables *bergères*, au lieu de ces paysannes dont *les bonnets de nuit*[3] vous font tant de peine. Toutes les jeunes filles sont coiffées en cheveux avec un bouquet de fleurs naturelles placé sur la tête du côté gauche; elles sont presque toutes jolies et surtout remarquables par l'élégance de leurs tailles.[4]

Figurez-vous les transports d'Adèle et de Théodore en voyant des objets si charmants et si nouveaux pour eux. Ils nous demandèrent la permission de courir dans la plaine et d'aller se promener sous les berceaux; et presque au même instant ils se trouvèrent à deux cents pas de nous. Théodore s'arrêta pour cueillir un bouquet, et sa sœur continuant sa course entra dans un petit sentier où je la perdis de vue. Je l'appelai deux ou trois fois; elle était trop éloignée pour m'entendre. J'envoyai Dainville la chercher; il revint un moment après et sans elle, mais en me criant qu'il l'avait trouvée et qu'elle allait revenir. Je doublai le pas, et Dainville s'approchant de moi, me dit en riant que nous ne partirions point d'Albenga sans pouvoir écrire sur notre journal une charmante aventure.

'Mais, où est ma fille?' interrompis-je.

'A deux pas d'ici,' reprit-il, 'avec une dame belle comme le jour.'

Comme Dainville achevait ces mots, Adèle parut en courant. Elle nous rejoignit; mais elle était si émue, si essoufflée, si transportée de *son aventure*, qu'elle ne pouvait répondre qu'en bégayant et par monosyllabes. Enfin, quand elle fut remise de son trouble, nous nous assîmes sur l'herbe, et elle nous conta, qu'aussitôt après nous avoir perdus de vue, elle avait aperçu de loin, dans une espèce de bosquet sur la gauche du chemin où elle était, une femme seule couchée sur le gazon. La curiosité ayant fait approcher Adèle, elle vit distinctement une belle femme lisant avec beaucoup d'attention; elle était vêtue d'une robe de gaze blanche. Elle avait l'air triste, mais une physionomie pleine de douceur et de majesté. Une jeune personne, qui paraissait une femme de chambre, était assise à dix pas d'elle. L'héroïne, au bruit que fit Adèle, leva les yeux et parut très surprise en la regardant. Adèle lui fit une profonde révérence et resta debout à sa place sans oser avancer.

Fig. 4: 'L'héroïne, au bruit que fit Adèle, leva les yeux et parut très surprise en la regardant. Adèle lui fit une profonde révérence.' Illustration dans la sixième édition d'*Adèle et Théodore* publiée en 1862 à Paris par Morizot. Gravure de Pégard d'après un dessin de Telory. (BnF)

L'inconnue la regarde toujours et lui sourit; alors Adèle enhardie s'approche. L'inconnue lui dit en italien qu'elle la trouve charmante, en ajoutant: 'Vous ne m'entendez sûrement pas.' Adèle lui répond en italien. Nouvelle surprise de l'inconnue, qui fait à Adèle quelques questions, l'embrasse tendrement plusieurs fois, ensuite se lève, appelle sa femme de chambre, et s'en va. Adèle ajouta que l'inconnue n'était pas de la première jeunesse, mais qu'elle était d'une beauté parfaite; et Dainville dit que, quoiqu'il ne l'eût vue que de loin, sa figure l'avait en effet singulièrement frappé.

Après ce récit, Adèle me conjura de coucher à Albenga, au lieu d'aller à Pietra, comme nous en avions le projet, et M. d'Almane y consentit. Nous sommes établis dans une assez jolie maison. Nous avons pris des informations sur notre inconnue; et d'après le portrait qu'en fait Adèle, on assure que ce ne peut être que la duchesse de C***, une personne aussi distinguée et aussi extraordinaire par ses vertus et ses malheurs, que par sa naissance et sa beauté. Elle est depuis quatre ans à Albenga, retirée dans une maison qu'elle a fait bâtir dans la partie la plus solitaire de la plaine. Elle vit dans la plus grande retraite, et l'on ajoute que sa bienfaisance et sa piété la rendent l'objet de l'admiration de tout le pays. Quant à son histoire, on ne la sait que très confusément, et les détails que j'ai pu recueillir sont si extraordinaires et si peu vraisemblables, que je ne les écrirai point encore. Vous croyez facilement que nous avons quelque curiosité de connaître plus particulièrement la duchesse de C***. Adèle surtout le désire avec passion. Ne sachant comment engager la duchesse à nous recevoir, nous avons enfin suivi le conseil de M. d'Almane, qui était d'avis qu'Adèle lui écrivît à ce sujet. Nous espérons quelques succès de la grâce enfantine et de la naïveté du billet d'Adèle. Il y a environ une heure qu'il est parti, et nous n'avons point encore de réponse.

* * *

Bonne nouvelle et grande joie. La réponse arrive dans l'instant: la duchesse de C*** consent à nous recevoir, et nous invite à souper. Comme elle mande à Adèle qu'elle soupe à sept heures, et qu'il en est près de six, nous allons partir dans l'instant.

Ah! Dainville avait bien raison de nous annoncer une charmante aventure. Nous ne savons plus quand nous partirons d'Albenga. Nous y resterons jusqu'à ce que nous ayons pu obtenir une connaissance un peu approfondie de l'histoire de la plus intéressante personne que j'aie jamais vue. Jugez vous-même, par le détail de notre première entrevue, si notre curiosité est fondée et doit être vive.

Nous sommes arrivés ce soir chez elle à six heures un quart. Sa maison est de la simplicité la plus élégante. Après avoir traversé deux antichambres et une assez longue galerie, nous entrons dans un petit cabinet. Adèle, apercevant la duchesse, me quitte et court à elle; la duchesse la prend dans ses bras et l'embrasse deux ou trois fois. Je m'approche. Je prie Adèle de me présenter, et Madame de C*** nous reçoit tous avec la grâce la plus obligeante. Nous nous asseyons; et, pendant que M. d'Almane parle de notre voyage et répond aux questions de la duchesse, j'examine cette dernière avec autant de plaisir que d'étonnement. Elle a trente-huit ou quarante ans, mais elle est en effet d'une beauté aussi régulière que frappante. Elle a des yeux noirs qui, par leur grandeur et leur forme, ressembleraient aux vôtres, si le regard en était moins languissant. Sa taille est de la plus belle proportion. Quoique, loin d'avoir la tête haute, elle ait au contraire l'habitude de la tenir un peu penchée en avant, elle a cependant l'air infiniment noble; et elle paraît véritablement majestueuse quand, par hasard, elle tourne ou relève sa tête. Elle n'a rien de la vivacité italienne. Tous ses mouvements sont lents; elle parle doucement, et s'exprime même avec quelque difficulté. On s'aperçoit, au bout d'un quart d'heure, qu'elle est d'une extrême distraction; tout à coup, elle tombe dans une rêverie qui a quelque chose de sombre et de frappant; et lorsqu'elle en sort, elle regarde avec un étonnement stupide tout ce qui l'entoure. Sa physionomie est également douce, intéressante et triste; elle a habituellement l'air souffrant. Ses manières sont affectueuses et caressantes. Et, autant qu'une visite de deux heures peut en faire juger, je crois qu'elle est d'une excessive sensibilité, que son imagination est très vive, et qu'elle a beaucoup d'esprit.

Pendant le souper, elle m'a fait plusieurs questions sur ma fille. Elle m'a dit qu'elle en avait une aussi qui faisait son bonheur et que je la verrais à Rome. Je lui ai témoigné ma surprise de la distance qui l'en séparait; elle m'a répondu que sa fille venait tous les ans passer deux ou trois mois avec elle; et après cette réponse, elle a soupiré et changé de conversation.

En sortant de table, j'ai remarqué que sa maison était plutôt illuminée qu'éclairée; car tous les appartements sont remplis de lustres, de torchères et de girandoles. 'Ah, madame, m'a dit la duchesse, si vous saviez combien je dois apprécier la clarté, et à quel point je dois haïr l'obscurité et les ténèbres!' En prononçant ces mots, ses yeux se sont remplis de larmes, et au même instant elle est tombée dans la plus profonde rêverie.

Nous avons pris congé d'elle à neuf heures. Quand je l'ai quittée, elle m'a dit qu'elle pensait avec peine que je partirais le lendemain. Alors j'ai répondu que, si elle voulait me recevoir encore, je resterais. Elle m'a serré la main, et m'embrassant, elle dit: 'Albenga attire peu de voyageurs. Cependant, depuis quatre ans, j'ai su que plusieurs étrangers s'y sont arrêtés; j'ai refusé de les voir, mais je voudrais, madame, pouvoir vous fixer ici. Ainsi, du moins promettez-moi donc de venir demain dîner chez moi.' Vous jugez bien que j'ai accepté avec plaisir, et que je serai exacte à me trouver au rendez-vous. Oh, si je pouvais obtenir d'elle quelques détails sur son histoire! Ce qu'il y a de certain, c'est que je ne quitterai point Albenga sans avoir fait à cet égard toutes les tentatives imaginables.

* * *

Continuation du journal de la baronne.

D'Albenga, ce mercredi au soir.

Je la possède enfin—cette histoire si désirée, si intéressante, si extraordinaire! Ce précieux manuscrit, écrit de la main même de la duchesse de C***, il m'est confié pour vingt-quatre heures, et j'ai la permission de le traduire et d'en prendre une copie! Je l'ai lu, et je ne quitterai sûrement pas, sans un regret inexprimable, l'héroïne d'une semblable histoire! Cette femme aussi vertueuse, aussi touchante, qu'elle fut infortunée! Oh, quelle destinée que la sienne! Mais reprenons le fil de mon récit. Pendant que M. d'Almane et Dainville sont enfermés et traduisent en français l'histoire de la duchesse de C***, je vais vous rendre compte de la journée qui nous a valu cet inestimable présent.

Nous sommes arrivés ce matin chez la duchesse à onze heures. Elle nous a proposé un tour de promenade avant le dîner et nous a conduits à un petit belvédère duquel on découvre un point de vue si charmant, que mes enfants et Dainville ont eu envie de le dessiner. Ils en ont fait une légère ébauche, et la duchesse désirant voir des ouvrages d'Adèle, j'ai envoyé chercher son portefeuille. La duchesse étonnée qu'un enfant de douze ans et demi sût plusieurs langues et dessinât d'après nature aussi bien, j'ajoutai qu'elle chantait et jouait de la harpe; il fallut faire venir sa harpe. Adèle avait grande envie de plaire, elle y réussit, et réellement la duchesse parut enchantée d'elle.

Après le dîner, elle me proposa une nouvelle promenade— c'est-à-dire, de sortir hors de la maison, car elle ne peut marcher ni longtemps, ni vite. Nous nous assîmes toutes deux seules sur un banc de gazon, et elle me parla encore d'Adèle: 'Elle me paraît bien sensible,' me dit-elle.

'Oui,' répondis-je, 'elle l'est extrêmement.'

'Ah! Madame,' reprit la duchesse, 'mettez tous vos soins à garantir son cœur des funestes impressions de l'amour; qu'elle ne connaisse jamais cette passion fatale qui peut produire tant de malheurs et tant de crimes!' Elle prononça ces paroles d'un ton qui me fit frémir. Elle s'en aperçut et, prenant affectueusement ma main, elle dit: 'Je ne sais si l'on vous a parlé de mon histoire.'

'Ah!' repris-je vivement, 'Quel serait mon bonheur si je la tenais de votre bouche!'

'De ma bouche,' s'écria-t-elle. 'Ah! Madame, elle est si terrible, qu'il me serait impossible d'avoir le courage de la conter; mais j'ai eu celui de l'écrire. J'ai désiré laisser à mes petites filles, encore dans la plus tendre enfance, un détail qui peut leur être utile un jour—une leçon frappante qui leur apprendra deux importantes vérités: la première, que les passions peuvent nous précipiter dans le plus profond abîme des misères humaines; et la seconde, qu'il n'est point de maux que la religion ne puisse faire supporter.'

'O Ciel!' interrompis-je. 'Ce précieux manuscrit existe, et jamais Adèle ne le lira!'

'Non, madame,' reprit la duchesse, 'ce n'est point à une mère telle que vous, que je pourrais le refuser; restez encore deux jours ici, et je vous le confierai.' A ces mots, j'éprouvai un mouvement si vif de reconnaissance et de joie, qu'il me fut impossible de l'exprimer autrement qu'en embrassant la duchesse avec un transport qui dut lui faire connaître tout le prix que j'attachais à une semblable grâce. 'Ce n'est point,' reprit-elle, 'une marque de confiance que je vous donne, ce n'est qu'une preuve d'amitié. Mon histoire n'est ignorée de personne; on pourra vous en dire à Rome toutes les particularités. Mais je pouvais seule vous instruire de mes sentiments et de mes réflexions, et sans doute ce détail ne sera pas pour vous le moins intéressant.'

Après cet entretien, nous rentrâmes dans la maison. La duchesse me conduisit dans son cabinet. Elle ouvrit une petite armoire et, en tirant deux gros cahiers d'une écriture très fine, elle me dit: 'Tenez, emportez ce manuscrit; si vous l'en jugez digne, faites-le copier, et offrez-le de ma part à la charmante Adèle. Elle ne le lira point, j'en suis sûre, sans répandre quelques larmes. Puisse-t-il offrir à sa jeunesse une utile leçon, et fortifier encore, s'il est possible, tous les principes qu'elle tient de vous!'

Enfin, à cinq heures je m'arrache d'auprès de la duchesse pour aller lire le trésor qu'elle m'a confié. Je ne vous parlerai point de l'impression qu'a produite sur moi cette lecture, vous en jugerez vous-même. Depuis que je vous écris, M. d'Almane et Dainville ont traduit plus de la moitié de l'histoire de la duchesse. Ils auront fini demain. Alors, Brunel en fera deux copies, l'une pour Adèle et l'autre pour vous, et je vous enverrai la vôtre, avec mon journal de la Corniche,[5] aussitôt que je serai à Gènes.

* * *

D'Albenga, ce jeudi.

Nous soupâmes hier chez la duchesse. Avec quel profond attendrissement nous avons revu cette personne si intéressante. Elle nous avait priés de ne point lui parler de ses aventures, parce qu'elle ne peut supporter cet entretien; mais Adèle, en l'embrassant, a fondu en larmes, et toute la soirée la duchesse a seule fait les frais de la conversation, car nous ne pouvions que la regarder et penser à ses malheurs. Elle nous a fait promettre ce matin de passer encore demain toute la journée avec elle; ainsi, nous ne partirons que samedi après dîner. Je lui ai rendu son manuscrit, et Brunel m'apporte dans l'instant la copie que je vous destine et que je place à la suite de ce cahier de mon journal.

* * *

HISTOIRE DE LA DUCHESSE DE C***

Ecrite par elle-même[6]

Comment aurai-je la force de me rappeler avec détail des malheurs dont, pendant si longtemps, le seul souvenir excitait en moi de si terribles révolutions! Comment pourrai-je l'écrire, cette déplorable histoire? O mes filles, vous la lirez, elle pourra vous offrir d'utiles et de frappantes leçons; cette idée soutiendra mon courage.

Et toi, qu'un lien funeste, mais sacré, rendit l'arbitre de mon sort, toi, dont je vais à regret troubler la cendre et retracer les fureurs et les crimes, pardonne! Tes forfaits et mes malheurs ne sont que trop connus; s'ils étaient ignorés, j'aurais su respecter ta mémoire et m'imposer un silence éternel. Si cet écrit en renouvelle le souvenir, du moins n'y dissimulerai-je pas les imprudences et les fautes qui me précipitèrent dans ce gouffre de maux et m'attirèrent de si cruels châtiments.

Je naquis à Rome, unique héritière[7] d'une fortune immense et d'une des plus illustres maisons d'Italie; je reçus une éducation distinguée. Elevée par la meilleure des mères, chérie d'un père tendre et d'une famille dont j'étais la seule espérance, la fortune et la nature semblaient avoir tout fait pour moi. J'atteignis ma quinzième année sans avoir, jusqu'à cette époque, éprouvé un seul chagrin, sans avoir eu de maladie, sans avoir versé d'autres larmes que celles que l'attendrissement ou la joie font répandre; j'aimais à me rappeler le passé, je jouissais avec transport du présent, et je ne voyais dans l'avenir qu'un sort aussi brillant qu'heureux.

J'avais eu pour compagne de mon enfance une jeune personne, fille d'une amie de ma mère; je pris pour elle une amitié passionnée; elle était honnête, sensible, mais elle n'avait point d'expérience; elle ne pouvait ni me conseiller, ni me guider; cependant j'avais en elle une confiance sans bornes. Je chérissais, je respectais ma mère, mais je ne la regardais point comme mon amie, parce qu'elle m'en avait laissé prendre une autre; elle s'était même plu à former une liaison si dangereuse. Cette imprudence me coûta cher; elle fut la principale cause de tous mes malheurs.

Mon amie se maria, elle épousa le marquis de Venuzi, qu'elle aimait depuis un an; je savais ce secret, et cette confidence n'avait que trop exalté mon imagination et séduit mon cœur. Mon amie, deux jours après son mariage, partit pour la campagne; le marquis de Venuzi l'emmena dans une maison charmante, à trente milles de Rome. Ma mère fut de ce voyage, et me mena avec elle.

La marquise de Venuzi était plus âgée que moi de trois ans, elle paraissait également réfléchie et raisonnable; ainsi, quoiqu'elle ne fût que dans sa dix-neuvième année, ma mère nous laissa une entière liberté de nous voir seules à toute heure. Un soir la marquise, après souper, me proposa d'aller nous promener dans le parc; nous y fûmes tête à tête. Nous entrâmes dans un petit labyrinthe, et au détour d'une allée, nous vîmes très distinctement un jeune homme, assis sur un banc. Il se leva en nous apercevant, et la surprise qu'il témoigna en nous voyant, nous en causa une très grande. La lune donnait sur son visage; nous étions fort près de lui, et nous fûmes également frappées de la beauté de sa figure et de l'air de noblesse répandu sur toute sa personne. Après un moment de silence, comme il ne s'éloignait pas, la marquise lui demanda qui il était; il lui répondit avec autant de respect que de galanterie, mais il refusa de se nommer, et s'éloigna au même instant.

Fort étonnées de cette aventure, nous rentrâmes aussitôt, et nous la confiâmes au marquis de Venuzi; il sourit, et nous laissa pénétrer que ce jeune homme ne lui était pas inconnu. Et comme je lui montrais un vif désir d'en savoir davantage, il répondit: 'Tout ce que je puis vous dire, c'est que ce jeune homme est libre, qu'il est d'une naissance distinguée, que depuis longtemps il souhaitait passionnément de vous voir et que, s'il y consent, je vous dirai demain son nom.'

Le lendemain, je renouvelai mes questions, et je n'obtins que des réponses vagues. Le soir, lorsque ma mère fut couchée, je descendis chez mon amie, et je m'enfermai avec elle dans son cabinet. Nous parlions de l'aventure de la veille, quand tout à coup la porte s'ouvrit, et je vis entrer le marquis de Venuzi, tenant d'une main une lanterne sourde et conduisant de l'autre ce même jeune homme que j'avais tant d'envie de connaître. Je restai immobile de surprise. S'approchant de moi, le marquis me dit: 'Je vous présente mon prisonnier, auquel je crois,' continua-t-il en riant, 'qu'il ne me sera plus possible maintenant de rendre la liberté, puisqu'il a eu l'imprudence de vouloir vous voir une seconde fois.' A ces mots, je rougis et j'éprouvai le plus mortel embarras; malgré mon extrême jeunesse, je sentais confusément les conséquences d'une semblable aventure; je fus un moment tentée de sortir, d'aller trouver ma mère, de lui tout avouer, mais la curiosité me retint et me fit oublier mon devoir.

Prenant un air plus sérieux, le marquis nous dit qu'il allait nous confier un secret important: 'Je connais,' ajouta-t-il, 'votre discrétion à l'une et à l'autre, et je suis bien sûr que vous justifierez la confiance que vous savez inspirer.' Après ce préambule, le marquis me fit promettre un secret inviolable, et le jeune homme prenant la parole, nous apprit qu'il s'appelait le comte de Belmire; que son père, le marquis de Belmire, était frère du duc de C***, un des plus grands seigneurs de Naples; que ce dernier, l'aîné de sa maison, brouillé avec son frère, trouva le moyen de le perdre à la cour, et le persécuta avec tant d'acharnement qu'il le força de s'expatrier et d'aller s'établir en France, où le marquis de Belmire, au bout de quatre ans, eut une affaire malheureuse qui l'obligea à chercher encore une autre retraite; que le marquis de Venuzi, son ami intime, alors en France et sur le point de repasser en Italie, le décida à revenir secrètement aux environs de Rome, en lui offrant un asile dans sa maison de campagne; qu'il était caché depuis trois mois dans cette même maison que nous habitions; que le jeune comte de Belmire, ayant entendu parler de moi, n'avait pu résister au désir de me voir; qu'après m'avoir entrevue la nuit au clair de lune, il avait conjuré le marquis de Venuzi de lui procurer une entrevue à laquelle il attachait un si grand prix, et qu'enfin il partait le lendemain pour Venise avec son père.

Après avoir écouté ce récit, je me levai et, malgré les instances du marquis, je me retirai. Je remontai dans ma chambre, accablée de tristesse; je n'osais réfléchir à tout ce qui venait de se passer; je craignais d'interroger mon cœur et d'examiner ma conduite; je ne pouvais concevoir que j'eusse été capable d'écouter, à l'insu de ma mère, au milieu de la nuit, un jeune homme, un inconnu qui avait osé m'entretenir de sa passion; j'entrevoyais clairement que je devais me défier des conseils du marquis de Venuzi, et même que sa femme n'était pas en état de me guider; je frémissais du danger de ma situation. Un pressentiment affreux semblait m'avertir que j'allais perdre sans retour ma réputation, mon repos, enfin, tout le bonheur dont jusqu'alors j'avais joui. La marquise de Venuzi reprit bientôt sur moi son ascendant ordinaire; elle me parlait sans cesse du comte de Belmire. Ces dangereux entretiens achevèrent d'égarer ma raison, sans pouvoir cependant dissiper ma tristesse.

Nous restâmes trois mois à la campagne, au bout desquels nous retournâmes à Rome. Vers la fin de l'hiver, il y eut beaucoup de fêtes. Le marquis de Venuzi donna un bal masqué, et j'y fus avec ma mère. Sur les deux heures après minuit, la marquise me proposa d'aller changer d'habit dans sa chambre; nous sortîmes de la salle et, en traversant une petite galerie assez obscure, je remarquai qu'un masque nous suivait. Quelle fut ma surprise, lorsque ce masque s'approchant de moi et, tombant à mes genoux, nous fit reconnaître le comte de Belmire lui-même! Malgré mon saisissement et la joie secrète que j'éprouvais en le revoyant, mon premier mouvement fut de chercher à m'échapper; il me retint par ma robe, en me suppliant de lui accorder un moment d'entretien; il conjura la marquise de m'engager à l'écouter, elle s'unit à lui, et j'eus la faiblesse d'y consentir enfin.

Le comte me dit que l'affaire de son père était heureusement arrangée, que depuis six semaines il était à Naples, qu'il y avait revu le duc de C*** son frère, avec lequel il s'était sincèrement raccommodé. 'Mon père,' continua-t-il, 'part dans un mois pour la France; quelques intérêts relatifs à sa fortune l'y rappellent, mais il est absolument décidé à revenir dans sa patrie. Et moi, avant de le suivre dans ce dernier voyage, j'ai voulu savoir mon sort; je me suis échappé de Naples uniquement pour apprendre si les vœux que j'ose former ne sont point entièrement rejetés! Parlez, mademoiselle; si vous me haïssez, je vais vous dire un éternel adieu. Méprisé par vous, c'en est fait, je renonce à l'Italie; l'on ne m'y reverra jamais; parlez. Votre réponse me rappellera dans ma patrie, ou m'en exilera pour toujours.' Comme le comte prononçait ces dernières paroles, je ne pus retenir mes larmes; cette réponse ne

Fig. 5: 'Quelle fut ma surprise, lorsque ce masque s'approchant de moi, et tombant à mes genoux, nous fit reconnaître le comte de Belmire lui-même!' Gravure sur cuivre d'après le dessin intitulé *The Lover's Plea, The Princess of Palestrina and Count de Belmire at the Masquerade* (1788) de John Francis Rigaud (1742-1810). Illustration tirée d'une édition du roman de Genlis publiée en 1788 et réimprimée dans *Camille, ou Le Souterrain*, version plagiée de la nouvelle de Genlis publiée en 1844 sans nom d'auteur par Pierre Chaillot jeune à Avignon. (BnF)

fut que trop bien entendue. Le comte n'en demanda pas d'autres; il me répéta mille fois l'assurance d'un amour éternel; certain d'être aimé et de revenir à Rome dans six mois, fait pour prétendre à ma main, quoique sa fortune ne fût pas aussi considérable que la mienne, tout semblait justifier ses espérances; et cependant, malgré moi, mon cœur ne pouvait les partager.

Deux mois après cette entrevue, qui me ravit à jamais toute la tranquillité de ma vie, le duc de C*** vint à Rome, et je le vis à une conversation[8] chez l'ambassadeur de France. Quand on me le nomma, j'éprouvai une espèce de saisissement très extraordinaire, mais qui cependant pouvait venir de tout le mal que j'avais entendu dire de lui au marquis de Venuzi, qui, en me parlant de ses procédés avec le marquis de Belmire, m'avait dépeint le duc comme un homme d'un caractère également vindicatif et dissimulé. Le duc de C***, âgé alors de trente-six ans, était parfaitement beau; cependant on remarquait dans ses yeux et dans ses sourcils je ne sais quoi de sombre et de sinistre qui frappait au premier abord beaucoup plus que la noblesse et la régularité de sa figure; il avait un regard perçant, dur et farouche; et quand il voulait l'adoucir, il le rendait équivoque et faux; ses manières étaient en général dédaigneuses; et quoiqu'il ne manquât pas de politesse à certains égards, son ton était aussi tranchant qu'impérieux. Enorgueilli de sa naissance, de ses emplois, de sa fortune, de son crédit à la cour, et de ses succès auprès des femmes, il ne pensait pas que rien dût jamais s'opposer à ses volontés ou résister à ses désirs. Emporté, violent, corrompu par l'orgueil et par la prospérité, il ne savait ni vaincre ses passions, ni surmonter ses ressentiments; implacable par faiblesse et par vanité, il mettait sa gloire à ne pardonner jamais; il haïssait avec fureur et sacrifiait tout à l'affreux plaisir qu'il trouvait à se venger.

Tel était le duc de C***. Je me sentis pour lui une antipathie invincible dès la première fois que je le vis, et, pour mon malheur, je produisis sur lui une impression bien différente; il se fit présenter chez ma mère; et quinze jours après, mon père me déclara que le duc avait demandé ma main et que je devais me décider à l'épouser dans un mois. Mon père ajouta: 'J'ai donné ma parole sans vous demander votre consentement, car je n'ai pas douté que vous n'acceptassiez avec plaisir le plus grand parti de l'Italie, un homme qui vous adore, et dont le personnel est si agréable.'

Je reçus cette déclaration (qui me parut l'arrêt de ma mort) sans pouvoir proférer une seule parole; mon père m'aimait, mais il était absolu. D'ailleurs, que pouvais-je dire! Avais-je même la ressource de m'adresser à ma mère! De quel front avouer mes fautes! Comment oser lui déclarer enfin que j'avais disposé de mon cœur sans son aveu! Ce fut alors que je connus dans toute son étendue la fatale imprudence de ma conduite, et que je sentis que le plus grand malheur qui puisse arriver à une jeune personne, c'est de n'avoir pas toujours regardé sa mère comme sa confidente et sa véritable amie. Ne pouvant ni me plaindre, ni parler, renfermant au fond de mon âme et mes chagrins et mes regrets, j'évitai la marquise, dont je craignais les dangereux conseils. Je pensai que l'obéissance pouvait seule expier mes fautes. Je me soumis à ma destinée, et je sacrifiai mon bonheur au respect que je devais à la volonté de mes parents. J'épousai le duc de C***, et je partis presque aussitôt avec lui pour Naples.

En arrivant dans cette ville, en entrant dans le palais où je devais passer ma vie, séparée de ma mère, de mes amis, de ma famille, j'éprouvai un mouvement de désespoir dont je ne puis dépeindre l'amertume. Le duc, n'attribuant ma profonde tristesse qu'à mon affection pour mes parents, s'efforçait de m'en distraire par les protestations d'un sentiment qu'il n'était plus en mon pouvoir de partager. Je parus à la cour, et je m'aperçus bientôt que le duc était excessivement jaloux. Je m'en affligeai peu. J'aurais préféré la retraite au grand monde, mais la vanité du duc me retenait à la cour malgré mon goût et sa jalousie.

J'étais mariée depuis sept mois, lorsque j'appris que le marquis de Belmire était mort en France; qu'il avait nommé par son testament le duc de C*** tuteur de son fils, âgé seulement de dix-huit ans; et que ce dernier, en revenant en Italie, était tombé malade à Turin. Quinze jours après, le duc entrant dans ma chambre, me dit qu'il venait de recevoir des nouvelles de son neveu, dont la santé était rétablie. 'Il ne veut point venir à Naples,' ajouta le duc, 'et il vous écrit pour vous prier de m'engager à lui accorder la permission de voyager pendant deux ans; voici sa lettre.' A ces mots, le duc me donne une lettre sous un cachet volant; je la prends en tremblant, et je lis tout haut, d'une voix mal assurée, ce qui suit:

Madame,

Quoique je n'aie pas l'avantage d'être connu de vous, il me semble que je suis assez malheureux pour pouvoir espérer de vous inspirer quelque compassion! J'ai perdu le plus tendre, le meilleur des pères! La douleur, le désespoir, m'ont conduit sur le bord du tombeau! Des secours inhumains, des amis cruels, m'ont rappelé à la vie; mais quelle existence m'est rendue! J'ai perdu tout ce qui pouvait me la faire chérir. Pardonnez-moi, madame, de vous entretenir d'une douleur qui vous est étrangère, mon cœur en est si plein! Ah, daignerez-vous du moins m'excuser et me plaindre! Les dernières volontés de mon père me mettent dans l'entière dépendance de mon oncle, mais je ne puis obéir à l'ordre de revenir à Naples! Mon père y reçut le jour, il y vécut vingt ans. Tout m'y rappellerait des souvenirs déchirants! Non, je n'irai point! Je suis sûr, madame, que vous approuverez cette délicatesse, et que vous engagerez mon oncle à révoquer un ordre qu'il est au-dessus de mes forces d'exécuter. Obtenez-moi, madame, la permission de voyager, de fuir, de m'éloigner de Naples—enfin, la liberté de porter loin de l'Italie une douleur et des regrets que je conserverai jusqu'à mon dernier soupir.

> Je suis avec respect,
> Le comte de Belmire

Je ne puis donner une idée du trouble affreux et de l'effroi que j'éprouvai en lisant cette lettre: il me semblait qu'il était impossible de n'en pas pénétrer le double sens. D'ailleurs, le duc était le plus défiant et le plus soupçonneux de tous les hommes; cependant, ignorant que son neveu eût été à Rome, convaincu que je n'avais jamais pu le voir, il n'eut pas le plus léger soupçon de la vérité. Pour moi, ne pouvant plus renfermer au fond de mon cœur des sentiments qui le déchiraient, j'écrivis le lendemain à la marquise de Venuzi une lettre dans laquelle j'osais enfin me plaindre de mon sort et gémir sur la funeste passion dont je ne pouvais triompher. La marquise, dans sa réponse, me questionnait sur la conduite du duc. Je lui répondis avec franchise, et je ne lui cachai pas que je découvrais chaque jour, dans le duc, des défauts, des vices, et une certaine férocité de caractère qui ne justifiait que trop l'antipathie que j'avais pour lui. C'est ainsi que, par de nouvelles imprudences, j'achevais de creuser l'abîme entr'ouvert sous mes pas.

Vers ce temps, je jouis du bonheur de revoir mon père et ma mère. J'étais au moment d'accoucher; ils vinrent à Naples pour mes couches. Je donnai le jour à une fille; je demandai et j'obtins la permission de la nourrir. Cette douce occupation, tout le temps qu'elle dura, suspendit mes chagrins et me rendit insensible aux mauvais traitements du duc, qui, depuis longtemps, cessait de se contraindre et me laissait voir toute la violence et l'inégalité de son caractère.

Le lendemain du jour où j'eus sevré ma fille, le duc entra chez moi et me dit qu'il fallait partir dans l'instant pour une terre qu'il avait à douze lieues de Naples.[9] Ma fille était auprès de moi; je la pris dans mes bras, et, sans dire une seule parole, je me levai et je suivis le duc. Nous montâmes en voiture. Je tenais ma fille sur mes genoux; je la caressais. Le duc gardait le silence, et, pendant toute la route, il parut plongé dans la plus profonde rêverie.

En arrivant à son château, nous passâmes sur un pont-levis, le bruit des chaînes du pont me fit tressaillir. Dans ce moment, je regardai le duc. 'Qu'avez-vous,' me dit-il, 'l'aspect antique de ce château paraît vous surprendre? Quoi donc! Croyez-vous entrer dans une prison?' Il prononça ces paroles avec un sourire aussi forcé qu'amer, et je remarquai dans ses yeux une joie si cruelle, que j'en fus épouvantée. Voulant cacher mon effroi, je penchai ma tête sur celle de ma fille, et je ne pus retenir mes larmes. Ma fille les sentant couler sur son visage, se mit à crier. Ses cris me pénétrèrent jusqu'au fond de l'âme. Je la serrai contre mon sein avec le mouvement de tendresse le plus passionné, et mes sanglots redoublèrent.

Dans cet état, je descendis de voiture. Le duc arrachant, pour ainsi dire, ma fille de mes bras, la donna à un de ses gens, et saisissant une de mes mains, il me conduisit, ou plutôt m'entraîna vers le château. Il me fit monter un escalier au haut duquel nous trouvâmes une longue galerie. Le jour commençait à tomber. La galerie que nous traversions était excessivement vaste et sombre. Le duc marchait d'une vitesse extrême, lorsque, s'arrêtant tout à coup, il me dit: 'Vous tremblez; d'où peut venir cette frayeur? N'êtes-vous pas avec un époux que vous aimez, qui doit vous chérir?'

'O Ciel,' m'écriai-je. 'Que signifie cet air sombre, égaré, ce son de voix terrible!'

'Venez, venez,' reprit-il, 'nous allons achever cette explication.'

A ces mots, me portant presque dans ses bras, car je ne pouvais ni le suivre ni marcher, il me traîna hors de la galerie, et me conduisit dans une grande chambre à coucher. Je me jetai sur une chaise, et je donnai un libre cours à mes larmes. Il sortit et revint presque aussitôt, en tenant une lumière qu'il posa sur une table vis-à-vis de moi et auprès de laquelle il s'assit. Je n'osais le regarder, respirant à peine. Pénétrée de terreur, les yeux baissés, j'attendais, en tremblant, qu'il rompît le silence. Toutes mes fautes se retraçaient à la fois à ma mémoire. Je craignais confusément que le fatal secret de mon cœur n'eût été pénétré; ce cœur rempli d'une passion criminelle palpitait d'effroi et frémissait devant un juge irrité. O combien l'innocence m'eût donné de courage! Mais je me sentais coupable, et je n'avais pas la force de supporter des pressentiments affreux, causés surtout par mes remords.

Enfin, prenant la parole, le duc dit: 'C'est assez jouir du trouble secret de votre conscience; il est temps de porter au comble la confusion qui vous accable. Lisez ces lettres que j'ai copiées moi-même.' Alors il me donna un paquet de papiers, et voyant que j'hésitais à le prendre, il en tira une feuille, et lit tout haut. Dès les premiers mots, je reconnus une des lettres que j'avais écrites à la marquise de Venuzi, et dans laquelle je lui parlais sans déguisement et du sentiment qui remplissait mon âme et de mon invincible aversion pour le duc.

'Ah, je suis perdue!' m'écriai-je.

'Perfide,' reprit le duc, 'je n'ai pu faire votre bonheur! Je vous avais choisie, préférée. Je vous adorais, et vous me haïssiez, et vous vous trouviez infortunée. Je vous inspire *une invincible aversion!* Ah, je justifierai votre haine! Vous aurez désormais le droit de me haïr! Trahi, déshonoré par vous, croyez-vous que je puisse souffrir impunément tant d'outrages?'

'Arrêtez', interrompis-je, 'vous pouvez m'accuser, et me punir sans me calomnier. Je suis coupable en effet; mais si je n'ai pu triompher d'une passion malheureuse, du moins votre honneur et le mien sont sans tache, et je n'ai à me reprocher que les imprudents aveux que l'amitié sut m'arracher.'

'Parjure!' reprit le duc avec fureur, en reprenant une des lettres, 'écoutez votre condamnation.' Alors il lut la phrase suivante:

Cet objet, que rien ne peut arracher de mon cœur, hélas! Il est aussi à plaindre que je le suis moi-même! Ne sait-il pas à quel excès il est aimé! Ne sait-il pas à quel excès je me reproche un aveu qui me rend aujourd'hui si coupable et si malheureuse!

Je ne me rappelai que trop ce passage d'une de mes lettres. Je me rappelai parfaitement aussi que, dans aucune de mes lettres, non seulement je n'avais nommé le comte de Belmire, mais que même je n'avais parlé de lui que d'une manière si vague, qu'il était impossible de savoir par ces lettres dans quel temps ou à quelle époque la passion que j'avouais avait pris naissance. Le duc, violemment jaloux, dès le commencement de mon mariage, de deux hommes de la cour de Naples dont les sentiments pour moi avaient éclaté, ne doutait pas que l'un des deux ne fût l'objet que j'aimais. Cette supposition me rendait véritablement criminelle à ses yeux; car, d'après la phrase qu'il venait de me citer, il semblait prouvé que j'eusse avoué mes sentiments depuis mon mariage. Il fallait, pour me justifier, lui déclarer qu'en lui donnant ma main, mon cœur déjà n'était plus à moi. Mais je n'ignorais pas combien il méprisait les femmes, et combien il était susceptible de former les plus odieux soupçons. D'après cette connaissance, l'intérêt même de ma fille me fermait la bouche. Je n'avais quitté Rome que six semaines après mon mariage. Le duc, en apprenant que j'aimais avant de le connaître, n'était que trop capable de concevoir d'injurieuses défiances sur la naissance de sa fille. D'ailleurs, cet aveu pouvait aussi le conduire à pénétrer l'entière vérité. Il pouvait tout à coup se rappeler mille circonstances faites pour l'éclairer: la lettre que j'avais reçue de son neveu, mon trouble en la lisant, ma rougeur toutes les fois qu'il m'avait prononcé son nom. Il pouvait enfin découvrir les liaisons du marquis de Venuzi avec le père du comte de Belmire. En un mot, lui ôter la préoccupation qui fixait tous ses soupçons à Naples, c'était risquer un secret qu'il m'était impossible de trahir sans exposer ce que j'aimais à toutes les fureurs de son ressentiment, d'autant plus redoutable, que le comte de Belmire dépendait absolument de lui, puisqu'il n'avait pas dix-neuf ans, et que le duc était son oncle et son tuteur.

Toutes ces réflexions se présentèrent à la fois à mon imagination et me plongèrent dans le plus mortel embarras. Ne pouvant me justifier, je n'osais répondre. Le duc prit mon silence pour l'aveu tacite qui confirmait son déshonneur et ma honte. Alors son emportement n'eut plus de bornes. Il se leva, et s'approchant de moi avec un visage enflammé de fureur et des yeux étincelants: 'Ainsi donc,' dit-il, 'vous ne pouvez plus rien alléguer pour votre défense?'

'Hélas! répondis-je, êtes-vous en état de m'entendre? Je suis innocente, j'en atteste le ciel.'

'Vous, innocente!' interrompit-il. 'Osez-vous le soutenir? N'avez-vous pas écrit vous-même que votre amant *sait à quel excès il est aimé?'*

'Et cependant,' repris-je, en versant un torrent de larmes, 'je suis innocente, oui, je le suis!'

'O monstre d'imposture,' s'écria le duc, 'frémis de la vengeance prête à tomber sur toi!'

A ces mots, prononcés d'une voix menaçante et terrible, je crus entendre l'arrêt irrévocable de ma perte. Je me jetai à genoux et levant les bras au ciel, je m'écriai: 'O, Dieu! Dieu, mon seul recours, protégez-moi!'

'Levez-vous,' me dit alors le duc avec un ton plus calme. 'Asseyez-vous, et écoutez-moi.' J'obéis, en le regardant d'un air timide et suppliant. Il fut quelques instants sans parler. Ensuite, poussant un profond soupir, il dit: 'Vous devez comprendre à quel point je suis offensé! Vous, qui m'accusiez d'être *féroce* et *vindicatif*; vous, ingrate, à qui, jusqu'ici, je n'ai donné que des preuves d'amour, vous êtes en droit maintenant de craindre les effets d'un ressentiment si fondé. Cependant, il m'est possible encore de vous pardonner, mais votre sincérité seule peut désarmer ma colère. Songez-y. Désormais le moindre déguisement vous perdrait sans retour. Je puis me contenter d'une victime, mais il m'en faut une. Nommez-moi, sans hésiter, le vil séducteur qui vous a fait trahir et vos serments et vos devoirs les plus sacrés.'

'Non,' interrompis-je, 'non, je n'ai trahi ni mes serments, ni mes devoirs.'

'Je veux,' reprit le duc en élevant la voix, 'je veux savoir le nom de votre amant. Je vous ordonne de me le dire.'

Dans cet instant, je pressentis toute l'horreur de mon sort. Mais, avec mon danger, je sentis mes forces s'accroître; et préférant la mort même à la lâcheté qu'on me proposait, je répondis: 'S'il vous faut une victime, immolez celle que vous tenez en votre pouvoir. Faites tomber sur moi tout le poids de votre vengeance; car ce nom que vous me demandez, vous ne le saurez jamais.'

Etonné, confondu de ma hardiesse et de ma fermeté, le duc reste un moment immobile. Il ne trouve point d'expression qui puisse rendre sa rage et son indignation. Enfin, éclatant impétueusement, il dit: 'Malheureuse, je ne le saurai jamais! Ah! Je le vois, vous n'avez point d'idée des excès où je puis me porter. Vous ne me connaissez point encore!'

'Je m'attends à tout, et je suis assez infortunée pour savoir braver la mort.'

'La mort! Cesse de te flatter. Va, ce n'est pas la mort que je te destine. Depuis un an, je renferme au fond de mon âme et ma haine et ma fureur. Depuis un an, je médite le châtiment de ton infidélité, et tu crois que la vengeance d'un instant pourrait me satisfaire! Non, tu ne mourras point! Ta tombe en effet est préparée, mais c'est vivante qu'il y faudra descendre, et tu n'y trouveras point la mort que tu désires.' A cet affreux discours, je sentis tout mon sang se glacer; mes yeux se fermèrent, et je perdis entièrement l'usage de mes sens.

En reprenant ma connaissance, je me trouvai dans les bras de mes femmes. Je demandai avec empressement celle qui m'était le plus attachée, et la seule que j'eusse amenée de Rome. On me répondit qu'elle était restée à Naples. Je compris que c'était par les ordres du duc, qui sans doute avait craint un témoin importun et vigilant, et cette circonstance mit le comble à ma terreur.

Je passai la nuit entourée de mes femmes, gênée par leur présence, et redoutant de me trouver seule, n'osant ni me plaindre devant elles, ni les renvoyer, et souffrant intérieurement tous les tourments que peuvent causer le repentir, l'effroi et l'attente d'une affreuse catastrophe. Sur les six heures du matin, je demandai qu'on me conduisît dans l'appartement de ma fille. Elle dormait encore; je renvoyai ses femmes, et je m'assis auprès de son berceau. Sa vue, loin d'adoucir mes peines, les accrut encore.

'Hélas, chère enfant,' disais-je, 'tu dors paisiblement. Tu goûtes les douceurs du repos; tu ne peux ni sentir, ni partager les chagrins déchirants de ta malheureuse mère! Je te vois peut-être pour la dernière fois. O, reçois mes plus tendres bénédictions! O Dieu,' poursuivis-je en me jetant à genoux, 'je me résigne à mon affreuse destinée, mais que ma fille soit heureuse! Qu'elle vive innocente et paisible! S'il est vrai qu'on ait la barbarie de me l'arracher, grand Dieu, protégez-la, tenez-lui lieu de sa mère!' A ces mots, des sanglots redoublés me coupèrent la parole. Dans cet instant, la porte de la chambre s'ouvrit brusquement, et le duc parut. Je frémis en le voyant, et mes larmes s'arrêtèrent. Je me levai, mais ne pouvant me tenir sur mes jambes, je retombai dans le fauteuil.

'Eh bien,' dit le duc, 'la réflexion vous a-t-elle rendue plus raisonnable? Sentez-vous enfin tout ce que vous risquez en résistant à mes volontés?' Un profond soupir fut toute ma réponse. 'Ce nom que je vous ai demandé,' reprit-il, 'êtes-vous encore décidée à ne jamais me le dire?' Je levai les yeux au ciel, et je continuai toujours à garder le silence. 'Je veux une réponse positive,' dit le duc, '*me le nommerez-vous ou non?*'

'Je ne le puis,' répondis-je.

'Ah,' s'écria le duc, 'c'est ta sentence que tu prononces! Regarde cet enfant, et dis-lui un éternel adieu.'

'Non,' interrompis-je, 'vous n'aurez point la barbarie de m'en séparer. Ah, laissez-moi ma fille! Que du moins je puisse la voir quelquefois, et je supporterai sans murmure tout ce que votre haine voudra m'imposer. Eh, quoi donc! Votre cœur est-il en effet inaccessible à la pitié? Ah, s'il était vrai, quel que soit le sort que vous me prépariez, vous seriez encore plus à plaindre que moi!

The Duchess of C___

Fig. 6: Le duc s'emparant de l'enfant de la duchesse. Frontispice de la traduction anglaise de la nouvelle de Genlis, *The Affecting History of the Duchess of C.*, publiée à Londres par S. Bailey vers 1800. Artiste inconnu. (Copyright Chawton House Library)

Mais je ne puis le croire. Non, vous ne m'arracherez point ma fille pour toujours!' Dans ce moment, ma fille se réveilla, elle ouvrit les yeux, et, regardant son père, elle sourit, et leva vers lui ses deux petites mains presque jointes. 'Hélas,' dis-je, 'elle semble vous implorer pour moi. O ma fille, ma chère fille, que ne sais-tu parler, tu fléchirais ton père!'

Alors je voulus la prendre dans mes bras; mais le duc la saisissant, dit: 'Laissez-la, elle n'est plus à vous.'

'Ah,' m'écriai-je, 'arrachez-moi la vie ou rendez-moi ma fille! Faut-il, pour vous fléchir, tomber à vos genoux? Vous m'y voyez.' En disant ces paroles, je me précipitai à ses pieds, je les arrosai de larmes, j'embrassai ses genoux. Rien ne coûtait à mon orgueil; je demandais ma fille. Le barbare parut jouir de mon abaissement. Il me contempla un instant dans cette situation; ensuite il me repoussa avec fureur, et fit quelques pas vers la porte. Je me traînai toujours sur mes genoux, en criant: 'Ma fille, ma fille!' L'enfant, d'un air effrayé, fit un cri plaintif en me tendant les bras. Elle semblait me dire un douloureux adieu. Hélas! Au même instant, je la perdis de vue. Le duc sortit impétueusement de la chambre, et me laissa au comble du désespoir.

Au bout d'un moment, il revint et me força d'aller dans mon appartement. Alors, composant son visage, il dit: 'Vous me croyez un cœur impitoyable, et cependant ….' Il s'arrêta et baissa les yeux—ces yeux dont le regard sinistre et farouche aurait pu découvrir son horrible artifice. J'étais en son pouvoir; j'ignorais ses affreux projets; je ne lui voyais aucun intérêt à dissimuler; je n'avais que dix-huit ans. Je crus qu'en effet il se reprochait l'excès de sa cruauté, et que du moins il adoucirait la vengeance qu'il avait méditée d'abord. Un rayon d'espoir vint ranimer mon cœur. Je reparlai de ma fille. Le duc m'écouta d'un air sombre, mais sans témoigner de colère. Il feignit même d'éprouver un attendrissement qu'il voulait cacher. Il me fit entendre que sa passion pour moi causait seule les fureurs auxquelles il s'était livré, et il finit par me dire que, si je prenais soin de ma santé, je pourrais revoir ma fille. Une espérance si chère me fit oublier tout ce que j'avais souffert. Voyant le duc moins cruel, je me trouvai plus coupable. Je sentis qu'en effet il devait me haïr, et que, d'après mes lettres, il pouvait me croire véritablement criminelle. Enfin, j'excusai ses fureurs, et je fus profondément touchée de la compassion qu'il me laissait entrevoir. Et tandis que le repentir le plus sincère faisait couler mes larmes, le cruel auteur de mes maux s'applaudissait en secret du succès de ses noirs artifices, et préparait tout pour ma perte.

Cependant une fièvre assez considérable, causée par des chagrins si violents, me força de me mettre au lit. Le duc parut alors éprouver la plus vive inquiétude. Il dépêcha un courrier à Naples, et en fit venir deux médecins. Il ne quitta plus le chevet de mon lit. Il me donna, devant mes femmes, les plus grands témoignages de tendresse. Il me dit en particulier tout ce qui pouvait me persuader que sa passion l'emportait sur son ressentiment, et il m'assura positivement que je reverrais ma fille aussitôt que je serais sans fièvre. A cette promesse, j'oubliai tout ce qu'il m'avait fait souffrir. Je saisis une de ses mains, je la serrai dans les miennes, et j'arrosai des larmes de la reconnaissance cette main barbare qui devait, dans quelques heures, m'entraîner et me précipiter au fond d'un horrible cachot.

Les médecins assurèrent que ma maladie n'était point dangereuse, et pressés de retourner à Naples, ils partirent au bout de deux jours. Le matin même de leur départ, le duc affecta un redoublement d'inquiétude sur mon état; et quoique je n'eusse plus de fièvre, il me força de rester dans mon lit. Comme il avait obligé toutes mes femmes à me veiller les trois jours précédents, elles étaient accablées de lassitude. Il les envoya se reposer pour la journée entière, déclarant qu'il me garderait, avec un de ses valets de chambre et une vieille femme, concierge du château. Ces deux témoins n'étaient pas choisis sans dessein; il leur donna la préférence sur tous les autres, parce qu'il les connaissait pour être l'un et l'autre aussi crédules que bornés. Les rideaux de mon lit étaient tirés; je me croyais toujours gardée par mes femmes, lorsqu'à midi je m'aperçus que je n'avais dans ma chambre que les deux personnes dont je viens de parler. J'en témoignai ma surprise. Le duc s'approcha de mon lit, en me disant que je n'en serais pas moins bien servie, et qu'il ne me quitterait point.

'Eh pourquoi donc?' repris-je avec émotion. 'Je ne suis pas plus mal.'

A cette question, pour toute réponse, il me pria de ne point parler et de tâcher de me tranquilliser. Il s'assit au chevet de mon lit. Sans savoir pourquoi, je me sentis troublée, et mes yeux se remplirent de pleurs. Le duc parut inquiet, agité, et je remarquai sur son visage une altération extraordinaire.

Vers les trois heures après midi, il me demanda mon bras. Je le lui donnai en tremblant. Il me tâta le pouls; et, tout à coup, il fut vers mes deux gardes, et tout haut il dit au valet de chambre de courir aux écuries pour envoyer un courrier à Naples chercher un médecin et à la vieille femme d'aller chercher le chapelain et de l'amener. Après avoir donné ces ordres, il ajouta d'un ton désespéré: 'Elle se meurt! Elle se meurt!' Qu'on se figure, s'il est possible, l'excès de ma surprise et de mon effroi. Mon premier mouvement fut de me lever, de fuir; mais je retombai sans force sur mon lit, avec un battement de cœur qui m'ôtait la respiration et une terreur qui me glaçait et me rendait immobile.

Mes deux gardes, après avoir reçu chacun une commission qui les éloignait au moins pour trois quarts d'heure, partent, et je me trouve seule avec le duc. Alors il s'approche de moi, et, me présentant une tasse, dit d'une voix étouffée: 'Tenez. Prenez cette boisson.' A ces paroles, mes cheveux se dressèrent sur ma tête, et une sueur froide inonda mon visage. Je crus être aux derniers instants de ma vie, car je ne doutais point qu'il ne m'offrît du poison. 'Buvez donc,' reprit-il.

'Ah!' répondis-je. 'Que me donnez-vous?'

'Ce qu'il faut que vous preniez.'

'Laissez-moi donc le temps d'implorer la miséricorde éternelle.'

'Qu'osez-vous soupçonner? M'accusez-vous d'un crime?'

'Hélas! J'accuse surtout mon imprudence et ma destinée! O mon Dieu,' continuai-je en joignant les mains, 'pardonne-moi, pardonne à mon persécuteur. Console ma mère, mon père, et protège mon enfant!' Après cette courte prière, je sentis tout mon courage se ranimer. J'osai croire que ma résignation me rendait digne de paraître devant Dieu. Je jetai sur le duc un œil assuré. Il était pâle, interdit et tremblant; il balbutia quelques mots entrecoupés, et d'une main soulevant ma tête, de l'autre il approcha le vase de mes lèvres. Alors, sans résistance, je bus toute la liqueur qu'il me présentait, et, croyant avoir reçu la mort, je retombai sur mon oreiller, ayant fait entièrement le sacrifice de ma vie.

Quelques minutes après, mes yeux appesantis se fermèrent. Un engourdissement total m'ôta jusqu'à la faculté de parler et de penser, et je tombai dans le sommeil léthargique le plus profond. Au bout d'une demi-heure, la vieille femme et le valet de chambre revinrent. Le duc, les cheveux en désordre, le visage baigné de larmes, courut au-devant d'eux, et leur dit que je venais d'expirer. Il les ramena dans ma chambre, afin, ajouta-t-il, d'acquérir la confirmation de son malheur, ou de me secourir si j'avais encore quelques restes de vie. Il s'approcha de mon lit. Ayant eu le soin d'en fermer les rideaux et de rendre ma chambre extrêmement obscure, il feignit de me donner tous les secours imaginables. Ensuite il parut se livrer au plus violent désespoir.

Le chapelain arriva, il lui ordonna de réciter les prières pour les morts. Pendant ce temps, mes femmes réveillées et tous les domestiques accoururent. Le duc était à genoux à mon chevet; mes deux gardes contaient à toute la maison rassemblée tout ce qu'on avait tenté pour essayer de me rappeler à la vie. Après ce récit, le duc entrouvrit un instant mes rideaux, on me vit pâle et sans mouvement, et personne ne douta de ma mort. Le duc fit retirer tout le monde dans la chambre prochaine. Il resta dans la mienne et garda avec lui le chapelain, vieillard âgé de quatre-vingt ans; il fit continuer les prières des morts jusqu'à minuit; alors il envoya tous ses gens se reposer. Il déclara qu'il ne me ferait ensevelir que le lendemain au soir, et que ne pouvant s'arracher d'auprès de moi, il y passerait le reste de la nuit. Il ferma toutes les portes de mon appartement. Il établit le chapelain et mes deux gardes dans une antichambre séparée de ma chambre par trois grandes pièces. Il leur dit qu'il ne me quitterait qu'à sept heures du matin, et qu'il voulait rester seul chez moi, afin, ajouta-t-il, de n'être distrait ni dans sa douleur ni dans ses prières.

Toute la maison, excédée de fatigue et de veilles, profita avec empressement de la permission d'aller se reposer. Tout le monde dormait profondément à quatre heures après minuit, lorsque, sortant par degrés de ma léthargie, je me réveillai. En ouvrant les yeux, et reprenant l'usage de mes sens, j'aperçus le duc debout à côté de mon lit. Sa vue me fit tressaillir, quoique cependant je n'eusse aucun souvenir de tout ce qui m'était arrivé. Ensuite, le regardant fixement, je me rappelai confusément qu'il était irrité contre moi. J'éprouvai un mouvement de frayeur. Je détournai la tête, et voulant me recueillir, afin de rappeler les idées du passé, mille images vagues et fantastiques s'offrirent à mon imagination, et je tombai dans une rêverie stupide qui fut suivie d'une espèce d'assoupissement. Alors le duc me fit respirer une eau spiritueuse et avaler quelques gouttes d'une liqueur qui me ranima entièrement. Je me soulevai, je regardai autour de moi avec surprise. Mes idées se débrouillant peu à peu, je me rappelai que j'avais cru prendre du poison, et je doutais presque de mon existence.

'O, quel miracle me rend à la vie!' m'écriai-je enfin.

'Vous n'avez éprouvé qu'une vaine terreur,' dit le duc, 'calmez-vous, et bannissez ces craintes outrageantes.' Je n'osai répondre, j'entrouvris mon rideau, je regardai dans la chambre, et voyant que j'étais seule avec le duc, je fus d'autant plus effrayée, que j'avais repris toute ma connaissance.

'Pourquoi donc', lui demandai-je, 'me veillez-vous?'

'Vous le saurez,' répondit-il. 'Levez-vous maintenant.' A ces mots, il me présente une robe, il m'aide à la passer, et me soutenant dans ses bras, il me conduit ou plutôt me porte dans un fauteuil. Comme il me vit également faible et tremblante, il me fit prendre encore de la liqueur dont j'avais déjà bu; et après un moment de silence, il me dit: 'Je ne vous cacherai rien à présent: La boisson que vous prîtes hier était un breuvage assoupissant.'

'Et pourquoi?'

'Ecoutez-moi sans m'interrompre. Vous m'avez trahi, déshonoré; je vous offrais votre pardon, vous l'avez refusé. Convaincue d'infidélité, vous nourrissez toujours au fond de l'âme une passion criminelle. Ma colère et mes menaces n'ont pu vous décider à me déclarer le nom de votre amant. Vous avez cru peut-être que ma considération pour votre famille m'empêcherait de vous arracher votre fille et de vous priver de la liberté. Vous pensiez sans doute (car il n'est point de crime dont votre haine ne me juge capable), vous pensiez que le seul moyen que j'eusse de me venger de vous, était d'attenter en secret à votre vie, et cette *invincible aversion* que vous avez pour moi vous déterminait facilement à mourir! Mais sachez enfin que vous vivrez, et que vous serez pour jamais soustraite à vos parents, à vos amis, à vos domestiques, au monde entier!'

'O Ciel!' m'écriai-je. 'Et croyez-vous, cruel, que je ne sois redemandée ni par un père tendre ni par la meilleure des mères?'

'Ils recevront demain,' reprit le duc, 'la fausse nouvelle de votre mort.'

'Grand Dieu! Et comment pourrez-vous?'

'J'ai déjà annoncé votre mort dans ce château. Durant votre assoupissement, tous mes gens vous ont vue.'

'Hélas!' interrompis-je en fondant en larmes. 'Je n'existe donc plus que pour vous? Ah, je vois à présent toute l'horreur de ma destinée!'

'Vous ne savez pas tout encore,' dit le duc. 'Apprenez que j'ai dans ce château de vastes souterrains inconnus à tout le monde, où le jour ni pénétra jamais.'

'O Dieu!' m'écriai-je. 'C'en est donc fait, je suis perdue sans ressource!'

'Non," reprit le duc, 'votre sort est encore dans vos mains; je puis aller dans un moment réveiller mes gens, et déclarer que vous n'étiez qu'en léthargie. Je n'ai point fait partir ma lettre pour votre père, je puis encore vous faire reparaître et vous pardonner. Je n'exige de vous qu'un mot, un seul mot; il me faut une victime, je vous l'ai dit. Nommez-moi votre amant, et vous rentrez dans tous vos droits, et je vous rends au monde, à la vie!'

'Que me proposez-vous,' interrompis-je? 'De livrer à votre ressentiment un objet, je vous le répète, qui ne vous a point outragé? Ah, je serais indigne de vivre si j'avais la lâcheté d'y consentir!'

'Pensez-y bien,' dit le duc, en me lançant un affreux regard. 'Encore un refus, et je vous traîne dans la demeure ténébreuse d'où rien ne pourra vous arracher. Il faut que demain votre père, votre mère se désespèrent de votre perte, ou se réjouissent de votre convalescence. Demain vous reverrez votre fille et le jour, ou vous serez à jamais privée de la lumière, gémissante au fond d'un horrible cachot. Demain, enfin, l'on vous verra dans ce château, jouissant d'une santé parfaite, ou l'on fera vos funérailles. Songez-y; ce moment passé, plus d'espoir de pardon; en vain votre repentir l'implorerait, je n'aurais plus la possibilité de vous l'accorder.

A ce discours pressant et terrible, je me lève éperdue. Je tourne avec effroi mes yeux du côté de la porte et, poussant un cri lamentable, 'Eh quoi, m'écriai-je, 'suis-je donc abandonnée de l'univers entier! Ma fille! Je vivrais, et je ne la reverrais plus! Mon père, ma mère, demain vous pleureriez ma mort! Ma fille! Ah, laissez-moi voir ma fille encore une fois!'

'Dites un mot,' répondit le duc, 'et dans un quart d'heure votre fille sera dans vos bras.' A ces mots, je sentis mon cœur se déchirer. Je gardai le silence un moment. Je pensai que le comte de Belmire était absent, qu'il ne devait revenir que dans un an; que, pendant cet espace, il me serait facile de le faire prévenir; que d'ailleurs, un aveu naïf ferait connaître mon innocence; mais tout à coup, songeant à la cruauté de mon persécuteur, je rejetai promptement cette légère tentation. Qui m'assurait qu'un tel aveu pût me rendre et ma fille et ma liberté? Ne devais-je pas croire au contraire que le duc, certain de ma haine, ne renoncerait point à la vengeance qu'il avait méditée, ou que du moins il se contenterait d'en adoucir l'inhumaine rigueur? Et dans ce doute, pouvais-je être tentée de livrer à sa fureur l'objet que j'aimais? Toutes ces réflexions se présentèrent à mon esprit avec une extrême rapidité.

Le duc crut que je balançais. Il me pressa de nouveau, en ajoutant: 'Le jour bientôt va paraître, il est temps de vous décider; je vais réveiller mes gens, et leur annoncer que vous vivez, ou je vais vous conduire dans votre tombe. Parlez! Voulez-vous me nommer l'auteur de vos maux et des miens?'

A cette question, je levai les yeux au ciel, et rassemblant toutes mes forces: 'Je ne le puis,' répondis-je.

'Que dites-vous, malheureuse!' interrompit le duc.

'Non,' repris-je, 'perdez cette espérance, je ne le nommerai jamais.'

'Perfide,' s'écria le duc, 'ainsi donc tu préfères ton amant à ta fille, à la liberté, à la vie! A l'univers! Tremble maintenant: l'instant de la vengeance est arrivé enfin!'

Comme il achevait ces mots, il voulut me saisir par le bras. Pénétrée d'épouvante et d'horreur, je m'échappai, je courus à l'autre bout de la chambre, et passant mes deux bras autour d'une des colonnes de mon lit, je m'y attachai fortement. En faisant ce mouvement, ma coiffure de nuit se détacha, et mes cheveux tombèrent sur mes épaules. Le duc, qui venait à moi, s'arrêta; il parut surpris, frappé, et me regarda un instant en silence. Ensuite, m'arrachant de la colonne, il me porta vis-à-vis d'une glace.

'Infortunée,' dit-il, 'contemple pour la dernière fois cette beauté que d'affreuses ténèbres vont cacher pour toujours! Lève les yeux, regarde-toi. Ne sois pas plus barbare que je ne le suis moi-même. Songe à ta jeunesse, à tes charmes, prends pitié de ton sort. Tu pourrais encore le changer!'

Alors je ne pus me défendre de jeter sur la glace un regard craintif et languissant. Je fermai les yeux aussitôt, et je sentis quelques larmes s'échapper à travers mes paupières.

'Eh bien,' reprit le duc, 'êtes-vous toujours inébranlable?'

'Ah!' répondis-je, 'ne m'avez-vous pas vainement offert de revoir ma fille!'

A peine eus-je prononcé ces paroles, que le duc, transporté de rage, m'enleva dans ses bras, et m'emporta hors de la chambre. Je n'opposai nulle résistance; l'excès de ma terreur me rendait immobile et muette. Après avoir traversé deux ou trois pièces, il me fit descendre un petit escalier dérobé, et je me trouvai dans une grande cour, au bout de laquelle était une porte que le duc ouvrit. Nous sortîmes, et je vis que nous étions dans le jardin.

Dans cet instant, le duc s'apercevant que le jour paraissait: 'Cette aurore,' dit-il, 'est la dernière que tes yeux verront jamais!'

Je me jetai à genoux, et levant la tête vers le ciel: 'O Dieu,' m'écriai-je, 'Dieu qui connaissez mon innocence, souffrirez-vous que je sois enterrée vivante, et privée pour jamais de la clarté des cieux?' Comme je disais ces mots, le duc m'entraîna vers un rocher à vingt pas de nous, et posant une clef derrière une énorme pierre, tout à coup une espèce de trappe s'abattit. Je frémis.

Le duc s'arrêta: 'Ce moment vous reste encore,' me dit-il. 'Voici votre tombe, elle n'est qu'entr'ouverte. Repentez-vous enfin, montrez-moi vos remords par un aveu sincère, et je suis prêt à vous pardonner. Vous croyez peut-être,' continua-t-il, 'qu'à l'instant de consommer ma juste vengeance, j'en crains les suites pour moi-même, mais je la médite depuis longtemps; tout est prévu, et rien ne peut m'arrêter.' Alors il entra dans l'affreux détail de toutes les précautions qu'il avait prises; il m'apprit qu'il avait fait faire une figure de cire pâle et livide qu'il placerait dans mon lit, et que, sous le prétexte de vouloir remplir un acte de piété, il l'ensevelirait, avec l'aide de la vieille femme dont j'ai déjà parlé, sans être obligé de mettre cette femme dans sa confidence, qui ne serait que spectatrice et témoin de cette action. 'Enfin,' ajouta-t-il, 'acceptez-vous le pardon que je daigne vous offrir encore pour la dernière fois? Parlez, sacrifiez votre amant à mon ressentiment, apprenez-moi son nom, ou renoncez pour jamais à la liberté, au monde, à la lumière.'

A ces mots, je tendis les bras vers le soleil naissant, comme pour lui dire un éternel adieu. Le ciel, chargé de nuages brillants et majestueux, offrait l'aspect le plus imposant. Cette contemplation éleva mon âme, et me rendit tout mon courage. Je jetai avec mépris mes regards sur la terre, et me tournant vers le duc: 'Prenez votre victime,' lui dis je d'un ton ferme. Au même instant il m'entraîne. Mon cœur palpite avec violence, je tourne la tête pour voir encore une fois le jour que j'abandonne pour jamais. Nous descendons dans une obscure caverne. Mes jambes tremblantes ne peuvent me soutenir; agitée par d'affreuses convulsions, je me débats dans les bras de mon cruel persécuteur, et je tombe à ses pieds sans mouvement et sans connaissance.

J'ignore combien de temps je restai dans cet état. Hélas, je ne devais revenir à la vie que pour abhorrer une si funeste existence! Comment dépeindre l'horreur dont je fus saisie, lorsqu'en ouvrant les yeux, je me trouvai seule dans ces vastes souterrains, environnée d'épaisses ténèbres, et couchée sur des nattes de paille! Je pousse un cri plaintif, et du fond de la caverne, l'écho, en le répétant, me fait tressaillir et redouble encore l'épouvante et la terreur qui m'oppressent! 'O Dieu,' m'écriai-je, 'voilà donc désormais la seule voix qui me répondra, le seul son que j'entendrai!' Cette idée me fit répandre un déluge de larmes.

Dans ce moment, j'entendis ouvrir la porte de ma prison, et le duc parut, une lanterne à la main. Il posa à côté de moi une cruche remplie d'eau et un pain: 'Voici,' dit-il, 'quelle sera désormais votre nourriture. Vous la trouverez chaque jour dans le tour que vous voyez vis-à-vis de vous; je vous l'apporterai moi-même, je la mettrai dans ce tour,[10] et je ne rentrerai plus dans cet affreux cachot.'[11]

A ces mots, je regardai autour de moi. Je vis une caverne immense dont l'œil ne pouvait embrasser toute l'étendue. La partie que j'occupais était tapissée de grosses nattes de paille, afin de préserver du froid et de l'humidité; car la barbarie qui me précipita dans cette horrible demeure avait pris aussi toutes les précautions qui pouvaient m'y conserver la vie. Après avoir considéré, en frémissant, tout ce qui m'entourait, je me retournai vers mon cruel geôlier; et faisant éclater enfin une haine si longtemps cachée et si fondée dans ce moment, j'osai lui reprocher l'excès de sa barbarie, et lui peindre toute l'horreur et tout le mépris qu'il m'inspirait. Il m'écouta quelque temps avec une fureur concentrée; ensuite, ne pouvant plus se contenir, il se livra à l'emportement le plus terrible, et tout à coup il me quitta brusquement.

Depuis ce jour, il n'entra plus dans ma prison. Lorsqu'il venait m'apporter ma nourriture, il frappait au tour jusqu'à ce que j'eusse répondu, et il s'en allait sans proférer une seule parole. Je me repentis bientôt d'avoir, par mes reproches, augmenté encore, s'il était possible, sa haine et son ressentiment. Je me ressouvins qu'il était le père de ma fille, que cet enfant si cher était entre ses mains. D'ailleurs, malgré l'horreur de ma situation, l'espérance n'était point encore absolument anéantie dans mon cœur; plus j'y réfléchissais, moins il me semblait vraisemblable qu'il eût en effet le projet de me retenir à jamais dans cette affreuse captivité. Je me flattais même qu'il n'avait annoncé ma prétendue mort ni dans sa maison ni à ma famille, qu'il avait trouvé quelque autre moyen de me soustraire à leurs recherches, et qu'il s'était réservé la possibilité de me faire reparaître quand il le voudrait. Comment pouvais-je imaginer enfin qu'il eût pu s'imposer à lui-même la pénible nécessité de m'apporter tous les deux jours les choses nécessaires à la vie, et par conséquent qu'il se fût réduit au triste esclavage de ne pas s'absenter de son château plus de deux ou trois jours, puisqu'il était mon seul geôlier, et qu'il n'avait mis personne dans sa confidence? Hélas, je ne croyais pas que la haine, pour se satisfaire, fût capable de s'imposer des chaînes que l'amour le plus passionné porterait à regret! D'après mes réflexions, je parvins à me persuader qu'il mettrait un terme à sa vengeance. Remplie de cette idée, toutes les fois qu'il frappait au tour, je lui parlais; et quoiqu'il ne me répondît point, j'implorais sa compassion, et je l'assurais de mon innocence.

Comme j'étais absolument privée de la lumière, je ne puis dire combien de mois, combien de temps je conservai l'espérance, mais enfin je la perdis. Alors la raison m'abandonnant entièrement, j'accusai la providence, je murmurai contre ses décrets éternels; mon âme abattue, flétrie par la douleur, perdit sa force et ses principes, et je tombai dans le plus sombre et le plus funeste désespoir. J'osai croire que l'excès de mon malheur me donnait le droit de disposer de ma vie, comme si l'on pouvait rompre un lien sacré, parce qu'il cesse d'être agréable! Décidée à mourir, je fus près de deux jours sans prendre de nourriture et sans l'aller chercher au tour. En vain le duc frappait et m'appelait, je m'obstinais à ne lui pas répondre; enfin, il entra dans ma prison. Quand il parut, sa lanterne à la main, malgré l'horreur que m'inspirait sa présence, je sentis un mouvement de joie en revoyant de la lumière, mais je ne lui parlai point. Il m'offrit d'adoucir ma captivité, de me donner de la lumière, des livres, une meilleure nourriture, si je voulais enfin lui dire ce nom si souvent demandé.

A cette proposition, je le regardai fixement avec le plus profond mépris: 'Maintenant,' lui dis-je, 'que vous avez rompu tous les liens funestes qui nous unissaient, mon cœur est libre; il se livre sans remords aux sentiments qu'il a jadis vainement combattus. Cet objet, dont vous ne me demandez le nom que pour l'immoler à votre ressentiment, je l'aime plus que jamais; mon dernier soupir sera pour lui. Jugez à présent si je vous le dénoncerai!'

'Ainsi donc,' reprit le duc, 'tout sentiment de religion est éteint dans votre âme? Vous nourrissez au fond du cœur une flamme adultère, et vous renoncez à la vie?'

'Barbare,' interrompis-je, 'suis-je encore votre femme? Osez-vous le dire, vous qui m'avez précipitée dans cet abîme, vous qui portez mon deuil? Il est vrai, je n'ai plus le courage de supporter la vie, mais ce Dieu qui nous entend et qui nous juge ne punira que vous du désespoir où vous me réduisez. Dans l'état où je suis, si je commets un crime, vous seul en serez responsable. Nul être vivant ne peut entendre mes plaintes et mes cris! Mais quel antre profond, quelles épaisses voûtes peuvent dérober à l'Eternel les gémissements du faible injustement opprimé? Tremblez, il nous voit, il m'excuse, il est prêt à me pardonner! Et son bras vengeur est levé sur vous.'

A ces mots, le duc frémit et me regarda d'un air égaré. Je jouis un moment du plaisir d'avoir rempli d'épouvante et de remords son âme aussi faible que féroce. Pâle, interdit, troublé, les yeux baissés, il garda quelques instants un farouche silence. Enfin, prenant la parole, il dit: 'N'imputez qu'à vous-même les maux dont vous gémissez. Vous étiez criminelle, j'en ai les preuves certaines; vous n'avez pu les désavouer, et cependant je ne vous ai puni qu'après vous avoir cent fois offert votre grâce. Je vous propose encore d'adoucir votre châtiment, et vous me refusez! Oui, si vous l'eussiez voulu, malgré votre infidélité, malgré votre haine pour moi, vous seriez encore dans mon palais, vous y verriez votre fille!'

'O ma fille,' interrompis-je. 'Hélas! Vit-elle encore? Qu'est-elle devenue?'

'Elle est avec votre mère.'

'Elle n'est plus dans vos mains, est-il bien vrai?'

Alors le duc, voyant que cette idée me ranimait, tira de sa poche une lettre de ma mère, et me permit de la lire. Cette lettre, que j'arrosai de larmes, était conçue dans ces termes:

Ma petite-fille est arrivée hier au soir. O, comment vous dépeindre tous les sentiments qui ont déchiré mon cœur en l'embrassant! Vous me la donnez, elle est à moi. Je sens que déjà je l'aime avec excès; elle pourra m'attacher à la vie, mais non me consoler! Hélas! Maintenant puis-je, sans éprouver d'affreuses inquiétudes, jouir du bonheur d'être mère encore? Après la perte que j'ai faite, est-il sur la terre un bien sur lequel j'ose compter? J'irai vous voir et vous mener votre fille l'été prochain, nous passerons deux mois avec vous. Puisque vous ne pouvez vous arracher du triste séjour que votre douleur vous rend si cher, j'aurai le courage d'aller vous y chercher. Je verrai ce superbe monument que votre amour élève à la mémoire d'un objet si digne de nos regrets! Peut-être trouverai-je auprès de vous le terme de mes peines! Eh quoi donc, serait-il possible qu'une mère, sans mourir, pût embrasser le tombeau de sa fille? Cependant je veux vivre; la religion me l'ordonne, la nature même m'en impose la loi; je vivrai pour l'enfant que vous daignez me confier. Ah, comment reconnaîtrai-je jamais un tel bienfait, un tel sacrifice! A quel point vous devez la chérir cette enfant! Hélas, elle a tous les traits de sa mère, elle en a tous les charmes; c'est me rendre ma fille dans son enfance! O trop flatteuse illusion! Malheureuse mère, tu n'as plus de fille, et l'excès de ta douleur ne peut te délivrer de la vie!

A peine eus-je achevé cette lettre, que me jetant à genoux, je m'écriai: 'Dieu, ma fille est dans les bras de ma mère! Cette tendre mère consent à vivre pour ma fille! O Dieu, je te bénis, tu n'as frappé que moi! Eh bien, je me soumets enfin à mon sort. Pardonne-moi des murmures insensés, rends heureux tout ce que j'aime, et prolonge à ton gré ma pénible existence.' En achevant ces mots, je retombai sur ma paille, car j'étais si faible, que je ne pouvais me soutenir. Le duc saisit cet instant pour m'offrir quelques aliments que je pris au moment même, ensuite il me quitta; et, depuis cette époque, je ne l'ai jamais revu.

Cependant, fidèle au vœu que j'avais formé, je pris soin de ma vie. L'idée que mes prières et ma résignation attireraient sur ma mère et sur ma fille toutes les bénédictions du ciel, cette idée consolante eut le pouvoir de ranimer et de soutenir mon courage. Le souvenir de mes fautes devint ma peine la plus réelle. 'Hélas,' disais-je, 'tous mes malheurs sont mon ouvrage; j'ai manqué de confiance en ma mère; en cessant de la consulter, je me suis égarée: fille ingrate et coupable! Le ciel, pour me punir, aveugla mes parents dans leur choix; l'époux qu'ils me donnèrent ne pouvait faire mon bonheur. Cependant, sans de nouvelles fautes, les sentiments de la nature auraient pu me rendre heureuse. Mais loin de chercher à triompher d'une passion criminelle, je la nourrissais en secret; et j'osai même, dans les lettres imprudentes qui m'ont perdue, en parler, en peindre toute la violence, et me plaindre en même temps de l'époux que j'outrageais!'

Ces réflexions me faisaient répandre des torrents de larmes. Cependant je trouvais une sorte de douceur à pleurer sur mes fautes; j'aimais à les sentir aussi vivement; en gémir, c'est les expier. Le remords d'un crime doit flétrir l'âme, mais le repentir d'une faiblesse involontaire n'a rien de déchirant ni d'amer; ce sentiment vertueux nous console de nos fautes, et nous raccommode avec nous-mêmes. Dénuée de tout, séparée de l'univers, mon cœur fait pour aimer se livra bientôt tout entier à la passion sublime qui pouvait seule me rendre la vie supportable. La religion me fit connaître et goûter toutes les consolations inépuisables qu'elle peut offrir; insensiblement elle bannit de mon âme cet amour infortuné, le plus grand de mes maux. Elle sut enfin me donner tout ce que la sagesse humaine et la seule philosophie ne pourraient procurer, le courage de supporter, sans désespoir et sans murmures, neuf ans de captivité dans un cachot impénétrable au jour!

J'avouerai cependant que j'éprouvai, dans les deux ou trois premières années, des peines dont le seul souvenir me fait frémir encore. Le temps où je supposai (d'après le calcul que j'en avais pu faire) que ma mère et ma fille devaient être arrivées dans ce même château où j'étais prisonnière, ce temps s'écoula pour moi d'une manière bien douloureuse et forme l'époque la plus cruelle de ma captivité. Mon cœur se déchirait en pensant que ma mère et ma fille étaient si près de moi, sans qu'il me fût possible de conserver l'espoir de les revoir jamais!

'O ma mère!' m'écriais-je, 'vous gémissez de ma mort, et j'existe! Et quelle main, grand Dieu, choisissez-vous pour essuyer vos larmes! C'est dans le sein de mon persécuteur, de mon bourreau, que vous les répandez! Ah, ce n'est point où l'on vous conduit qu'est ma tombe! Hélas, vous la foulerez aux pieds sans la connaître, vous verrez d'un œil sec ces rochers qui la cachent! Peut-être, dans le silence de la nuit, ne pouvant goûter les charmes du sommeil, viendrez-vous errer autour de ma caverne! Peut-être en cet instant même, êtes-vous assise près de cette trappe affreuse qui ne s'ouvrira plus pour moi! Ah, s'il est vrai, sans doute vous pensez à votre malheureuse fille, vous la pleurez, et vous ne pouvez entendre ses cris et sa voix qui vous appelle!

Ces idées déchirantes m'arrachaient l'âme et souvent troublaient ma raison. A ces cruels accès de douleur succédait une espèce d'anéantissement stupide, plus affreux peut-être que le désespoir même. Mais, à mesure que la piété se fortifia dans mon cœur, ces violents transports s'affaiblirent. Je trouvai dans la prière des consolations inexprimables; toutes les méditations, qui communément attristent les hommes, étaient pour moi les plus agréables sujets de rêverie. Avec quel plaisir je réfléchissais à la brièveté de la vie! Avec quelle sérénité j'envisageais la mort!

'L'être le plus heureux,' me disais-je, 'est-il jamais pleinement satisfait de ce bonheur faible et fragile qu'on peut goûter sur la terre? Il est moins occupé des biens qu'il possède que de ceux qu'il attend; au sein de sa félicité trompeuse, son imagination se plaît à s'égarer dans l'avenir. Mais qu'importe que sa destinée soit fortunée ou malheureuse! Qu'importe que ses espérances soient satisfaites ou trompées! Ne formera-t-il pas toujours de nouveaux désirs? Sait-il jouir du présent, sait-il s'en contenter? Pourquoi donc regretterais-je avec tant d'amertume tous les biens dont je suis privée, puisqu'enfin ils ne peuvent procurer le bonheur! Je dois, il est vrai, passer ma vie dans ces affreuses ténèbres; l'avenir n'offre à mon imagination glacée qu'une longue et triste nuit! Eh bien, ne songeons qu'au réveil! Oublions cette vie périssable, ne voyons que l'éternité! Méprisons cette douleur d'un moment à laquelle doit succéder une immortelle félicité! Portons tous nos désirs, toutes nos espérances vers le seul objet digne de fixer et de remplir le cœur humain!'

C'est ainsi que, par de salutaires réflexions, je m'élevais au-dessus de mon sort, et que je parvins enfin à m'y résigner entièrement. Rendue à la raison, à moi-même, non seulement mes peines s'adoucirent, mais je m'accoutumai aux ténèbres, à ma captivité; je me formai des occupations. Ma prison était spacieuse. Je me promenais une grande partie de la journée (ou de la nuit). Je faisais des vers que je récitais tout haut. J'avais une belle voix; je savais parfaitement la musique; je composais des espèces d'hymnes, et un de mes grands plaisirs était de les chanter et d'écouter l'écho qui me répondait. Mon sommeil devint paisible, des songes agréables me représentaient mon père, ma mère, ma fille; je voyais ces objets si chers toujours satisfaits et heureux. Quelquefois je me trouvais transportée dans de brillants palais ou dans de charmants jardins; je revoyais les cieux, des arbres, des fleurs. Enfin, ces douces illusions me rendaient tous les biens que j'avais perdus. Je me réveillais en soupirant, il est vrai, mais je m'endormais avec plaisir. Même éveillée, la joie cessa d'être étrangère à mon cœur. Mon imagination s'exalta. Sous les yeux de l'Etre suprême, j'osais me flatter que ma patience et ma résignation n'offraient point à ses regards un spectacle indigne de lui. Témoin de toutes mes actions il m'entendait, il parlait à mon cœur, il le ranimait, l'élevait jusqu'à lui, et je ne me trouvais plus seule dans ma caverne.

Après la privation des objets que j'aimais, la seule chose que je regrettasse encore malgré moi, c'était la lumière et la vue du ciel. Je ne comprenais plus comment on pouvait se livrer au désespoir dans le plus triste esclavage, si l'on jouissait d'une fenêtre donnant sur la campagne. Enfin, je m'accoutumai tellement à ma situation, que, loin de désirer la mort, je connus plus d'une fois que je la craignais encore. Souvent je manquai de nourriture. Le duc m'en apportait quelquefois pour trois ou quatre jours. Je comprenais alors qu'il allait faire un petit voyage; et quand ma provision approchait de sa fin, j'éprouvais de l'inquiétude. La mort de mon tyran entraînait la mienne, et cette cruelle idée me forçait à former des vœux pour sa santé. Il est vrai que je n'avais plus d'aversion pour lui. La religion m'avait fait aisément renoncer à la haine; ce faible effort pouvait-il me coûter! N'avais-je pas déjà triomphé de l'amour!

Je plaignais mon persécuteur. Je me représentais l'état horrible de son âme, ses fureurs, ses craintes, ses remords, et je ne me trouvais que trop vengée. Dans les premiers temps de ma captivité, je ne l'entendais jamais arriver sans être au moment de m'évanouir de terreur. Peu à peu, ces mouvements violents s'affaiblirent. Il m'inspirait toujours une sorte d'émotion mêlée de quelque effroi. Cependant, je désirais qu'il vînt, non seulement pour l'intérêt de ma vie, mais aussi parce qu'il interrompait le silence effrayant et profond de ma solitude. Il me faisait entendre du mouvement, du bruit. Enfin, il me procurait une espèce de distraction qui ne me fut jamais agréable, mais qui me devint nécessaire. Je ne puis exprimer combien était vif en moi ce désir singulier d'entendre quelque bruit. Quand le tonnerre était excessif, je l'entendais. Il m'est impossible de rendre ce que j'éprouvais alors; il me semblait que j'étais moins seule. J'écoutais ce bruit majestueux avec autant de ravissement que d'attention; et lorsqu'il cessait entièrement, je tombais dans l'abattement et dans la tristesse la plus profonde.

Telle fut à peu près ma situation pendant six ou sept ans. Durant cet espace, je ne fus véritablement affectée que du chagrin d'ignorer absolument tout ce qui était relatif à la destinée de ma mère et de ma fille. En vain, à travers mon tour, je questionnais le duc à cet égard. Je n'en pus obtenir un seul mot de réponse; car, depuis sa dernière apparition dans mon souterrain, il ne me parla jamais. J'avais besoin de tout mon courage pour supporter cette cruelle incertitude sur un point aussi intéressant. Souvent, quand j'invoquais le ciel pour ma fille, pour ma mère, tout à coup mon cœur se serrait, mes larmes coulaient: 'Hélas! M'écriais-je, existent-elles encore? Je fais des vœux pour leur bonheur, et peut-être ai-je le malheur affreux de leur survivre!' Dans d'autres moments, l'espérance dans mon cœur était si forte à cet égard, que je n'éprouvais même pas la plus légère inquiétude; et dans cette heureuse disposition d'esprit, je me flattais encore qu'il n'était pas impossible qu'un événement extraordinaire pût m'arracher de ma prison. Cette idée s'imprima tellement dans ma tête, surtout la dernière année de ma captivité, que je promis à Dieu, si jamais je recouvrais ma liberté, de lui consacrer ma vie dans une solitude éloignée de Rome, et de m'y fixer jusqu'à la fin de mes jours, aussitôt que ma fille n'aurait plus besoin de mes soins.

Cependant, je touchais à l'époque la plus intéressante de ma vie. J'approchais du moment de ma délivrance, et bientôt la bonté divine allait me dédommager amplement de neuf ans de souffrance et de douleur. Depuis quelque temps, je jugeais que le duc habitait constamment son château, parce qu'il m'apportait régulièrement ma nourriture. Mais, un jour, me trouvant au moment d'en manquer, je l'attendais avec impatience. Il ne vint point, et j'achevai entièrement ma faible provision. Je m'endormis assez paisiblement. Le lendemain, j'attendis en vain les secours que chaque instant me rendait plus nécessaires; il fallut m'en passer. L'inquiétude, autant que la soif et la faim, me priva du sommeil, et je restai dans cette situation encore près d'un jour. Alors, absolument épuisée, je crus toucher enfin au terme de ma vie. J'envisageai la mort avec tranquillité. Cependant, le souvenir de tout ce qui m'était cher vint me troubler et m'attendrir.

'Fille et mère infortunée', m'écriais-je, 'dans quel funeste abandon s'écoulent mes derniers moments! Chers auteurs de mes jours, il faut donc mourir sans recevoir vos bénédictions! O, ma fille! Je ne puis te donner la mienne; je ne jouirai pas de la douceur d'expirer dans tes bras. Ma fille, tu ne peux même me regretter dans cet instant où ta malheureuse mère est prête à rendre son dernier soupir. Tu te livres sans doute aux amusements, aux plaisirs faits pour ton âge! Affreuse pensée! Je meurs, et tout ce que j'aime est depuis longtemps consolé de ma mort! Mais que dis-je, insensée. Je me plains, je murmure lorsque tous mes maux vont finir! Grand Dieu, pardonne-moi cette criminelle faiblesse! Mon cœur l'abjure et la désavoue. O mon juge et mon Père, daigne enfin m'appeler à toi! Pleine d'espoir et de confiance, sûre de jouir d'un bonheur immortel, j'attends la mort avec sécurité; je l'invoquerais même si tu ne me défendais de la désirer!' En achevant ces mots, je retombai presque expirante sur la paille qui me servait de lit. Je sentais au fond de mon âme un calme, une tranquillité dont jamais, jusqu'à cet instant, je n'avais goûté les charmes. Il me semblait qu'un baume salutaire guérissait subitement toutes les blessures de mon cœur.

L'excès de ma faiblesse confondant bientôt mes idées, je tombai doucement dans une rêverie vague et délicieuse, une espèce de sommeil durant lequel les images les plus ravissantes s'offrirent successivement à mon imagination. Je croyais voir autour de mon lit des anges brillants de lumière, des figures célestes. J'entendais de loin des voix harmonieuses, des concerts divins. Je voyais le ciel entr'ouvert; et l'éternel, sur un trône éclatant, m'appelant et me tendant les bras. Il veillait en effet sur moi, sa main paternelle allait briser ma chaîne.

Tout à coup, je me réveille en tressaillant. Je crois avoir entendu frapper au tour. J'écoute. On frappe encore. Mon cœur palpite. Mais, ô surprise, ô transport inouï, transport impossible à dépeindre! J'entends une voix, et cette voix n'est plus celle de mon tyran, c'est une voix nouvelle! Elle me parut celle d'un ange descendu du ciel pour me délivrer! Hors de moi, éperdue, je joignis les mains, avec le mouvement le plus passionné de la plus vive reconnaissance.

'O Dieu, m'écriai-je, c'est un libérateur que tu m'envoies! Ah, j'acceptais avec joie la mort, et tu me rends la vie! La vie est un de tes bienfaits, il m'est permis de la chérir!' En disant ces paroles, je veux me lever, m'approcher du tour, je ne puis, la force m'abandonne, et je retombe sur mon lit. Dans ce moment, ma porte s'ouvre et j'aperçois de la lumière. On entre. Je me soulève, je veux regarder, je ne distingue rien. Mes yeux, depuis si longtemps privés du jour, ne peuvent soutenir la faible clarté d'une lampe, et se ferment malgré moi. Cependant on approche.

Fig. 7: 'Je fixe un instant mes yeux sur son visage éclairé par la lampe. Ses cheveux paraissaient hérissés sur sa tête; il était pâle et tremblant. Mais je ne pus le méconnaître.' Gravure de Pégard d'après un dessin de Telory. Illustration dans la sixième édition d'*Adèle et Théodore* publiée en 1862 à Paris par Morizot. (BnF)

'O, qui êtes-vous?' m'écriai-je d'une voix entrecoupée. A ces mots, je rouvre avec peine mes yeux éblouis encore. Je vois un homme à genoux devant moi. Il passe son bras sous ma tête, il la soutient, et me présente des aliments. Alors, consumée d'une faim dévorante, je n'ai plus qu'une idée, celle de satisfaire ce besoin impérieux. Toutes mes autres pensées sont pour ainsi dire suspendues, et je me jette avec avidité sur la nourriture qui m'est offerte. Enfin, sentant ma force renaître, je me tournai tout à coup vers mon libérateur. Son visage était dans l'ombre, je ne pus distinguer ses traits: 'O, parlez-moi,' lui dis-je, 'êtes-vous le complice de mon persécuteur, ou venez-vous pour me délivrer?'

'O Ciel', interrompit l'inconnu. 'Quelle voix! ... Où suis-je, ô Dieu!' En achevant ces paroles, il se lève brusquement, et prenant la lumière, il revient à moi. Il me regarde avec une attention mêlée d'attendrissement et d'horreur. Je fixe un instant mes yeux sur son visage éclairé par la lampe. Ses cheveux paraissaient hérissés sur sa tête; il était pâle et tremblant. Mais je ne pus le méconnaître.

Je veux parler. Mes pleurs me coupent la parole. Je ne puis prononcer que le nom du *comte de Belmire*.[12]

C'était lui-même en effet. Il tombe à mes pieds; il les arrose de larmes. Il me regarde encore. Il bégaye des mots entrecoupés. Il accuse et bénit le Ciel. L'excès de sa compassion donne à sa joie l'apparence de la fureur et du désespoir. Nous parlons tous les deux à la fois, sans nous entendre, sans nous répondre. La caverne retentit de nos cris. Enfin, le comte se relevant impétueusement: 'O, le plus barbare des hommes,' s'écria-t-il, 'monstre exécrable, est-il un supplice assez affreux pour te punir de ton forfait? Et vous,' continua-t-il, en m'aidant à me relever, 'vous, victime infortunée des fureurs d'un tigre impitoyable, venez, vous êtes libre.'

A ces mots, mon premier mouvement fut de m'élancer vers la porte. Mais, m'arrêtant aussitôt. 'Ah,' dis-je au comte, 'vous êtes mon libérateur, je vous dois la vie, la liberté! Mais ces biens que vous me rendez, peuvent-ils encore faire mon bonheur? Hélas, je n'ose vous interroger: ma mère? ... mon père?'

'Ils vivent.'

'Ciel! ... Et ma fille?'

THE

DUTCHESS OF C——.

BY

MADAME LA COMTESSE DE GENLIS.

Publiſhed Octo.ʳ 8.ᵗʰ 1800, by George Nicholſon, College, Ludlow.
Sold by
Champante and Whitrow, 4, Jewry-Street, Aldgate, London;
and by all other Bookſellers.

Fig. 8: Couverture de la traduction de la nouvelle de Genlis, *The Dutchess of C---. Moral tale*, publiée par George Nicholson à Manchester, Angleterre, en 1800. Illustration de William Marshall Craig (1788-1828), gravée par William Hawkins (1784-1809). (Courtesy of Charles Deering McCormick Library of Special Collections, Northwestern University Library.)

'Elle est à Rome; elle sera bientôt dans vos bras.'

'O Dieu,' m'écriai-je en me prosternant, 'quelle reconnaissance pourra jamais m'acquitter envers toi! Ce moment seul m'a déjà payée de toutes mes souffrances! O vous, mon généreux protecteur,' poursuivis-je en m'adressant au comte, 'maintenant, pour votre récompense, apprenez que je suis innocente; mais avant de vous instruire des tristes détails de mon histoire, souffrez que je vous fasse une question: Sans doute le duc est malade?'

'Attaqué d'une maladie mortelle, il est sur le bord de la tombe et ne peut vivre plus de deux jours. Venez! Sortez de cet horrible cachot que le barbare, avant d'expirer, apprenne que la liberté vous est rendue.'

'Non,' interrompis-je, 'c'est mon père, ma mère, qui doivent m'arracher de ma prison; ce n'est que guidée par eux que j'en puis sortir.' Alors je conjurai le comte d'envoyer un courrier à mon père au moment même. Il me le promit; et me donnant un crayon et du papier, j'écrivis sur le champ un billet qui contenait ces mots:

> Mon père, ma mère, j'existe, je suis innocente! Venez, par votre présence, me rendre véritablement à la vie. Venez me tirer d'un affreux souterrain et me faire oublier tous les maux que j'ai soufferts.

Ce billet était à peine lisible. Je fus près d'un quart d'heure à l'écrire, car je ne savais plus former une lettre, et j'avais totalement oublié l'orthographe.[13] Le comte, voyant que j'étais irrévocable-ment décidée à rester dans ma prison jusqu'à l'arrivée de ma mère, me remit les clefs de toutes les portes. Il me quitta avec un regret inexprimable, après m'avoir donné sa parole de dissimuler avec le duc s'il vivait encore et de revenir le lendemain, aussitôt que la nuit serait tombée.

Quand je me retrouvai seule, je me sentis saisie d'une terreur presque aussi forte que celle que j'éprouvais jadis dans les commencements de ma captivité. Cependant j'avais de la lumière; le comte m'avait laissé une lampe et une lanterne sourde. Je lui avais demandé encore une montre, afin de pouvoir compter toutes les heures, car je n'espérais pas qu'il me fût possible de m'endormir un instant. Immobile à la place où le comte de Belmire m'avait laissée, je respirais à peine, je n'osais lever les yeux, et cependant je ne pouvais m'empêcher de jeter à la dérobée quelques regards autour de moi. La lumière, loin de me rassurer, ajoutait à ma frayeur, parce qu'elle me faisait distinguer ma triste et lugubre habitation. Enfin, ne pouvant supporter cet état, je me levai, je pris ma lumière, j'ouvris ma première porte, je sortis et j'entrai dans une espèce de long corridor et l'endroit du souterrain où le tour était placé. Je sentis déjà un grand soulagement en me voyant dans un lieu nouveau et qui me rapprochait de la dernière porte de ma prison. Je précipitai mes pas jusqu'au bout du corridor; j'ouvris encore sa porte d'entrée. Alors, je me trouvai au bas de l'escalier du souterrain, et n'étant plus enfermée que par la double porte qui donnait sur le jardin, je fermai celle du corridor, comme pour me séparer de mon affreuse caverne. Ensuite, montant rapidement l'escalier, je m'assis sur la dernière marche, et je commençai enfin à respirer.

Il semble qu'après un événement aussi heureux qu'inattendu, j'aurais dû ressentir la joie la plus vive et la plus pure. Mais j'avais souffert trop longtemps, j'avais été trop malheureuse, pour que mon cœur osât se livrer aux charmes séduisants des plus douces espérances. Je pensais, il est vrai, avec transport, que tout ce que j'aimais existait. Cependant, quand je réfléchissais au bonheur inexprimable que je goûterais en me retrouvant dans les bras de ma mère, en embrassant et mon père et ma fille, je ne pouvais me flatter qu'une félicité semblable dût jamais être mon partage! Mille idées funestes venaient troubler et noircir mon imagination, et dans cet état d'abattement et de mélancolie, je prenais pour des pressentiments toutes les craintes les plus chimériques.

Cette époque intéressante de ma vie, le jour où le comte de Belmire entra dans ma prison, fut le 3 juin 17**.[14] Il me quitta à minuit, et jusqu'à six heures du matin je fus dans la situation que je viens de décrire, quand tout à coup je crus entendre un léger bruit. J'appuyai l'oreille la plus attentive sur la porte de ma prison, et malgré son épaisseur et celle du rocher qui la couvrait, j'entendis assez distinctement le ramage des oiseaux éveillés par le jour naissant. Le mouvement de joie que j'éprouvai dans cet instant ne peut ni se peindre ni se concevoir. Toute ma mélancolie s'évanouit, mon cœur se rouvrit à l'espérance, au bonheur. Les plus douces larmes coulaient de mes yeux, quoique j'eusse cependant une

Fig. 9: Illustration de H. Brevière-Rouery dans *Camille, ou Le Souterrain*, version plagiée de la nouvelle de Genlis publiée à Rouen en 1816 par Lecrêne-Labbey sans nom d'auteur. (BnF)

extrême confusion d'idées, et que je ne fusse pas en état de réfléchir au changement inespéré de ma situation; car j'étais uniquement occupée du désir d'entendre ce qui se passait dans le jardin. L'oreille collée sur ma porte, retenant ma respiration, j'écoutais avec une attention dont nulle autre pensée ne pouvait me distraire. J'entendis des chiens aboyer, des hommes marcher et même parler confusément, et tous ces différents bruits me causaient un plaisir inexprimable.

Cependant, vers la fin du jour, je désirai vivement la nuit, afin de revoir le comte de Belmire et de le questionner sur mille choses dont je brûlais d'être instruite et qui se présentaient successivement à ma mémoire à mesure que mes idées se débrouillaient. Par exemple, je souhaitais apprendre combien de temps j'avais passé dans ma prison. Avant d'avoir vu le comte, je croyais avoir près de cinquante ans. L'air de jeunesse du comte de Belmire me prouvait que la douleur et l'ennui savent mal mesurer le temps, mais je ne pouvais savoir encore, à quatre ou cinq ans près, quel était mon âge.

Le comte vint à minuit précis. Je connus aisément, par l'excès de sa pâleur, par son trouble et son attendrissement, combien il était profondément affecté de l'événement qui changeait mon sort. Respectant ma situation qui me forçait à le recevoir seule au milieu de la nuit, respectant le nœud fatal, prêt à se rompre, mais qui me liait encore, il ne me parla ni des sentiments dont j'osai faire l'aveu dans des temps plus heureux, ni de ceux qu'il me conservait toujours. Après qu'il m'eut appris qu'il avait écrit à mon père, en lui envoyant mon billet, et que le duc était toujours à l'extrémité, je le priai de m'instruire des raisons qui avaient déterminé le duc à lui confier un secret si important pour lui. Le comte, prenant la parole, satisfit ainsi ma curiosité.

'Je voyageais depuis un an, lorsque je reçus la nouvelle de votre mort. J'appris en même temps que le duc était inconsolable de votre perte. Cette circonstance affaiblit beaucoup l'antipathie naturelle que j'avais pour lui. Je voyageai deux ans encore, et rappelé par des affaires, je revins enfin en Italie. Obligé de voir le duc, il fallut venir dans ce château, car il ne s'en absentait que très rarement, et seulement pour aller à Naples passer deux ou trois jours. Je vis ici votre tombeau, j'y vis votre portrait placé dans presque tous les appartements. Je m'attachai à cette habitation, je m'attachai même au monstre inhumain dont vous étiez la victime. Il montrait une douleur si vive, une tristesse si profonde, que bientôt préférant sa société à toute autre, je vins tous les ans passer cinq à six mois dans ce château.'

'Depuis un an, le duc, attaqué d'une maladie mortelle, s'aveuglait sur son état et faisait encore quelques voyages à Naples. L'hiver dernier, il cessa entièrement d'aller à la cour et m'écrivit à Rome pour m'engager à venir le voir. J'arrivai sur la fin de janvier, et je le trouvai mourant, quoiqu'il ne gardât point son lit et qu'il marchât toujours. Je crus même m'apercevoir que dans de certains moments, il n'avait pas entièrement sa tête. Dévoré de remords, la vie, depuis neuf ans, n'était pour lui qu'un fardeau insupportable, et cependant il ne pouvait en envisager le terme qu'avec horreur. Enfin, s'affaiblissant chaque jour, il tomba tout à coup dans des convulsions qui l'obligèrent de se mettre au lit. Il y resta trois jours, au bout desquels un de ses valets de chambre vint me dire, à neuf heures du soir, qu'il demandait à me parler. Cet homme ajouta que le duc, cette nuit même et la précédente, avait renvoyé ses gens pour essayer de se lever seul; mais que ne pouvant se soutenir, il les avait sonnés, et qu'on l'avait trouvé hors de son lit et à moitié habillé.'

'Je fus au même instant dans sa chambre. Il renvoya son médecin et ses gens, et m'annonçant qu'il allait me confier un important secret, il me fit jurer de le garder avec fidélité. Ensuite, me regardant d'un air égaré, il me dit: 'Des raisons de famille m'obligent à garder prisonnière dans ce château une femme criminelle et qui méritait la mort. Elle doit manquer de nourriture, allez-lui en porter. Frappez au tour qui sert à cet usage; si elle ne vous répond pas, entrez dans sa prison et secourez-la. Mais je vous préviens que cette femme est en démence; ne l'écoutez point. Donnez-lui de la nourriture, et revenez sur le champ. Je vous promets de vous dire un jour et son histoire et son nom.' Alors le duc m'apprit encore le secret de ses souterrains, et tirant de dessous son chevet un paquet de clefs, il me le donna en me recommandant d'exécuter sa commission sans délai. Le barbare, croyant que je ne vous avais jamais vue, pensait ne pouvoir mieux placer sa confiance et remit ainsi dans mes mains votre destinée et la mienne.'

Lorsque le comte de Belmire eut fini ce récit, il me conjura de lui apprendre mon histoire. Mais comme je ne pouvais la conter sans parler des sentiments que j'avais eu pour lui, je lui déclarai que je ne l'en instruirais qu'en présence de mon père et de ma mère.

D'après le calcul du comte de Belmire, mon père devait arriver sous deux jours au plus tard. Moins agitée, et plus en état de réfléchir, je goûtai pendant vingt-quatre heures tout le bonheur qu'une attente si chère devait me procurer. Ensuite, mon impatience augmentant à mesure que l'instant de ma délivrance approchait, bientôt elle n'eut plus de bornes et devint un tourment insupportable. Je n'ai jamais rien senti que je puisse comparer aux mouvements violents que j'éprouvai dans la nuit qui précéda le plus beau jour de ma vie. Les yeux fixement attachés sur ma montre, je considérais tristement le mouvement si lent, à mon gré, de ses aiguilles. A chaque instant je croyais entendre du bruit, je tressaillais. Je sentais mon sang bouillonner dans mes veines, et toutes mes artères battre avec violence. Ces vives agitations s'accrurent encore quand le chant des oiseaux m'annonça la naissance du jour, de ce jour fortuné où j'allais renaître en reprenant le titre et les droits chers et sacrés de fille et de mère!

Ce moment fait pour dédommager d'un siècle de souffrances, ce moment si passionnément désiré! Il approche! J'y touche enfin! Des cris redoublés, des voix tumultueuses se font entendre. Bientôt je distingue un bruit confus de voitures, de chevaux, de gens armés. Ce bruit redouble et se rapproche. Je tremble; je frissonne. Dieu! Quelle voix frappe mon oreille et retentit jusqu'au fond de mon âme! O ma mère! Elle appelle sa fille! Mon cœur s'élance vers elle! 'Dieu, qui me donna la force de supporter mes malheurs. Ah, ne permets pas que je succombe à cet excès de joie! Je sens que je me meurs; faudra-t-il expirer aux pieds de ma mère?' Comme j'achève ces mots, ma porte s'ouvre. Je me précipite hors de ma caverne. Malgré l'éclat brillant du jour qui frappe et blesse mes yeux éblouis, je vois, je reconnais ma mère, mon père. Je pousse un cri perçant, je me jette dans leurs bras, et j'y tombe évanouie.

O, qui pourrait décrire le ravissement, les transports que j'éprouvai en reprenant ma connaissance! Je me trouvais sur le sein de la mère la plus chérie, je sentais mon visage inondé de ses pleurs. Mon père, à genoux devant moi, pressait mes deux mains dans les siennes. Je revoyais le jour, le soleil. J'étais sûre enfin de

Fig. 10: 'Je me précipite hors de ma caverne [...]. Je reconnais ma mère, mon père, je pousse un cri perçant, je me jette dans leurs bras, et j'y tombe évanouie.' Gravure sur cuivre de Luigi Schiavonetti d'après la peinture à l'huile intitulée *The Duchess of C. coming out of the Cavern* de John Francis Rigaud (1742-1810). ©Trustees of the British Museum.

revoir bientôt ma fille. Cet instant réalisait toutes mes espérances les plus chères et satisfaisait tous les désirs de mon cœur. Je ne rendrai point compte de mes idées dans ces premiers moments. Je sentais trop pour qu'il me fût possible de penser et d'exprimer l'excès de ma joie autrement que par mes sanglots et mes larmes.

Enfin, mon père me soulevant dans ses bras me dit: 'Venez, ma chère fille, quittez cet affreux séjour où le crime a si longtemps opprimé l'innocence, venez.' A ces mots, je me levai. Je regardai autour de moi, et je vis avec surprise que nous étions entourés d'une troupe nombreuse de gens armés, parmi lesquels je reconnus beaucoup de parents et quelques anciens amis de mon père, qui m'apprit que les ayant tous rassemblés avant de quitter Rome, il les avait conduits directement à Naples. Là, mon père s'était jeté aux genoux du roi, et lui montrant mon billet, en avait obtenu, non seulement la permission de venir m'enlever à main armée, si la force était nécessaire, mais encore des troupes pour le seconder. 'En arrivant ici, continua mon père, j'ai appris que votre infâme persécuteur venait d'expirer.[15] Ainsi, ce jour heureux vous rend à tout ce qui vous chérit, vous délivre d'un tyran exécrable, et vous assure une parfaite liberté.'

A ce discours, pour toute réponse, j'embrassai mon père en pleurant. Au comble du bonheur, n'ayant plus rien à craindre, je ne pus m'empêcher de plaindre, au fond de mon âme, le sort du malheureux duc de C***. 'Hélas,' me disais-je, 'si je l'eusse aimé, il n'aurait point souillé sa vie par des fureurs si criminelles, il vivrait et serait heureux!' Cette réflexion, en excitant ma compassion, la rendit pénible et douloureuse, et pendant quelques instants, elle porta dans mon cœur une cruelle impression de tristesse, et corrompit ma joie. Enfin, nous partîmes, et le lendemain, mère aussi fortunée qu'heureuse fille, je retrouvai cette enfant si passionnément aimée. Je la serrai dans mes bras, je vis couler ses larmes, et je l'entendis m'appeler sa mère!

Je fus dans une espèce d'ivresse les deux premiers jours de mon arrivée à Rome, étourdie du bruit, étonnée de tout, et ne jouissant véritablement que du bonheur de revoir ma fille et de me trouver entre mon père et ma mère. Ensuite, mon cœur étant pleinement satisfait, je commençai à sentir le prix de tous les biens qui m'étaient rendus. Je trouvai, dans les choses les plus communes de la vie, des jouissances aussi agréables que nouvelles; tout était spectacle pour moi. La première fois que je me promenai au clair de la lune, j'éprouvai une admiration et un saisissement inexprimables en revoyant cette clarté si douce et si pure et les cieux parsemés d'étoiles. Je ne pouvais me promener dans la campagne ou dans un jardin sans m'arrêter à chaque pas pour examiner avec détail les objets qui s'offraient à ma vue. Je ne me lassais point de contempler les fleurs, les fruits, les arbres, la verdure, les nuages, le coucher du soleil et l'aurore, ce spectacle ravissant et sublime! 'O Dieu,' m'écriais-je, 'que de merveilles ta bonté créa pour nous, que de trésors elle nous prodigue, et l'homme ingrat pourrait les dédaigner! Et lorsqu'il jouit de tant de biens, il pourrait se croire malheureux!'

C'est ainsi que mon cœur se livrait avec transport à la félicité qui lui fut si longtemps ravie. Je goûtai aussi un plaisir extrême en me retrouvant dans le palais où j'étais née, et dans lequel s'écoulèrent les heureuses années de mon enfance et de ma première jeunesse. Mais j'avoue que je ne revis pas sans quelque peine la marquise de Venuzi, cette ancienne amie, et la première cause de tous mes malheurs.

Le comte de Belmire me suivit de près à Rome; et en présence de mon père, de ma mère, de la marquise de Venuzi et de quelques parents, je lui contai mon histoire. A peine l'eus-je finie, que se précipitant à mes genoux, il m'exprima, dans les termes les plus passionnés, l'excès de son attendrissement et de sa reconnaissance.

'Eh quoi,' s'écria-t-il, 'vous pouviez, en me nommant, vous soustraire à cette horrible destinée! C'est moi qui vous ai plongée dans cet abîme, et tandis que vous y gémissiez, je vivais, je voyais le jour dont vous étiez privée pour moi! M'est-il permis de me flatter encore que l'amour pourra vous dédommager des maux affreux qu'il vous causa? Ce cœur si noble et si tendre pourrait-il n'être pas fidèle? Vos malheurs vous auraient-ils fait abjurer des sentiments sans lesquels je ne puis vivre?'

A ce discours, mon père embrassa affectueusement le comte de Belmire, et me fit connaître par cette action qu'il approuvait ses sentiments. Mais, pour moi, ayant perdu jusqu'à l'idée d'une passion qui jadis eut tant d'ascendant sur mon cœur, je ne concevais même plus qu'on pût s'y livrer, et encore moins la possibilité que j'en fusse l'objet. Après un moment de silence, je pris la parole, et m'adressant au comte, je lui peignis si naturellement la situation de mon âme, qu'il perdit au moment même toutes ses espérances. Il s'éloigna de Rome pendant quelque temps. Mais le sentiment qui le faisait fuir l'y ramena bientôt; et consolé par l'amitié que je lui témoignais, il s'y fixa entièrement.

Cependant, loin de me blaser sur le bonheur que je goûtais, chaque jour semblait m'en faire mieux sentir le prix. Toutes les fois que je me réveillais, combien ma première pensée avait de charmes! J'éprouvais une joie si pure en jetant les yeux autour de moi, en voyant le lit de ma fille à côté du mien, en me retrouvant dans la demeure paternelle! Je ne comprenais plus comment j'avais pu supporter la privation de la félicité dont je jouissais et même celle des choses d'agrément et de commodité que l'habitude commençait à me faire paraître absolument nécessaires à la vie. Ces idées m'inspiraient la plus tendre compassion pour tous les infortunés. J'avais couché neuf ans sur de la paille, j'avais souffert la faim, la soif, le froid. Je devais du moins à mes malheurs le sentiment qui nous rapproche le plus de la divinité! Je n'écoutais point avec distraction les gémissements du pauvre, implorant ma pitié. Son sort me rappelait le mien; je voyais en lui mon semblable, et je trouvais la satisfaction la plus pure à le consoler, à le soulager! Ce n'était point assez pour moi de le recevoir, de l'accueillir; j'allais le chercher. Eh! qui mérite d'être prévenu, si ce n'est le malheureux qui souffre, et qui souvent n'ose demander le faible secours qui lui sauverait la vie! Ce désir de trouver des infortunés afin de changer leur sort n'était point en moi une vertu, c'était le besoin le plus pressant de mon cœur et le plus doux de mes plaisirs.

Mais plus je m'accoutumais moi-même à l'aisance qui m'était rendue, plus le souvenir de ma captivité me faisait d'impression, et bientôt il ne me fut plus possible ni de parler de mes malheurs, ni même d'écouter avec tranquillité les récits et les discours qui pouvaient me les rappeler ou m'en retracer l'image.[16] Cette faiblesse m'en donna beaucoup d'autres; je ne pouvais supporter les ténèbres ou bien une solitude absolue, ne fût-ce que pour un moment. Je me souviens qu'une nuit ma lumière s'éteignit; j'ouvris les yeux, et en me voyant dans une obscurité profonde, j'éprouvai un effroi que ma raison ne put ni vaincre, ni modérer. Je fis un cri perçant, on accourut et l'on me trouva pâle, défigurée, presque sans connaissance et agitée des plus effrayantes convulsions. Ces vaines terreurs, ces faiblesses involontaires, tristes fruits de mes malheurs et de ma captivité, ne furent pas pour moi les peines les plus sensibles. Je me trouvai absolument hors d'état de présider à l'éducation de ma fille. Il me fallut apprendre de nouveau à lire, à écrire et à compter. Mais, par une singularité assez remarquable, je n'avais presque rien oublié de tout ce que j'avais lu dans ma jeunesse; car n'ayant eu, durant neuf ans, aucune espèce de distraction, j'en avais cherché dans le passé, en me rappelant souvent, et avec détail, ce que les livres et la conversation avaient pu m'apprendre. Ainsi toutes ces choses étaient restées gravées dans ma mémoire, mieux peut-être que si je n'eusse jamais quitté le monde.

J'étais âgée de vingt-sept ans lorsque je sortis de ma prison, et alors ma fille en avait dix. Uniquement occupée d'elle, vivant dans la plus profonde retraite, toujours enfermée dans mon appartement, n'y voyant que mon père, ma mère et quelquefois le comte de Belmire, je vécus ainsi cinq ans. Ma fille atteignant enfin sa quinzième année, et se trouvant le plus grand parti de l'Italie, me fut demandée par tout ce qu'il y avait de plus distingué dans Rome. Depuis longtemps, mon choix était fait au fond de mon cœur. Je consultai ma fille, elle m'avoua que ses sentiments étaient d'accord avec mes désirs; mon père et ma mère approuvaient mon dessein, j'en pressai l'exécution. Le comte de Belmire, jeune encore, d'une figure charmante, aussi vertueux qu'aimable, possesseur d'une fortune considérable, avait constamment refusé les établissements les plus avantageux et les plus brillants. C'est à cet amant trop fidèle, cet ami si cher, mon libérateur enfin, que j'offris ma fille.

'Je vous la donne,' lui dis-je. 'Elle est à vous. Elle vous aime, elle a quinze ans, c'est l'âge où je vous vis pour la première fois; elle vous retrace tout ce que j'étais alors, et par sa figure et par ses sentiments. Le sort vous rend aujourd'hui ce qu'il vous ravit autrefois; et moi, n'étant pas née pour faire votre bonheur, je ne puis m'en consoler qu'en vous voyant heureux par ma fille.'

A ces mots, le comte de Belmire saisit une de mes mains, et la baigna de larmes. Et comme je le pressais de me répondre, il dit enfin: 'Ah! N'avez-vous pas le droit de disposer de ma destinée! Le soir même de cet entretien, les articles du mariage furent signés; et huit jours après, le comte de Belmire épousa ma fille.

Fig. 11: 'Je vous la donne. Elle est à vous. Elle vous aime [...]. Le sort vous rend aujourd'hui ce qu'il vous ravit autrefois.' Gravure sur cuivre de Gaetano Testolini (1700-1795) d'après la peinture à l'huile intitulée *The Dutchess of C. Giving Her Daughter to Count Belmire* de John Francis Rigaud (1742-1810). ©Trustees of the British Museum.

Je restai encore un an à Rome. Ensuite, voyant ma fille établie et parfaitement heureuse, je ne songeai plus qu'à me retirer dans une solitude, suivant le vœu que j'en avais fait dans ma prison. D'ailleurs, l'air de Rome étant très nuisible à ma santé, les médecins m'avaient ordonné d'aller respirer celui de Nice pendant quelque temps. J'entrepris ce voyage par la Corniche.[17] La situation d'Albenga me charma tellement, que je résolus de me fixer dans cet agréable séjour. J'y fis bâtir une maison simple et commode et, en revenant de Nice, je m'y établis pour toujours.

C'est ici que, depuis quatre ans, j'ai retrouvé une santé parfaite, et que ma vie s'écoule dans le plus délicieux repos. C'est ici que j'ai eu le courage d'écrire cette histoire, que je destine à mes petites-filles, lorsqu'elles seront en âge de la lire avec fruit. En abandonnant le monde, je n'ai pu renoncer aux objets qui me sont chers. Depuis que je suis à Albenga, j'ai déjà fait deux voyages à Rome pour y voir mon père et ma mère, et tous les ans ma fille et mon gendre viennent passer trois mois dans ma retraite. Enfin, je suis aussi parfaitement heureuse qu'on peut l'être. Chaque jour, je bénis le ciel et du bonheur que je goûte et même des maux que j'ai soufferts, puisqu'ils ont expié mes fautes, épuré mon cœur, et me font connaître tout le prix de la félicité qui m'est rendue.

* * *

Continuation du journal de la baronne.

Ce dimanche, de Pietra.

Quand vous aurez lu l'histoire de la duchesse de C***, vous comprendrez facilement la peine que nous avons eue à quitter Albenga; nous n'avons pu nous en arracher qu'aujourd'hui après dîner. Nous avons fait beaucoup de chemin à pied, et la conversation a toujours eu pour objet cette belle et touchante duchesse de C***. Nous remarquions que tous ses malheurs venaient uniquement d'avoir manqué de confiance en sa mère; et que sans la religion, son souterrain eût été son tombeau, ou qu'elle n'en serait sortie que stupide et folle. Ainsi Adèle et Théodore ont maintenant une juste idée de la religion. Ils ont vu à Lagaraye tout ce qu'elle peut produire de grand, de bienfaisant et d'héroïque;[18] et ils viennent d'apprendre encore qu'il n'est point de revers, d'infortunes, qu'elle ne fasse supporter avec courage et résignation. Ils n'oublieront jamais qu'elle est aussi consolante que sublime, qu'elle imprime au fond du cœur des vertus que nous ne pouvons tenir de la nature, et qu'enfin elle nous inspire un courage que la seule raison ne pourrait donner.[19]

NOTES TO THE FRENCH TEXT

[1] Albenga is an ancient coastal town in northwestern Italy on the Italian Riviera midway between Monaco and Genoa. In the notes to her edition of *Adèle et Théodore*, Isabelle Brouard-Arends points out that the itinerary followed by the d'Almanes was identical to that followed by Genlis on her trip to Italy with the Duchess of Chartres in the spring of 1776 and that the descriptions in the novel of the various places visited there, including Albenga, were taken directly from Genlis's travel journal. See *Adèle et Théodore, ou Lettres sur l'éducation*, ed. Isabelle Brouard-Arends (Rennes: Presses universitaires de Rennes, 2006), p. 652, n. 35. However, as Genlis explains in her memoirs, she did not actually visit the Duchess of Girifalco in Albenga, but instead saw her in Rome for only about fifteen minutes during a dinner party hosted by the duchess's father, the Prince of Palestrina. See Appendix C for the references to the Duchess of Girifalco found in Genlis's memoirs.

[2] In in his travel journal *Une année à Florence*, Alexandre Dumas père recalls an afternoon he spent in Albenga and mentions Genlis's tale of the duchess: 'Nous nous arrêtâmes pour déjeuner à Albenga, ville au doux nom, mais à laquelle ses remparts croulants et ses tours en ruines donnent un aspect des plus sombres. C'est à Albenga, s'il faut en croire madame de Genlis, que la duchesse de Cerifalco fut enfermée pendant neuf ans dans un souterrain par son mari.' [*Œuvres complètes d'Alexandre Dumas,* 17 vols (Paris: Au bureau du Siècle, 1850-57), VIII: *Impressions de voyage* (1851), p. 354.] This last sentence is incorrect, since the duchess was not imprisoned by her husband in Albenga, but (according to nineteenth-century historians Litta, Coppi, and Ademollo) in the castle of Girifalco in southern Italy. (See their accounts in Appendix G.) In Genlis's version of the duchess's story, the duke imprisons his wife in a castle near Naples, far from both Girifalco and Albenga.

[3] Genlis occasionally uses italics to indicate quotes within a quote. In this passage, Mme d'Almane is quoting the Viscountess de Limours, the friend to whom she is writing.

[4] *Note de Genlis*: Cette description n'est point exagérée; elle est absolument conforme à la vérité et prise du journal que l'auteur a écrit à Albenga même.

[5] La Corniche (or la Route des Corniches) is the name given to the narrow coastal road that crosses the Esterel mountain range (le Massif de l'Estérel) along the French Riviera from Saint-Rafael to the Italian border and then continues eastward along the Italian Riviera to the Gulf of Genoa, where Albenga is located. The road, much of which still exists

today, offers dramatic views of the Mediterranean and of the rugged, reddish mountain cliffs overlooking the sea.

[6] *Note de Genlis*: 'Le fond de cette histoire est parfaitement vrai: les neuf ans de captivité dans un souterrain où le jour ne pénétra jamais, la supposition de la mort de la duchesse, la manière dont cette dernière vécut et dont elle fut nourrie, sa délivrance—tous ces détails sont exactement vrais. Il n'y a d'invention dans cette histoire que l'amour et les personnages de l'amant et de l'amie. L'auteur, en 17**, a vu à Rome madame la duchesse de C*** et tous les jours dînait avec le père de cette personne intéressante.'

In the fourth edition published in 1804 by Maradan in Paris, we find a shorter, but more informative version of this footnote: 'Le fond de cette histoire est parfaitement vrai. L'auteur, en 1776, a vu à Rome madame la duchesse de Cerifalco, et tous les jours dînait avec le prince de Palestrine, père de cette personne intéressante.' The discrepancy between the two versions of this footnote is discussed in the section titled 'About the Text and Translation,' pp. 23-24.

[7] Contrary to Genlis's claim, the duchess was not the only child born to the Princess of Palestrina. Married at twelve in 1728, Cornelia Barberini bore seven children in the first nine years of marriage and two or three more children after that. Olimpia was her second daughter and eldest surviving child. See Caroline Castiglione, *Patrons and Adversaries: Nobles and Villagers in Italian Politics, 1640-1760* (Oxford & New York: Oxford University Press, 2005), pp. 108 and 181. See in particular the family tree on p. 181 that gives birth and death dates for Olimpia and her parents.

[8] *Note de Genlis*: On nomme ainsi en Italie une *assemblée*.

[9] According to *Le Petit Robert, une lieue* is roughly equivalent to 4 kilometers, so 12 *lieues* would have been about 48 km or 30 miles. Other sources give different equivalents, ranging from 3.98 to 4.4 km; this discrepancy is hardly surprising given that units of measure varied from region to region until the metric system was adopted. As for traveling times in the eighteenth century, Henri Sée remarks that 'sur les routes, les diligences ne font que deux lieues par heure, les carrosses huit à dix lieues par jour.' Given the difficulties of travel on the mountain roads around Naples (which Genlis describes in her novel), the journey by horse-drawn carriage from Naples to the duke's castle would probably have taken a full day. Henri Sée, *La France économique et sociale au XVIIIe siècle* (Paris: Armand Colin, 1967), p. 111.

[10] *Un tour* (turning-box) was a device traditionally found in convents. It consisted of a round cupboard embedded in the wall by which nuns received provisions from the outside without seeing or being seen. Inside the cupboard was a rotating circular shelf on which provisions and parcels were placed outside the wall and then moved to the inside compartment as the shelf was manually rotated. In French convents, the keeper of the turning-box was called *la tourière*.

[11] *Note de Genlis*: La malheureuse duchesse de C*** reçut aussi, dans la suite, assez régulièrement, par ce même tour, du linge et quelques vêtements, lorsqu'elle en avait un indispensable besoin.

[12] In her memoirs, Genlis claims that the imprisoned duchess was discovered by a valet who recognized her and released her from captivity. (Genlis, *Mémoires inédits,* III, p. 49.) Nineteenth-century chroniclers offer quite different versions of the duchess's rescue. Litta claims that two Capuchin monks passing by the castle one night heard her cries and sent for help. Coppi and Ademollo both dismiss this story as apocryphal and maintain that the duchess was able to get word of her plight to her father through her confessor, whom her husband allowed her to see during her captivity. See Appendix C for this and other passages in Genlis's memoirs concerning the duchess and Appendix G for nineteenth-century Italian accounts of her story.

[13] In her memoirs, Genlis describes the profound impression this note made on her when the duchess's father showed it to her during her stay in Rome: 'Le prince avait précieusement conservé le billet de sa fille; à mon instante prière, il me le montra; je ne pouvais me lasser de contempler ce petit morceau de papier; l'écriture, les paroles y les mots auxquels il manquait presque toutes les dernières syllabes, tout en était précieux à mes yeux. Une remarqué singulière, et qu'à ma connaissance on n'a point faite, c'est que dans des pertes de mémoire sans altération de la raison, ce sont toujours les dernières syllabes des mots qu'on oublie. Ce fut ainsi que John Selkirck, matelot anglais, retrouvé au bout de vingt-cinq ans dans une île déserte, parlait toujours fort bien anglais, à l'exception des dernières syllabes de chaque mot, qu'il avait oubliées. J'ai observé le même phénomène dans une personne jeune encore, mais aveugle depuis quatorze ans, à laquelle, comme je le dirai par la suite, je rendis la faculté d'écrire.' (Genlis, *Mémoires inédits,* III, p. 50.) See Appendix C for the complete French text and English translation of this passage.

[14] In a letter written to her friend Mrs Stokes on 9 August 1786, Anna Seward recalls the story her brother-in-law told her in 1764 about the duchess, who (he claimed) had recently been released from captivity: 'But what an interesting story is that of the imprisoned duchess! [...] When, in

1764, Mr Porter came over from Italy to marry my lovely sister, he told us that singular and almost incredible circumstance of a woman of fashion in that country having then been just discovered and rescued from a nine years confinement in a subterraneous dungeon.' [*Letters of Anna Seward: Written between the Years 1784 and 1807,* 6 vols (Edinburgh, Scotland: Archibald Constable, 1811), I, p. 399.] However, the dates given by Genlis in her memoirs and in her version of the duchess's story suggest that the duchess was released from captivity in 1759. Regarding the chronology of the duchess's story, see Appendix A.

[15] According to Luigi Russo, the Duke of Girifalco died on August 15, 1766, several years after his wife was rescued from captivity. (Russo, 'I Catasti Onciari di Orta e Casapuzzano,' in *Note e documenti per la storia di Orta di Atella*, ed. Franco Pezzella (Frattamaggiore: Istituto di Studi Atellani, 2006), pp. xlviii-lxi (p. lvi).

[16] We find this same detail in Pompeo Litta's account of the duchess's story: 'She never said a word about what had happened, nor did she ever permit anyone to speak to her about it.' [Pompeo Litta, *Famiglie celebri italiane*, 13 vols (Milan: Presso P. E. Giusti, 1819-1852), II (1838), folio 20 verso.] See Appendix G for the full Italian text and translation.

[17] See note 5 above.

[18] Genlis is referrring here to an episode earlier in the novel (recounted in vol I, letter 63, and vol II, letter 2, of the 1782 edition) regarding the Lagarayes, whom the d'Almanes had visited before returning from Paris to their country estate in Languedoc. After losing their only child, the Lagarayes had renounced their comfortable society life to study medicine in Montpellier. They had then returned to Languedoc, where they transformed their ancestral château of Lagaraye into a hospital and hospice that served the poor and provided jobs to the local population. In a footnote, Genlis explains that this episode is based on a true story. The parallels between the Lagarayes's experience and that of the Duchess of C*** are clear, as Genlis herself points out: Both stories serve to illustrate to the d'Almane children—and to Genlis's readers—the power of religious faith to overcome misfortune and to inspire a desire to help others less fortunate than oneself.

[19] An additional paragraph is found at the end of a translation of the duchess's story published in 1798 in Manchester by George Nicholson under the title *Moral tale. The Dutchess of C—:* 'How unfortunate has been this amiable, this virtuous, this affecting woman! How severe her sufferings! Ah, may we guard our hearts against the fatal impressions of

love! May a passion never be known that can produce such misery and guilt! And let us not fail to deduce from the narrative of the Duchess of C*** two important truths: the first, that an indulgence of the passions may plunge us into the deepest abyss of human woe; and the second, that there is no calamity that religion cannot help us bear.' This passage does not appear in the original French text of the novella published in 1783, nor is it found at the end of the duchess's narrative in *Adèle et Théodore*. It appears to have been drawn from a passage in *Adèle et Théodore* preceding the duchess's story in which she speaks privately with Mme d'Almane. See the discussion of this passage at the end of the introductory section titled 'About the Text and the Translation.'

STORY OF THE DUCHESS OF C***

TRANSLATED BY

MARY S. TROUILLE

THE

DUTCHESS OF C——.

BY

MADAME LA COMTESSE DE GENLIS.

Publifhed Octo.ʳ 8.ᵗʰ 1800, by George Nichollon, College, Ludlow.
Sold by
Champante and Whitrow, 4, Jewry-Street, Aldgate, London;
and by all other Bookfellers.

Fig. 12: Title vignette from *The Dutchess of C----. Moral tale*, translation of Genlis's novella published by G. Nicholson in Manchester, England, in 1800. Illustration by William Marshall Craig (1788-1828) engraved by William Hawkins (1784-1809). (Courtesy of Charles Deering McCormick Library of Special Collections, Northwestern University Library.)

STORY OF THE DUCHESS OF C***

From the baroness's journal

Albenga, Tuesday

My journal is at last becoming interesting; and surely, my dear friend, nothing I can send you from Venice and Rome will give you as much pleasure as what I am about to relate. I don't wish to tell you about it in advance, so that when you read my journal, you will share the surprise I experienced myself.

The road from Saint-Maurice to Albenga[1] is full of very frightening passes. But it also offers magnificent views, including the view from the top of the mountain overlooking the town of Languella. The descent is very steep and quite dangerous. We walked down it on foot, practically barefoot, since the rocks we had been climbing for three days had so worn out our shoes that the soles were almost entirely gone. Not anticipating that we would have to walk so much, we had not taken the precaution of bringing several pairs. At ten in the morning, we had the men carrying our sedan-chairs stop at the top of a mountain. From there, we could see the town of Albenga,[2] in the center of a lovely plain. Its location is most unusual in this coastal region, where all the other towns are located on the mountainsides.

After descending the mountain, we found ourselves in a vast and fertile plain, surrounded by boulders and majestic mountains, some of which are snow-capped. The barrenness of the rocky cliffs and the imposing aspect of the mountains form a striking contrast to the enchanting beauty and fertility of the plain. The pastures are dotted with pansies, lilies, and wild rhododendrons. The fields are surrounded by trellis-covered walkways planted with grapevines. Through the delicate latticework, one looks out at the flowers, fruit trees, and other greenery enclosed within these charming arbors. The archways are adorned with elegant garlands of grapevine, which sway in the gentlest breeze. In this delightful place, it seems as though the land is cultivated not for people's needs, but only for their pleasure. Everything is lovely to behold. There, my dear

105

women whose *nightcap-like bonnets*[3] you found so ugly. Instead of bonnets, the young women all place a little bouquet of fresh flowers on the left side of their head. Nearly all of them are pretty, and they are particularly remarkable for the elegance of their figures.[4]

You can imagine Adele and Theodore's delight at these sights that were so charming and so new to them. They asked us for permission to run in the fields and to wander under the arbors; and in an instant they were far ahead of us. Theodore stopped to gather a bouquet, but his sister continued running ahead and then entered a narrow path where I lost sight of her. I called out to her two or three times, but she was too far away to hear me. I sent Dainville to look for her; he returned a moment later without her, but called out to me that he had found her and that she was on her way back. I hurried on and, as he drew closer to me, Dainville laughed and said that we would not leave Albenga without a delightful episode to add to our journal.

'But where is my daughter?' I cried.

'Very close to here,' he replied, 'with a lady as lovely as the day.'

Adele appeared as Dainville finished speaking. She was running and soon joined us. But she was so out of breath and so excited by her *adventure* that she stammered and could only answer in monosyllables. When she finally recovered from all the excitement, we sat down on the grass. Adele explained to us that, after she lost sight of us, she had spotted, in the distance, a woman seated alone on the grass in a kind of grove to the left of the path. Drawn closer out of curiosity, Adele caught sight of a beautiful woman in a white gauze dress, reading intently. She had a sad expression on her face, but her appearance was full of gentleness and majesty. A young woman, who seemed to be her chambermaid, was seated a short distance from her. Hearing Adele's footsteps, the heroine lifted her gaze and appeared very surprised to see her. Adele curtsied deeply and then stopped short, not daring to move closer. The stranger continued to look at her and smiled. Encouraged by this, Adele approached. Speaking to her in Italian,

Fig. 13: 'Hearing Adele's footsteps, the heroine lifted her gaze and appeared very surprised to see her. Adele curtsied deeply.' Illustration from the sixth edition of *Adèle et Théodore* published in 1862 in Paris by Morizot. Engraving by Pégard from a drawing by Telory. (BnF)

the stranger said that she found her charming and then added: '*You surely don't understand me.*' She was quite surprised when Adele answered her in Italian. She asked Adele some questions, embraced her tenderly several times, then rose, called her chambermaid, and left. Adele said that, although the stranger was no longer young, she was still very beautiful; and Dainville said that, even though he had only seen the stranger from a distance, he had found her appearance most striking.

After telling her story, Adele begged me to stay in Albenga that night, instead of continuing on to Pietra as we had planned, and M. d'Almane agreed. We have settled here in a rather pretty house and have made inquiries about our lovely stranger. Based on Adele's description of her, we have been assured that she can be none other than the Duchess of C***, a person as remarkable for her virtues and misfortunes as for her birth and beauty. She has been living in Albenga for four years, in a house that she built in the most isolated part of the valley. She leads a most solitary existence, yet she is greatly admired by all for her charity, generosity, and piety. There is a great deal of confusion and uncertainty about her past life; the details that I've been able to gather are so extraordinary and so unbelievable that I will not write them to you yet. As you can imagine, we are very curious to make the duchess's acquaintance. And Adele is especially eager to see her again. Not knowing how to persuade her to receive us, we finally decided to follow M. d'Almane's advice that Adele should write to her. We hope that the childish grace and simplicity of her note will bring us success. The note was sent about an hour ago, but we have not yet received an answer.

* * *

Good news and great joy! The answer has just arrived: the duchess has agreed to see us and has invited us to supper. She mentioned in her note to Adele that she dines at seven o'clock. Since it is nearly six, we are leaving at once.

* * *

Ah! Dainville had good reason to promise us a charming adventure. We no longer know how long we'll stay in Albenga. We won't leave until we've gained a better understanding of the duchess's story; for she is surely the most intriguing person I ever encountered. Based on my description of our first meeting, you can judge for yourself how keen our curiosity must be and whether it is justified.

At a quarter past six in the evening, we arrived at her house, which is furnished with the most elegant simplicity. After passing through two antechambers and a rather long gallery, we were shown into a small boudoir. Catching sight of the duchess, Adele left me and ran to her. The duchess took her in her arms and kissed her two or three times. I drew closer and asked Adele to introduce me. Madame de C*** received us all most graciously. We sat down; and while M. d'Almane was giving her an account of our trip and answering her questions, I examined her with as much pleasure as astonishment. She is thirty-eight or forty years old, but is still quite striking due to the classic beauty of her features. She has dark eyes that resemble yours in size and shape, but with a more languid expression. Her figure is beautifully proportioned. Although she tends to stoop her head a bit, she has a most noble air; and when by chance she turns or lifts her head, she appears truly majestic. She is utterly lacking in Italian vivacity; she moves slowly and speaks softly, even expressing herself with some difficulty. After spending a quarter hour with her, one realizes that her mind wanders easily. She suddenly falls into a reverie, a kind of trance that is both somber and unsettling. And when she comes out of it, she looks at everything around her with dazed astonishment. Her countenance is sweet and captivating, but melancholy at the same time, with the air of someone who has suffered much. She is affectionate and demonstrative toward others. And, as much as one can judge from a two-hour visit, I believe that she is extremely sensitive, that her sensibility is keen, her imagination vivid, and her mind very clever.

During dinner, she asked me several questions about my daughter. She added that she too had a daughter who was her greatest joy, and that I would see her in Rome. When I expressed my surprise at the distance separating them, she explained that her daughter spent two or three months every year with her, after which she sighed and changed the subject.

As we left the table, I observed that her house seemed illuminated, rather than simply lit; for all the rooms were filled with chandeliers, candelabra, and girandoles. 'Ah, Madame,' exclaimed the duchess, 'if you knew what reason I have to cherish light and to hate obscurity and darkness!' As she spoke these words, her eyes filled with tears, and she immediately fell into a deep reverie.

We left her at nine o'clock. As we were leaving, she told me that it saddened her greatly that I was to leave the following day. I replied that, if she wished to see me again, I would prolong my stay. She squeezed my hand and embraced me. 'Albenga attracts few visitors,' she explained. 'Although several strangers have stopped here over the past four years, I refused to receive them. But I wish it were in my power to keep you here. At least promise me that you will come dine with me tomorrow.' As you can imagine, I accepted this invitation with pleasure and look forward eagerly to our next visit. Oh, if only she would share some details of her story with me! What is certain is that I will not leave Albenga without doing all I can to satisfy my curiosity.

* * *

Continuation of the baroness's journal

Albenga, Wednesday evening

I have it at last—this fascinating, extraordinary story I've desired so ardently to hear! This precious manuscript, written by the duchess herself, has been entrusted to me for twenty-four hours, and I have permission to translate and copy it. I've now read it, and I surely will be very sorry to part from the heroine of so moving a story! This woman as virtuous and touching as she was ill fated— oh, what a destiny she has had to bear! But, let us return to my journal and, while M. d'Almane and Dainville are busy translating the duchess's story into French, I will tell you about the experiences today that brought us this priceless gift.

We arrived at the duchess's house this morning at eleven. She proposed a walk before lunch and led us to a little belvedere. The view from there was so charming that Dainville and the children wanted to sketch it. After they did a quick drawing, the duchess asked to see Adele's other drawings, so I sent for her sketchbook. The duchess was surprised that a twelve and a half-year-old child could speak several languages and draw so well. I added that she also could sing and play the harp; so we had to send for the harp as well. Adele was very eager to please, and she succeeded. The duchess seemed truly enchanted with her.

After lunch, the duchess proposed another walk to me. It was only a short stroll just outside the house, for she cannot walk very fast, nor for very long. We sat down, just the two of us on a garden bench, and she spoke to me again of Adele. 'She appears to have great sensibility,' she remarked.

'Yes, she does indeed,' I replied.

'Oh, Madame, you must do all you can to protect her heart from the deadly impressions of love! May she never know that fatal passion that can cause such unhappiness and so many crimes!' She spoke these words in a tone of voice that made me shudder. She noticed this and, affectionately taking my hand, she confided: 'I don't know whether you have heard my story.'

'Oh!' I eagerly replied, 'how happy I would be to hear it from your lips!'

'From my lips!' she cried. 'Ah, Madame, it is so dreadful that I would never have the courage to tell it out loud; but I did have the courage to put it in writing. I wished to leave for my granddaughters, who are still very young, an account that may be useful for them some day—a striking lesson that will teach them two important truths: the first, that passions can plunge us into the deepest abyss of human miseries; and the second, that there are no misfortunes, no suffering so great that religion cannot help us bear.'

'Oh, heavens!' I interjected. 'This precious manuscript exists, and Adele will never read it?'

'No, Madame,' the duchess replied, 'I could not keep it from a mother such as you. Stay here two days longer, and I will entrust it to you.' At these words, I felt such a strong feeling of gratitude and joy that was impossible for me to express in any way except by embracing her with a fervor that must have shown her how greatly I valued such a favor. 'I am not offering my story to you confidentially, but simply as an expression of friendship,' she explained. 'Everyone knows my story; in Rome, they will tell you all the details of what happened. But I alone can tell you of my feelings and reflections, which will no doubt be of even greater interest to you.'

After this conversation, we entered the house again. The duchess led me to her study, where she opened a small armoire, from which she took out two thick notebooks covered with very neat handwriting. 'Here, take this manuscript,' she said. 'If you find it worth reading, have it copied and offer it to the charming Adele for me. I am sure she will not read it without shedding a few tears. May it prove a useful lesson to my young friend and strengthen, if possible, all the principles you have taught her!'

At five o'clock, I finally left the duchess to read the treasure she had entrusted to me. I will not try to describe the impression reading her story made on me; you will judge for yourself. While I've been writing to you, M. d'Almane and Dainville have translated more than half the duchess's story; they will have finished by tomorrow. Brunel will then make two copies: one for Adele and the other for you. I'll mail it to you as soon as we reach Genoa, along with my travel journal about our trip on the narrow coastal road the French call la Corniche.[5]

* * *

Albenga, Thursday

We dined at the duchess's house last night. How deeply moved we were to see her again after reading her story. She had asked us please not to speak to her of her experiences because she could not bear to discuss them. But Adele could not help bursting into tears when she embraced her. The duchess was obliged to keep the conversation going by herself the whole evening; for we could only gaze at her and think of her misfortunes. This morning, she made us promise to spend the entire day tomorrow with her; so we will not leave Albenga until Saturday afternoon. I returned her manuscript to her, and Brunel has just brought the copy I intend for you, which I'll place at the end of my journal entry for today.

STORY OF THE DUCHESS OF C***

Written by herself[6]

How shall I find the courage to recall in detail my misfortunes, when for so long, the slightest memory of these experiences caused me such deep distress! How can I find the strength to write this dreadful story? Oh, my daughters, you will read it, and the fact that it may offer you useful and persuasive lessons will sustain my resolve.

And you, who became master of my destiny through an ill-fated but sacred tie, whose ashes I reluctantly am about to disturb by describing your violent passions and crimes, forgive me! Your misdeeds and my misfortunes are only too well known; were they not, I would have respected your memory and sworn myself to an eternal silence. Although this account recalls what you did, at least it will not conceal my own errors in judgment and behavior that plunged me into that abyss of misery and led to such cruel punishments.

I was born in Rome into one of the most illustrious families in Italy. Sole heiress[7] of an immense fortune, I received a refined education. Brought up by the best of mothers, cherished by a loving father and by a family that placed all its hopes in me, I seemed to be supremely favored both by destiny and by nature. I turned fifteen without ever experiencing a single sorrow, without having once been ill, without having shed any tears but those caused by joy or compassion. I loved to recall the past, I keenly enjoyed the present, and I envisaged a future that was bright and happy.

The daughter of a friend of my mother's had been my childhood companion, and I was deeply attached to her. She was virtuous and sensitive; but lacking experience of the world, she could not advise or guide me. I nevertheless had boundless confidence in her. I loved and respected my mother, but I did not look upon her as my friend and confidante because she had allowed me to take another; she was even pleased at my forming such a dangerous attachment. This lack of prudence cost me dearly and was the chief cause of all my misfortunes.

My friend married the Marquis of Venuzi, with whom she had secretly been in love for a year. I was in on the secret, which only served to stir my imagination and soften my heart. Two days after the wedding, the Marquis of Venuzi took his new bride to a charming villa in the countryside thirty miles from Rome. My mother was among the guests invited to accompany them, and she took me with her.

The Marquise of Venuzi was three years older than I; she seemed both prudent and sensible. So although she was only in her nineteenth year, my mother gave us complete freedom to see each other at any time of day. One evening after dinner, the marquise suggested that we take a stroll in the garden. Walking alone, we entered a labyrinth made of bushes. As we turned a corner, we caught sight of a young man sitting on a bench. He rose when he saw us, and we were startled by his expression of surprise. We were very close to him and, as the moon shone on his face, we were both struck by his beauty and noble air. He remained standing before us and, after a moment of silence, the marquise asked him who he was. He answered with the utmost courtesy and respect, but refused to give his name and then quickly left.

Greatly surprised by this encounter, we returned home immediately and told the marquis what had happened. He smiled and led us to understand that this young man was not a stranger to him. When I expressed a strong desire to know more about him, the marquis replied: 'All I can tell you is that the young man is not married, that he is of noble birth, and that he has long been most anxious to meet you. If he agrees, I will tell you his name tomorrow.'

The following day, I asked more questions, but received only vague replies. That night, after my mother went to bed, I went to my friend's bedchamber and we shut ourselves in her dressing room. As we spoke of the previous night's adventure, the door suddenly opened and the Marquis of Venuzi came in, holding a dimly lit lantern in one hand and, with the other, leading the same young man I so longed to meet. I was dumbstruck and motionless with surprise. Approaching me, the marquis declared: 'Please allow me to introduce you to my prisoner.' Laughing, he added: 'I fear that it will no longer be possible to restore his freedom to him now that he has imprudently dared to see you a second time.' At these words, I blushed and felt tremendous confusion. Despite my young age, I sensed what the consequences of such an encounter might be. For a moment, I was tempted to go find my mother and tell her everything; but curiosity got the better of me and led me to forget my duty.

Adopting a more serious tone, the marquis told us that he was about to entrust us with an important secret: 'I know how discreet you both are and feel certain that you will fully justify the confidence you inspire.' After this prologue, the marquis made me promise absolute secrecy. The young man then spoke up and told us that his name was the Count of Belmire and that his father, the Marquis of Belmire, was younger brother to the Duke of C***, head of one of the most powerful families of Naples. He explained that the duke, after quarrelling with his brother, had conspired to ruin his reputation at court and had persecuted him so relentlessly that he was forced to leave the country. The marquis had settled in France where, four years later, an unfortunate affair had obliged him to seek another refuge. His close friend the Marquis of Venuzi, who was in France at the time and about to return to Italy, convinced him to return secretly with him and offered him a safe haven in his country house near Rome. For three months, he and his son had been hiding in the same house where we were now staying. After hearing about me, the young count had felt an irresistible desire to see me and, after our moonlit encounter in the garden, had begged the Marquis of Venuzi to arrange this meeting with me, to which he attached such great importance. He concluded by saying that he was leaving the next day for Venice with his father.

After listening to this account, I stood up and, despite the marquis's entreaties, said goodnight. I went up to my bedroom, overwhelmed by feelings of sadness. I dared not reflect on what had just happened, afraid to probe my heart or to examine my conduct. I could not conceive how—in the middle of the night, without my mother's knowledge—I could have listened to a young man I did not know, who had dared express his love to me. I clearly saw that I should be wary of the Marquis of Venuzi's advice and that even his wife was unprepared to guide me. I shuddered at the danger of my situation. I had a terrible premonition that I risked losing my reputation and my peace of mind forever—in short, all the happiness that I had enjoyed until then. The Marquise of Venuzi soon regained her influence over me and spoke to me constantly of the Count of Belmire. These dangerous conversations led me further astray, but without easing my melancholy.

We remained in the country for three months and then returned to Rome. Toward the end of the winter, there were many parties. The Marquis of Venuzi gave a masked ball, which I attended with my mother. At two in the morning, the marquise suggested that we go to her room to change. We left the ballroom and, as we crossed a rather dark corridor, I noticed that a person wearing a mask was following us. Imagine my surprise when the masked stranger approached me, fell on his knees before me, and revealed himself to be the Count of Belmire! Despite my astonishment and my secret joy at seeing him again, my first impulse was to try to escape. He caught the hem of my gown to keep me from leaving and begged to let him speak to me for a few moments. He implored the marquise for her help, she added her entreaties to his, and in the end I foolishly agreed.

The count told me that his father had settled his affairs, that he had been in Naples for six weeks, that he had seen his brother the Count of C*** again and been sincerely reconciled with him. 'My father,' he continued, 'is leaving for France in a month to take care of some business related to his fortune, but he is absolutely determined to return to his homeland. Before accompanying him on this last trip, I wanted to know my fate and so I came secretly from Naples to Rome to learn whether the tender vows I've dared to make are entirely rejected. Speak, Mademoiselle; if you scorn my love, I will bid you an eternal farewell. If I am rejected by you, then my fate is sealed and I will never return to Italy. Speak! Your answer will bring me back to my homeland or will banish me forever.' As the count uttered these last words, I could not hold back my tears; that response was only too well understood, and the count asked for no other. He assured me over and over of his eternal love. Although his fortune was not as considerable as mine, everything seemed to justify his hopes, now that he was certain of my affection and would be able to return to Rome in six months in a position to ask for my hand in marriage. And yet, my heart could not share his optimism.

Fig. 14: 'Imagine my surprise when the masked stranger approached me, fell on his knees before me, and revealed himself to be the Count of Belmire!' Copper engraving from the oil painting titled *The Lover's Plea, The Princess of Palestrina and Count de Belmire at the Masquerade* (1788) by John Francis Rigaud (1742-1810). Illustration from a 1788 edition of Genlis's novel and reprinted in *Camille, ou Le Souterrain*, plagiarized version of Genlis's novella published in 1844 without the author's name by Pierre Chaillot jeune in Avignon. (BnF)

117

Two months after this meeting, which shattered my peace of mind forever, the Duke of C*** came to Rome; I saw him at a social gathering in the home of the French ambassador. When I heard his name, I felt a cold chill run through my body that made a deep impression on me. My reaction simply may have been due to the extremely negative portrait the Marquis of Venuzi had drawn of him. In describing his dealings with the Marquis of Belmire, he had described the duke as a man who was as vindictive as he was deceitful. The Duke of C*** was thirty-six at the time and undeniably handsome; yet his eyes and eyebrows had a somber, sinister quality difficult to describe that, on first glance, made a much stronger impression than the regularity of his features and his noble air. He had piercing, fierce-looking eyes that appeared false and shifty when he tried to soften their expression. His manner was generally arrogant and disdainful; and although in certain respects, he was not lacking in social graces, his tone was both sharp and imperious. Haughtily proud of his high birth and fortune, of his position and influence at court, and of his success with women, he believed that nothing should ever oppose his will or resist his desires. Hot-tempered, violent, corrupted by pride and prosperity, he was incapable of controlling his passions or overcoming his resentments. Through weakness and vanity, he had become ruthless and incapable of forgiveness. Indeed, he prided himself on never forgiving anyone. His hatred was fierce, and he sacrificed everything to the dreadful pleasure he found in revenge.

Such was the Duke of C***. I felt an overwhelming aversion to him the moment I laid eyes on him. Unfortunately for me, I made quite a different impression on him. He came to our home to pay his respects to my mother. Two weeks later, my father announced to me that the duke had asked for my hand in marriage and that I was to marry him within a month. 'I gave my word without asking for your consent,' he added, 'because there was no doubt in my mind that you would gladly accept the finest match in all of Italy, a man who adores you and who is so attractive.'

This declaration seemed like a death sentence to me, and I listened to it in silence, unable to utter a single word. My father loved me, but he was inflexible and stern. Besides, what could I have said? Could I even ask my mother for help? How could I ever dare admit my mistakes to her and confess that I had pledged my heart without her permission! It was only then that I fully understood the fatal imprudence of my behavior and realized that the greatest misfortune that could befall a young woman was to have failed to regard her mother as her true friend and confidante at all times. Unable to voice my distress, I buried my sorrow and regrets deep in my heart, and I avoided the Marquise of Venuzi, whose dangerous advice I feared. I felt that the only way to make up for my transgressions was through obedience and respect for my parents' wishes. I resigned myself to my fate and sacrificed my happiness to them. I married the Duke of C*** and left almost immediately with him for Naples.

When we arrived in the city and entered the palace where I was to spend my life separated from my mother, my friends, my family, I experienced feelings of despair painful beyond description. The duke attributed my deep sadness to my affection for my parents and strove to ease my suffering by protestations of feelings that were not in my power to share. I appeared at Court and soon discovered that the duke was excessively jealous. This bothered me very little, and I would have preferred to withdraw from Court; but out of vanity, the duke obliged me to remain there, despite his jealousy and my preference for a quieter life.

I had been married for seven months when I learned that the Marquis of Belmire had died in France, that in his will he had named the duke guardian to his son, who was only eighteen years old at the time, and that the latter had fallen ill in Turin on his way back to Italy. Two weeks later, the duke entered my room and said that he had just heard from his nephew, who had recovered from his illness. 'He does not wish to come to Naples,' the duke added, 'and he has written to you to ask for your help in obtaining my permission to travel for two years. Here is his letter.' At these words, the duke handed me a letter, with the seal broken. Trembling, I took it and, in a faltering voice, read aloud what follows:

Madame,

Although I do not have the honor of your acquaintance, I hope that my misfortunes are sufficient to rouse your compassion for me! I have lost the most tender and best of fathers. Grief and despair brought me to the brink of the grave! The unwelcome aid of cruel friends recalled me to life. But what a life has been restored to me! I have lost all that could give it meaning. Forgive me, Madame, for troubling you with sorrows that have nothing to do with you, but my heart is overflowing with grief. Will you at least deign to excuse and pity me! My father's last will and testament has made me entirely dependent on my uncle, but I cannot obey his command to return to Naples. My father was born in Naples and spent the first twenty years of his life there. Everything in that place would recall painful memories to me. No, I will not return! I am sure, Madame, that you will approve my decision and that you will persuade my uncle to withdraw an order that is beyond my strength to obey. Secure for me, Madame, permission to travel, to flee, to go far away from Naples—in short, the freedom to carry far from Italy the sorrows and regrets that I will carry with me to my last breath.

Yours respectfully,
The Count of Belmire

I can in no way describe the dreadful agitation and terror I experienced reading this letter. It seemed impossible not to guess its double meaning. The duke was the most mistrustful and suspicious of men; yet unaware that his nephew had been in Rome and convinced that I never met him, he had not the slightest inkling of the truth. No longer able to repress feelings buried deep in my heart that were tearing it apart, I wrote the following day to the Marquise of Venuzi. In my letter, I dared at last to lament my unhappy lot and the ill-fated passion I could not overcome. In her response, the marquise questioned me about the duke's behavior. I answered her candidly and did not hide the fact that, each day, I discovered flaws, vices, and a certain ferocity of character that justified only too well the aversion I felt for him. In this way, through further indiscretions, I deepened the abyss opening beneath my feet.

Around this time, I enjoyed the happiness of seeing my mother and father again. I was nearing the end of my pregnancy, and they came to Naples to be with me for the delivery. I gave birth to a daughter and was allowed to breastfeed her. During all the time I nursed her, this sweet and gentle occupation gave a respite to my sorrows and made me impervious to mistreatment by the duke, who for a long time had ceased to restrain himself, revealing all the violence and volatility of his character.

The day after I weaned my daughter, the duke entered my bedchamber and said that we needed to leave at once for an estate he owned in the country a day's journey from Naples.[8] My daughter was beside me. I took her in my arms and, without uttering a word, rose and followed the duke. Once in the carriage, I held my daughter on my lap and caressed her. The duke remained silent and, throughout the entire trip, appeared lost in the deepest thought.

When we arrived at his castle, we crossed a drawbridge, and the rattling of the chains made me shudder. At that moment, I glanced at the duke. 'What's wrong?' he asked. 'You seem startled by this castle's ancient appearance. Come now! do you think you're entering a prison!' He uttered these words with such a forced and bitter smile, his eyes sparkling with such cruel joy, that I was terrified. In an effort to hide my fear, I bent my head over my daughter in my lap, and could not hold back my tears. Feeling my tears trickle down on her face, the child began to cry. Her cries pierced the very bottom of my soul. I pressed her to my bosom with the most tender affection, and my sobs increased.

Still crying and trembling with fear, I stepped out of the carriage. The duke snatched my daughter from my arms and gave her to one of his attendants. Then, seizing one of my hands, he led—or rather dragged me—toward the castle and made me go up a flight of steps, at the top of which was a long passageway. Night was beginning to fall, and the gallery that we were crossing was very large and dark. The duke was walking extremely fast. Suddenly he stopped and exclaimed: 'You're trembling. Why are you so afraid? Aren't you with a husband whom you love and who must love you dearly?'

'Oh, heavens!' I cried. 'What's the meaning of these wild-eyed, somber looks and this frightening tone of voice!'

'Come with me, and we'll finish this discussion.'

At these words, the duke led me out of the long passageway into a large bedchamber. He practically had to carry me in his arms, because I was unable to walk on my own. I sank into a chair and gave free rein to my tears. The duke left the room, but returned almost at once, holding a candle that he placed in front of me on a table at which he then sat down opposite me. I dared not look at him, and—hardly breathing, filled with terror, eyes downcast— waited for him to break the silence. All my missteps and errors of judgment ran through my mind. I was afraid the duke had somehow guessed the fatal secret of my heart, which filled with a criminal passion, now trembled with fear before an angry judge. Oh! If only if I had been blameless, how that innocence would have given me courage! But I felt guilty and lacked the strength to bear the terrible sense of foreboding caused by my remorse.

The duke spoke at last: 'I've enjoyed watching the signs of your guilty conscience long enough. It's time now to bring to a head the sense of shame that's tormenting you. Read these letters that I copied myself.' With this, he handed me a bundle of papers. Seeing that I hesitated to take it, he pulled out one sheet of paper and read it aloud. At the first words, I recognized one of the letters written to the Marquise of Venuzi, in which I had candidly expressed both the love that filled my heart and my invincible aversion for the duke.

'Oh, I'm lost!' I cried.

'You faithless creature!' replied the duke. 'I chose you and preferred you above all others, but wasn't able to make you happy. I adored you, yet you hated me and lamented your fate. I fill you with *an invincible aversion*! Well, I'll justify your hatred. From now on, you'll have the right to hate me! Betrayed and dishonored by you, do you think that I could tolerate such outrageous offenses without punishing them?'

'Stop!' I cried, interrupting him. 'You can accuse and punish me, but don't slander me. It's true that I'm guilty, but although I could not overcome my unfortunate passion, at least your honor and my own remain unsullied. I blame myself only for the imprudent confessions that friendship drew from me.'

'Liar!' shouted the duke, in a fit of anger. Picking up one of the letters, he declared: 'Listen to this proof of your guilt.' He then read the following passage:

> That object that nothing can tear from my heart—alas!—he is as much to be pitied as I am! For surely he knows how deeply he is loved and yet how much I regret the confession of my feelings that makes me feel so guilty and miserable today.

I recalled this passage from one of my letters only too well. But I also clearly remembered that I had not mentioned the Count of Belmire's name in any of them. In fact, I had spoken of him in so vague a manner that it was impossible to guess from these letters when my passion had begun. Early in our marriage, the duke had been violently jealous of two men at the Court of Naples who had openly expressed their feelings for me; he presumed that one of these two men was the one I loved. This supposition no doubt made me appear truly criminal in his eyes, since the passage he had just quoted seemed to prove that I had engaged in an adulterous liaison after my marriage to him. To justify myself, I would have had to admit that I was already in love with someone else when I married him—that in giving him my hand, I had no heart to offer. But knowing how much he scorned women and how likely he was to form the most odious conjectures, I remained silent for my daughter's sake. Although I had not left Rome until six weeks after our wedding, the duke was only too capable of forming offensive suspicions concerning his daughter if he learned that I had been in love before I met him. Besides, this confession could have led him to discover the whole truth. He might suddenly have recalled a thousand circumstances that could shed light on what really happened: the letter that I had received from his nephew, my confusion in reading it, the fact that I blushed every time he mentioned his name to me. He might also learn of the Marquis of Venuzi's friendship with the Count of Belmire's father. All these factors might well have led him to cast his suspicions beyond Naples, thereby risking a secret that was impossible to betray without exposing the object of my affections to the full fury of the duke's rancor. This prospect was all the more alarming, given that the Count of Belmire, who was only eighteen, was entirely dependent on the duke, his uncle and guardian.

All these reflections came flooding into my mind all at once and plunged me into the most terrible quandary: unable to justify myself, I dared not answer. The duke took my silence as a tacit confession of guilt that confirmed his dishonor and my shame. His rage then knew no bounds. He arose and, approaching me with a face enflamed and eyes flashing with fury, he cried: 'So, you have nothing more to allege in your defense!'

'Alas,' I replied. 'Are you in any state of mind to hear me out? I'm innocent, as heaven is my witness.'

Interrupting me, he exclaimed: 'You, innocent? How dare you make that claim! Didn't you yourself write that your lover *knows how deeply he is loved*'?

'And yet, I am innocent, yes, I am!' I insisted, shedding a torrent of tears.

'Monster of deceit!' shouted the duke. 'Tremble at the vengeance that is about to strike you!'

These words, spoken in a threatening and terrible voice, struck me as the irrevocable sentence of my destruction. I threw myself on my knees and, lifting my arms to heaven, I cried: 'O God, my sole refuge! God, protect me!'

'Get up,' said the duke in a calmer voice. 'Now sit down and listen to me.' I obeyed, looking at him with a timid and humble expression. He remained silent for a few minutes; then, with a deep sigh, he said: 'You ought to understand how deeply offended I am! You, who accuse me of being *fierce* and *vindictive*—ungrateful wretch to whom, until now, I've given only proofs of love—you're right now to fear the effects of my well-founded resentment. It's still possible for me to forgive you, but your sincerity alone can disarm my anger. Think about this carefully: From now on, the least attempt to mask the truth will seal your fate. I can be satisfied with a single victim, but I must have one. Tell me, without delay, the name of the vile seducer who led you to betray your vows and your most sacred duties.'

'No!' I cried, interrupting him. 'No, I did *not* break my vows, nor did I betray my duties.'

Raising his voice, the duke declared: 'I insist on knowing your lover's name, and I order you to tell me.'

At that moment, I sensed all the horror of my fate. But as the danger of my situation increased, so too did my resolve, and preferring death to the cowardly solution proposed to me, I declared: 'If you must have a victim, then sacrifice the one you hold in your power; let the full weight of your vengeance fall upon me; for you will never know the name you are seeking.'

Startled by my boldness and determination, the duke stood still for a moment; no words can express his rage and indignation. Exploding impetuously at last, he exclaimed: 'Miserable wretch! I'll never know his name! Ah! I see that you have no idea of the extreme lengths to which I can go. No, you don't yet really know me!'

'Wretched as I am, I'm prepared for anything, even to face death,' I replied.

'Death! Stop deluding yourself. I don't intend for you to die. For a year now, I've buried my hatred and fury deep within my soul. For a whole year, I've been carefully planning the punishment for your infidelity, and you really believe that one moment of revenge could satisfy me! No, you will not die. It's true that your tomb is ready, but you must descend into it alive, without finding the death you desire.' Hearing these dreadful words, I felt the blood freeze in my veins; my eyes closed, and I fell into a deep swoon.

When I regained consciousness, I found myself in the arms of my female attendants. I asked anxiously for the only chambermaid I had brought from Rome, the one most devoted to me. I was told that she had remained in Naples. I guessed that this had been arranged by the duke, who no doubt feared a troublesome and vigilant witness. This discovery increased my terror to a fever pitch.

I spent the night surrounded by my female servants, feeling constrained by their presence, but afraid to be alone—not daring to complain in front of them, nor to send them away—and inwardly tormented by remorse, dread, and anticipation of a terrible catastrophe. Around six in the morning, I asked to be taken to my daughter's room. She was still asleep. I sent her nursemaids away and sat down beside her cradle. The sight of her, far from easing my anguish, only increased it further.

'Alas, dear child,' I murmured, 'as you sleep peacefully in sweet slumber, you are oblivious to your mother's bitter sorrows! I may be seeing you for the last time. Receive my most tender blessings!' Falling on my knees, I cried, 'O God, I resign myself to my dreadful fate, but let my daughter be happy! May she live in peace and innocence! If they have the cruelty to take her from me, may the good Lord protect her and be like a mother to her!' As I uttered these words, my sobs intensified and kept me from continuing. At that moment, the bedroom door suddenly opened, and the duke appeared. I shuddered at the sight of him, and my tears stopped. I rose, but unable to support myself, I fell into an armchair.

'So, are you more reasonable, now that you've had time to reflect?' he asked. 'Do you finally realize everything you risk by opposing my will?' A deep sigh was my only response. 'Are you still resolved never to tell me the name I asked you for?' I raised my eyes to heaven and maintained my silence. 'I demand a definite answer,' insisted the duke. 'Will you name him or not?'

'I cannot,' I replied.

'Ah,' exclaimed the duke. 'You're pronouncing your own sentence! Look again at this child and bid her an eternal farewell.'

'No!' I cried, interrupting him. 'You won't have the cruelty to separate me from her. Let me have my child! Or at least let me see her from time to time, and I'll be able to bear without complaint whatever punishment your hatred can inflict on me. What! Is your heart completely closed to pity? If that is true, then regardless of the fate you've prepared for me, you deserve more pity than I do! But I can't believe that you would take my daughter away from me forever!' At that moment, my daughter awoke and opened her eyes. Seeing her father, she smiled at him and reached out to him, her little hands almost joined together. 'Alas!' I said. 'She seems to be pleading for me and imploring your pity! O, my dear child, if only you could speak, you would soften your father's heart!'

The Duchess of C___

Fig. 15: The duke snatching the duchess's baby from her arms. Frontispiece from *The Affecting History of the Duchess of C.*, English translation of Genlis's novella published in London by S. Bailey circa 1800. Artist unknown. (Copyright Chawton House Library)

127

I wanted to take her in my arms, but the duke seized her. 'Let her be,' he ordered. 'She's no longer yours.'

'Oh, give me back my daughter or take my life,' I cried. 'To soften your heart, must I beg you on my knees? So be it.' As I spoke these words, I threw myself at his feet and bathed them with my tears, my arms around his knees. I would have suffered any mortification; I was begging for my child. The brute seemed to take pleasure in my humiliation. He gazed at me for a moment; then, pushing me away angrily, he headed for the door. I followed him on my knees crying 'My child! My child!' Frightened by this, the baby gave a plaintive cry and stretched out her arms to me. She seemed to be bidding me a sad farewell. I then lost sight of her as the duke hastily left the room, leaving me in the depths of despair.

A while later, the duke returned and led me to my bedchamber. Adopting a hypocritical expression of sympathy, he said, 'You consider me ruthless, with an unfeeling heart, and yet....' He broke off and lowered his gaze. The fierce, sinister look in his eyes might have revealed his cunning artifice, had I been less naïve. But I was only eighteen and in his power. Unaware of his dreadful intentions, I saw no reason why he would dissemble. I imagined he reproached himself for his extreme cruelty and that he might soften the vengeance he had originally planned. A ray of hope revived my heart. I spoke to him again of my daughter. The duke listened with a gloomy expression on his face, but without showing any anger. He even feigned a tenderness for me that he wished to hide. He gave me to understand that his passion for me was the sole reason for his violent conduct, and he ended by saying that if I took care of my health, I might see my daughter again. So fond a hope made me forget all I had suffered. Now that the duke seemed less cruel, I felt more in the wrong. I felt that he was justified in hating me and, based on my letters, in believing me guilty. Deeply touched by the compassion he seemed to show for me, I excused his earlier outbursts. And as I shed tears of sincere remorse, the cruel author of my misfortunes was secretly congratulating himself on the success of the diabolical trap in which he was about to ensnare me.

A high fever, brought on by my deep sorrows, forced me to take to my bed. The duke appeared deeply worried and sent immediately to Naples for two doctors. He never left my bedside and, in the presence of my attendants, displayed the greatest affection for me. When we were alone, everything he said served to persuade me that his love for me outweighed his resentment, and he assured me that I would see my daughter again as soon as my fever was gone. Hearing this promise, I forgot all he had made me suffer. I seized one of his hands, pressed it in mine, and bathed in tears of gratitude that barbarous hand which, only a few hours later, was to drag me away and cast me into the depths of a horrible dungeon.

The doctors assured us that my illness was not dangerous and, anxious to return to Naples, they left in the morning two days later. Soon after their departure, the duke feigned greater anxiety concerning my health. Although my fever was gone, he forced me to stay in bed. As he had obliged all my attendants to watch over me the three preceding nights, they were overcome with fatigue. He sent them away to rest the whole day, declaring he would look after me, along with one of his valets and the castle's old housekeeper. These two witnesses were not chosen randomly. The duke gave them preference over all the other servants because he knew they were both as credulous as they were ignorant. Since the curtains of my bed were drawn, I thought that my women were still keeping watch over me. At noon, I realized that no one was in my bedchamber besides the two people I just mentioned. When I expressed surprise at this, the duke came to my bedside and assured me that I would still be well attended and that he would not leave me.

'Why, since I am no longer ill?' I asked, rather alarmed.

His only reply was to ask me not to speak and to try to remain calm. He sat down by my bedside. Without knowing why, I felt uneasy, and my eyes filled with tears. The duke appeared anxious and agitated, and a strange expression came over his face.

About three in the afternoon, the duke asked for my arm to take my pulse. Trembling, I obeyed. After feeling my pulse, he hurried over to my two attendants. He told the valet to run to the stables to send a messenger to Naples for a physician, and he told the old woman to quickly fetch the chaplain. After giving these orders, he cried in a tone of desperation: 'She's dying! She's dying!' Imagine, if you can, how shocked and terrified I was. My first impulse was to get up and try to escape; but paralyzed with fear and unable to breathe due to the pounding of my heart, I sunk back helplessly onto the bed.

After receiving orders that would occupy them for at least three quarters of an hour, my two attendants departed, leaving me alone with the duke. He came over to me and, handing me a cup, said in a muffled voice that was barely audible, 'Here, drink this.' At these words, my hair stood on end and a cold sweat ran down my face. I thought I had come to the last moments of my life, for there was no doubt in my mind that he was giving me poison. 'Drink it!' he said again.

'Oh! What are you giving me?' I asked.

'What you must take,' he insisted.

'Then give me time to beg for God's mercy.'

'What do you suspect! Do you dare accuse me of plotting a crime?'

'Alas, it's my fate and my own imprudence that I blame above all.' Clasping my hands together, I cried, 'Oh, Lord! Forgive me, forgive my persecutor, comfort my father and mother, protect my child!' After this short prayer, I felt all my courage return. I dared to hope that my resignation would make me worthy to appear before God. With an air of self-assurance, I looked at the duke. He was pale, disconcerted, and trembling. He stammered a few halting words; then, raising my head with one hand, he brought the cup to my lips with the other. Without resisting, I drank all the potion he gave me and, believing I had received my death and fully resigned to my fate, I fell back on my pillow.

After few moments, my eyes grew heavy and closed; I was overcome with a feeling of lethargy and numbness that prevented me from thinking or speaking, and I fell into a deep sleep. About half an hour later, the valet and old woman returned. With hair disheveled and his face bathed in tears, the duke ran to meet them and told them I had just died. He brought them again into my bedchamber, in order, he explained, to have them confirm his misfortune or to assist me if I were still alive. Before their arrival, he had taken the precaution to close my curtains and to make the room extremely dark. In their presence, he approached my bed and pretended to give me all possible assistance. He then appeared to abandon himself to the most violent grief.

The chaplain arrived, and the duke ordered him to recite the prayers for the dead. Meanwhile, my women, who had just awakened, came running to my room along with all the servants. With the duke kneeling by my bedside, the housekeeper and valet told the assembled household all that had been done to try to save me. After this account, the duke partially opened my curtains for a moment. Seeing me pale and lifeless, no one doubted my death. The duke had everyone move to an adjoining room, except for the chaplain, an old man of eighty, who remained with him in my bedchamber and continued the prayers for the dead until midnight. He then announced that he would not bury me until the following evening and told everyone to go rest. He added that, unable to tear himself away from me, he would spend the rest of the night in my room. He then locked all the doors, after ordering the chaplain and my two attendants to await his orders in an antechamber separated from my bedroom by three large rooms. He told them that he would not leave me until seven in the morning and that he wished to remain alone with me, so as not to be disturbed in his grief and his prayers.

Everyone was exhausted from lack of sleep and eagerly took advantage of the permission to rest. At four in the morning, when the entire household was asleep, I slowly emerged from my lethargy and awoke. Opening my eyes and recovering use of my senses, I caught sight of the duke standing by my bedside. Although I had no memory of what had happened to me, I shuddered at the sight of him. Looking carefully at him, I had a confused recollection that he was angry with me. A feeling of terror came over me, and I turned my head away. As I tried to compose myself and to make sense of what had happened, a thousand vague, fantastic images flooded my mind, and I sunk into a dazed reverie, followed by a kind of stupor. The duke gave me smelling salts and then some drops of a potion to revive me. I sat up and looked around me with astonishment. My thoughts gradually grew less confused; I recalled that I thought I had taken poison, and I almost doubted my existence.

'Oh,' I cried at last, 'what miracle has saved my life!'

'It was only an imaginary terror that you felt,' replied the duke. 'Calm yourself and banish these outrageous fears.' I dared not answer. I opened my bedcurtains part way and looked around the room. Seeing that I was alone with the duke, my fears increased, especially now that I had entirely recovered my senses.

'Why then are you here with me alone?' I asked.

'You will soon know,' he replied. 'Now get up.' At these words, he brought me a gown and helped me put it on. Supporting me in his arms, he led—or rather carried—me to an armchair. Noticing that I was still weak and trembling, he made me take more of the drops he had just given me. Then, after a moment's silence, he said: 'I will conceal nothing from you now. What you drank yesterday was a sleeping potion.'

'But why?' I asked.

'Listen to me without interrupting. You have betrayed and dishonored me; I offered you my forgiveness, but you refused to accept it. Guilty of infidelity, you still harbor an adulterous passion deep in your soul. Neither my anger nor my threats were able to persuade you to reveal your lover's name. You thought perhaps that my regard for your family would stop me from taking your child from you and depriving you of your freedom. You thought, no doubt—for your hatred will judge me capable of any crime—that my only means of revenge was to murder you in secret. Indeed, the *invincible aversion* you feel for me made you welcome death! But understand now that you will go on living, separated forever from your family, your friends, your servants, the entire world!'

'Oh heavens!' I cried. 'How cruel and heartless you are! But do you really believe that my parents, devoted as they are to me, won't ask what has become of me?'

'Tomorrow they will receive the false news of your death.'

'Good heavens! And how can you possibly succeed?'

'I have already announced your death in the castle. During your deep sleep, the entire household saw you and thought you were dead.'

Alas!' I cried, interrupting him and bursting into tears. 'Then I no longer exist, except for you? I see now all the horror of my fate!'

'You don't yet know everything,' declared the duke. 'Beneath this castle of mine, there are vast underground chambers unknown to the world where the light never penetrates.'

'Oh, God!' I cried. 'So there's no hope for me. I'm lost forever!'

'No,' replied the duke, 'your fate is still in your own hands. I can instantly go and awaken everyone and declare that you were only in a deep sleep. I have not yet sent my letter to your father. I can still forgive you and restore you to the world. I ask you only for one word, a single word. I must have a victim, as I told you before. Name your lover, and I will restore you to your rank, to the world, to life!'

'What are you proposing to me?' I cried, interrupting him. 'To sacrifice to your vengeance someone who has not harmed or offended you in any way? Ah! I would be unworthy to live if I had the baseness to consent to it!'

'Think carefully about this,' warned the duke, with a menacing look on his face. 'One more refusal, and I will drag you down to that dark abode from which nothing can release you. Tomorrow your father and mother will either mourn your death or rejoice at your recovery. Tomorrow, you will once again see your daughter and the sun or you will be forever deprived of daylight, groaning at the bottom of a ghastly dungeon. In short, tomorrow we will see you in this castle, enjoying perfect health, or we will attend your funeral. Consider the choice carefully. Once this moment has passed, there will no hope of forgiveness. You will repent in vain, because I will no longer be able to pardon you.'

Hearing this ominous warning, I stood up, overcome with shock and terror. I turned my eyes toward the door and, with a plaintive cry, exclaimed: 'Alas, has the whole world abandoned me? Am I to live without ever seeing my daughter again! Tomorrow my mother and father will mourn my death! My daughter! Oh, let me see my child one more time!'

'You have only to say one word,' replied the duke, 'and your daughter will be in your arms.' These words tore my heart to pieces, and I remained silent for a moment. It occurred to me that the Count of Belmire was out of the country and not due to return for a year; during that time, it would be easy for me to warn him of the danger. And besides, a frank confession might demonstrate my innocence. But then, recalling the cruelty of my persecutor, I quickly rejected this temptation. Who could assure me that if I made such a confession, my child and my freedom would be restored to me? Quite to the contrary, shouldn't I fear that the duke, certain of my hatred for him, would never give up the vengeance he planned and that he might only soften its cruel rigor? Given that doubt, could I dare abandon the man I loved to his rage? All these reflections ran through my mind with extreme rapidity.

The duke thought I was hesitating and once again urged me to confess. 'It will soon be daylight. It's time for you to come to a final decision. I will either wake the household and tell them that you are alive or I will lead you to your tomb. Speak up! Will you name the author of your misfortunes and of mine?'

At this question I lifted up my eyes to heaven, and summoning all my strength, I answered, 'I cannot.'

'What are you saying, wretched woman!' cried the duke, interrupting me.

'No, give up that hope, for I will never name him.'

'You faithless woman!' exclaimed the duke. 'So you prefer your lover to your daughter, to freedom, to life, to the whole world! Tremble at your fate. The moment of vengeance has at last arrived!'

As he finished these words, he tried to seize my arm. Filled with terror, I fled to the other end of the bedroom, threw my arms around one of the bedposts, and clasped it tightly. All this agitation caused my nightcap to fall off, and my hair tumbled loosely about my shoulders. The duke, who was coming toward me, suddenly stopped; he appeared surprised, evidently struck by what he saw, and stared at me silently for a moment. Then, pulling me from the bedpost, he stood me in front of a mirror.

'Miserable woman,' he said. 'Gaze for the last time upon this beauty that the most horrid darkness will soon conceal forever. Lift your eyes and look at yourself. Don't be crueler than I am myself. Think of your youth, your charms! Take pity on yourself! It's still within your power to change the fate awaiting you!'

I could not help casting an anxious and mournful look at the mirror. Closing my eyes, I felt some tears trickle down my cheeks.

'So, is your resolution still unshaken?' asked the duke.

'Didn't you already falsely promise to let me see my daughter again?' I replied.

Scarcely had I finished uttering these words that the duke, in a fit of rage, caught me in his arms and carried me out of the room. I made no attempt to resist; my extreme terror left me motionless and mute. After crossing two or three rooms, he led me down a narrow, hidden staircase, and I found myself in a spacious inner courtyard at the end of which was a door that the duke opened. We went through the doorway, and I saw that we were in the garden.

Seeing that day was breaking, the duke declared: 'This is the last dawn your eyes will ever behold!'

I threw myself down on my knees and, raising my head upward toward heaven, I cried: 'O God! You who know my innocence, will you let me be buried alive and deprived forever of the light of day?' As I uttered these words, the duke dragged me about twenty steps to a rock cliff. He inserted a key into a keyhole hidden behind a boulder, and a trapdoor suddenly sprang open. I shuddered.

The duke paused. 'There is still time,' he urged. 'Here is your tomb, but it is only half open. If you finally repent and show me your remorse by a sincere confession, I am ready to forgive you. You may think that, on the verge of satisfying my just vengeance, I may dread possible consequences to myself. However, I have long meditated my plan; I have been attentive to every eventuality, and nothing can stop me.' He then recounted, in chilling detail, all the precautions he had taken. He explained that he had had a deathly white wax figure made that he would place in my bed; under the pretence of fulfilling an act of piety, he would bury it alone with the assistance of the old housekeeper, who would be a witness to the burial, without his being obliged to take her into his confidence. 'And so, I'm asking you for the last time: Will you accept the pardon I'm offering you? Speak up, sacrifice your lover to my rancor and tell me his name, or forever renounce freedom, the world, and the light of day.'

Hearing these words, I extended my arms toward the rising sun, as if to bid it an eternal farewell. The heavens were filled with bright, majestic clouds, forming a most glorious sight that exalted my soul and restored my courage. I cast a look of disdain upon the earth, and turning toward the duke, I declared in a resolute voice: 'Take your victim!' Immediately after, he dragged me through the doorway. With my heart beating violently, I turned my head to gaze one last time at the sunlight that I was leaving behind forever. As we descended into a dark cavern, my legs trembled so much that they were unable to support me. Shaking uncontrollably, I struggled in the arms of my cruel persecutor and then fell motionless and unconscious at his feet.

I have no idea how long I remained in this condition. Alas, I regained consciousness and came back to life again only to abhor it. How can I describe the horror that gripped me when I opened my eyes and found myself alone in that vast dungeon, lying on a bed of straw and encircled by impenetrable darkness! I let out a plaintive cry; the echo reverberating from the innermost recesses of the cavern made me shudder and intensified the terror that oppressed me. 'Oh, God!' I cried. 'Is this the only voice that will answer me, the only sound I will hear from now on?' This thought caused me to shed a torrent of tears. At that instant, I heard the door of my prison open, and the duke appeared with a lantern in his hand. He placed by my side a pitcher of water and some bread.

'Henceforth, this shall be your only nourishment. You will find it each day in the turning-box[9] opposite you. I will put it there myself, and so never again will I need to enter this dreadful dungeon.'[10]

At these words, I looked around me and saw a cavern so immense that my eyes could not see the end of it. The walls of the part I occupied were hung with coarse straw mats to insulate it from the cold and damp; for the monster who had cast me into this dreadful place had taken every possible precaution to prolong my life in it. Trembling with horror, I gazed at the dismal scene around me. I then turned toward my cruel jailer and gave free rein at last to a hatred so long concealed, but so well founded. I dared to criticize his extreme cruelty and to express, without reserve, the deep revulsion and contempt he inspired in me. The duke listened to me for awhile, seething with a concentrated rage; but then, no longer able to contain himself, he flew into a terrible fit of anger and then abruptly left.

From that day on, whenever the duke came to bring me food, he knocked at the turning-box until I answered him and then went away without entering my prison or speaking a single word to me. I soon regretted having thus, by my tirade against him, increased still more, if it was possible, his hatred and resentment toward me. I reminded myself that he was my daughter's father and that this dear child was in his care. And despite the horror of my situation, hope was not yet entirely extinguished in my heart. The more I thought about it, the less likely it seemed that the duke truly intended to keep me forever in that terrible captivity. I even deluded myself into thinking that he had not really announced my death to his household or to my family, that he had found some other way to elude their inquiries, and that he had reserved the possibility of having me reappear when he chose. How could I have imagined that he would impose on himself the tedious necessity of bringing me food and water every other day, of reducing himself to the miserable bondage of never leaving the castle for more than two or three days at a time, since he was my only jailor and had taken no one into his confidence? I could not believe that, to satisfy a desire for vengeance, hatred was capable of imposing chains on itself that the most passionate love would bear only with regret! These reflections persuaded me that he would one day give up his vengeance. Convinced of this, I spoke to him every time he knocked at the turning-box; and, although he never answered me, I begged him to take pity on me and assured him of my innocence.

Since I was completely deprived of light, I cannot tell how many days and months I sustained this hope, but I eventually lost it. My sanity then completely abandoned me; I accused Providence and railed against its decrees. My dejected soul, weighed down by grief, lost its fortitude and principles, and I sank into the darkest, most dreadful despair. I dared to think that my extreme misfortune gave me the right to dispose of my life, as if one could break the most sacred tie when it ceased to be agreeable! Resolved to die, I refused to eat for two days or to take any provisions from the turning-box. In vain the duke knocked and called to me; I stubbornly refused to answer him. He eventually entered my prison. When he appeared, with the lantern in his hand—despite the horror that his presence inspired in me—I felt a secret joy in seeing light again. But I did not speak to him. He offered to soften the rigor of my captivity and to give me a lantern, some books, and better food, if I would at last tell him the name he had so often demanded.

Hearing this proposal, I looked at him intently with an expression of the deepest scorn: 'Now that you have broken all the fateful ties that bound us together, my heart is free and has yielded completely and without remorse to the feelings that it resisted in vain before,' I declared. 'This person whom you ask me to name simply to sacrifice him to your vengeance, I love him more than ever, and my last breath shall be for him. So you are mistaken if you think I'll ever denounce him to you!'

'Have you lost all sense of religion?' the duke replied. 'You're harboring an adulterous flame deep in your heart, and you're resolved to die?'

'Monster!' I cried, interrupting him. 'How can you dare say that I'm still your wife—you who have cast me into this abyss, you who even now are wearing mourning clothes for me? It's true that I no longer have the courage to go on living, but the Lord who hears and judges us will punish you alone for the despair to which you have reduced me. If I commit a crime, you alone will be responsible. No other living being can hear my moans and cries! But can the deepest cavern, the thickest dungeon walls keep God from hearing the plaintive cries of the weak and unjustly oppressed? Tremble, because he is watching us. He is ready to forgive me, and his vengeful arm is raised above you ready to strike!'

The duke shuddered as I spoke and looked at me with a wild look of consternation on his face. I took pleasure for a moment in filling his fierce, but cowardly heart with terror and remorse. Pale and visibly troubled, with eyes downcast, he remained stormily silent for a few minutes. At last he spoke: 'You have only yourself to blame for your misfortunes. You were guilty; I have irrefutable proof that you could not deny, yet I did not punish you until after repeatedly offering to pardon you. Now I am proposing to lighten your punishment, and yet you refuse! Yes, if you had wished it— despite your infidelity, despite your aversion for me—you might still be in my palace, where you would see your daughter!'

'Oh, my child!' I cried, interrupting him. 'Alas! Is she still alive? What has become of her?'

'She is with your mother,' he replied.

'Is it really true that she is no longer in your care?' Seeing that this idea seemed to revive me, the duke took a letter from my mother out of his pocket and let me read it. This letter, which I bathed with my tears, contained the following words:

My granddaughter arrived here yesterday evening. Oh! how can I describe all the emotions that tore at my heart when I embraced her! You have given her to me; she is mine. I already love her so much that I feel she will give me a reason to go on living, but without consoling me. Alas! how can I enjoy the happiness of being a mother again, without feeling terrible uneasiness? After the loss I have I suffered, is there a felicity on earth on which I can depend? Next summer, I will come see you with your daughter and spend two months with you. Since you cannot tear yourself from the melancholy place your grief has rendered so dear to you, I will find the courage to join you there. I will see the magnificent monument that your love has erected to the memory of one so worthy of our tears. Perhaps I will find an end to all my sufferings there! Alas, is it possible that a mother can embrace the tomb of her daughter without dying? And yet, I wish to live. Religion commands me to, as does nature itself. I will live for the child you have deigned to entrust to my care. Oh! how can I ever express my gratitude for so great a gift to me and such a sacrifice on your part? How tenderly you must love this child! She has all her mother's features and all her charms! It is as if my own daughter has been restored to me in her infancy! Oh, such a flattering illusion! Wretched mother, you no longer have a daughter, and the violence of your grief cannot free you from the burden of living!

Hardly had I finished this letter, when falling upon my knees, I cried: 'My daughter is in my mother's arms, and that tender mother agrees to live for my child! Thank you, God! You have afflicted only me alone! I now submit willingly to my fate. Forgive my wild complaints, ensure the happiness of those I love, and prolong my painful existence as long as you wish.' As I finished these words, I fell back again on my bed of straw; for I was so weak that I could not support myself. The duke seized that instant to offer me some nourishment, which I very readily took. He then left me and, after that, I never saw him again.

Faithful to the vow I had made, I took care to preserve my life. The idea that my prayers and resignation could bring the blessings of heaven to my mother and daughter—this consoling thought had the power of reviving and sustaining my courage. The memory of my faults now became my greatest cause of distress. 'Alas,' I murmured to myself. 'All my misfortunes are my own doing. I lacked confidence in my mother; in ceasing to confide in her and to seek her advice, I was led astray. To punish me for my ingratitude and disloyalty to my parents, heaven blinded them in their judgment: the husband they chose for me was incapable of making me happy. And yet, had it not been for new errors in judgment, love for my family could have made me happy. But far from trying to overcome a guilty passion, I secretly fostered it. And in the imprudent letters that were my downfall, I even dared to express all the violence of that passion while complaining of the husband I was offending!'

These reflections caused me to shed a flood of tears. And yet I felt a certain sweet, soothing pleasure in crying over my faults and in regretting them so deeply. In true contrition, one finds expiation and healing. Remorse for a crime withers the soul, but repentance for an involuntary weakness brings neither heartache nor bitterness. It is a virtuous feeling that consoles us for our faults and reconciles us to ourselves. Deprived of everything and everyone, separated from the world, my naturally tender heart soon devoted itself wholly to that sublime passion that alone could make my life bearable. Religion taught me to know and enjoy the infinite consolations it can offer. Little by little, it banished from my heart the ill-fated passion that had been the greatest misfortune of my life. And, in the end, it granted me what human wisdom and mere philosophy could never give: the fortitude to endure, without despair or complaints, nine long years of captivity in a dungeon impenetrable to the light of day!

I will confess, however, that, for the first two or three years, I experienced periods of depression so extreme that, even now, the mere recollection of them makes me shudder. The times when I guessed (from the best calculations I could make) that my mother and daughter might be staying in the same castle where I was imprisoned—these periods passed for me in the most agonizing manner and formed the cruelest part of my captivity. My heart was torn to pieces at the thought that my mother and daughter were so near to me, without the hope of ever seeing them again.

'Oh, mother,' I cried, 'you are mourning my death, and I exist! And—good Lord!—what hand have you chosen to wipe away your tears? It's on the bosom of my persecutor, my executioner, that you shed them! The tomb to which he leads you is not mine! Alas, without realizing it, you tread on the ground above my prison, and you look upon the rocks that conceal it without a tear! Perhaps, in the silence of the night, unable to taste the sweet comfort of sleep, you will wander about near my dungeon. Perhaps, at this very moment, you are sitting near that dreadful trapdoor that will never again open for me! Ah, if it is so, you are thinking, no doubt, of your wretched daughter; you weep for her and cannot hear her plaintive cries, nor her voice calling you!'

Such painful thoughts tore at my heart and often clouded my mind. These cruel fits of grief were followed by a kind of dazed insensibility and feeling of bleak emptiness even more dreadful than despair itself. But as my religious faith gradually strengthened in my heart, these violent episodes diminished in frequency and intensity. I found ineffable consolation in prayer. Ideas that normally sadden people became favorite subjects of meditation for me. I reflected on the shortness of life with pleasure and envisaged death with the greatest serenity.

'Is the happiest person ever truly satisfied with the fragile and fleeting joys this world can offer?' I asked myself. 'He is less concerned with the blessings of the present hour than with those he anticipates in the future. He delights in wandering amidst the illusory visions of future happiness conjured up by his imagination. But what difference does it make whether his destiny is filled with joy or misery? What does it matter if his hopes are realized or not; won't he always be forming new desires? Will he ever know how to enjoy the present and be content with it? Why then should I regret so bitterly all I have been deprived of, since it cannot bring happiness? It's true that I am destined to spend my life in this horrible darkness; the future offers nothing to my frightened imagination but a long and gloomy night. Well then, let us think only of the awakening! Let us forget this transitory life and direct all our thoughts toward eternity. Let us scorn these momentary sufferings that are to be followed by everlasting joys; and let us henceforth focus all our desires, all our hopes on that object who alone is worthy of occupying the human heart!'

These salutary reflections enabled me to fully accept my fate and to rise above it. Restored to reason and to myself, I found not only that my sufferings eased, but that I became accustomed to darkness and to my captivity. I even devised activities for myself. My prison was spacious. I walked about the greater part of the time I was awake, composing poems that I repeated aloud. I had a fine voice and an excellent knowledge of music, and I made up hymns. One of my greatest pleasures was to sing them and to listen to the echo that answered me. My sleep became peaceful with pleasant dreams of my beloved father, mother, and daughter, who always appeared satisfied and happy to me. In my dreams, I was sometimes transported to magnificent palaces or lovely gardens. I again beheld the skies, trees, and flowers. These sweet illusions restored to me all that I had lost. I awoke, it is true, with a sigh; but I fell asleep content. Even when I was awake, joy ceased to be a stranger to my heart; my imagination was raised into a kind of sweet enthusiasm. I dared to flatter myself that my patience and resignation found favor in God's eyes and that, witness to all my actions, he was listening to me. I felt that he spoke to my heart, renewed it, and raised it up to himself, and I no longer felt alone in my dungeon.

Besides being deprived of those I loved, the only thing I still missed, in spite of myself, was daylight and a view of the sky. I no longer understood how people could give way to despair even in the bleakest bondage if only they could enjoy the view from a window that looked out on the countryside. In the end, I became so accustomed to my situation that, far from desiring death, I realized more than once that I still feared it. Often I lacked food and water.

Sometimes the duke brought me enough for three or four days; I understood then that he was leaving on a short trip. And when my supply was nearly exhausted, I became anxious; the death of my tyrant would lead to my own, and this cruel thought forced me to pray for his health. It's true that I no longer felt any aversion toward him; my religious faith had made it easy for me to renounce all hatred. This hardly cost me any effort. Hadn't I already triumphed over love!

I felt sorry for my persecutor. When I imagined the terrible state of his soul—his fury, fears, and remorse—I felt that I was only too well avenged. In the first days of my captivity, I never heard him approach without nearly fainting with terror; but these violent reactions gradually subsided with the passage of time. He still inspired a bit of fear in me, and yet I wanted him to come, not only for the preservation of my life, but also because he broke the deep and frightful silence of my solitude. Thanks to him, I heard sound and movement. In short, he provided a kind of distraction that, although never pleasant, became necessary to me. I cannot express the intensity of the desire I felt to hear some sound. When the thunder was extremely loud, I heard it and the sound filled me with an emotion that is impossible to describe. It made me feel less alone. I listened to that majestic sound in rapt attention; and when it ceased, I sunk into the deepest melancholy.

This was more or less my situation for six or seven years. During that time, nothing really troubled me much except for the distress I felt at not knowing what had become of my mother and daughter. In vain, I asked the duke about them through the turning-box whenever he approached it. I could not obtain a single word in response; for since his last appearance in my dungeon, he never spoke to me again. I needed all my fortitude to bear this cruel uncertainty on a subject so dear to me. Often, when I prayed for my mother and daughter, my heart would feel as if it were breaking and my tears would flow. 'Alas!' I cried, 'are they still alive? Here I am praying for their happiness, and perhaps I have the dreadful misfortune of surviving them!' At other times, the hope in my heart was so strong that I did not even feel the slightest anxiety on their account. In those happy moments, I flattered myself that some unexpected event might yet extricate me from my prison. This thought made such a deep impression on me, particularly during the last year of my captivity, that I vowed to God that if I ever recovered my freedom, I would devote the rest of my life to him in a solitary place far from Rome and would spend the remainder of my days there, as soon as my daughter no longer needed my care.

In the meantime, I was approaching the most interesting period of my life—the moment of my deliverance. God in his goodness was about to make up amply for the nine years of suffering and grief I had endured. For some time now, I had presumed that the duke was living in his castle all the time, because he brought food to me regularly. But one day, when my reserves were nearly exhausted and I was impatiently waiting for him, he failed to come. I finished my meager supply and fell asleep rather peacefully. The next day, I waited in vain for the help that was becoming more necessary with each passing moment; but I was forced to do without. My anxiety, as well as my hunger and thirst, made it impossible to sleep. I remained in this situation for yet another day. Then, completely overcome for lack of food and water, I believed that the end of my life was drawing near. I looked upon death calmly; yet the memory of all those dear to me troubled me and softened my heart.

'Hapless daughter and mother that I am!' I lamented. 'In what terrible solitude am I doomed to pass my final moments! Dear parents, must I die without receiving your blessing? And oh, my child, I cannot give you my own blessing, nor will I enjoy the sweet satisfaction of dying in your arms! You will not even grieve for me! At this moment when your wretched mother is about to breathe her last breath, you no doubt are enjoying the amusements and pleasures of childhood. How dreadful it is to think that I am dying, while all those I love have long been consoled for my death! But what am I saying? How ungrateful I am for complaining when all my miseries are about to end! Great God, forgive me this grievous weakness! My heart rejects and disavows it. Oh, my judge and Father, call me at last to heaven! Full of hope and confidence, certain of enjoying immortal bliss, I await death with a feeling of peace and security. I would even have wished for it, if you did not forbid me from desiring it.' As I concluded these words, I fell back almost lifeless onto my bed of straw. I felt a serenity of soul, the charms of which I had never tasted until that moment. A salutary balm suddenly seemed to heal all the wounds of my heart.

My extreme weakness soon clouded my mind, and I drifted gently into a hazy reverie, a kind of sweet slumber during which the most enchanting images appeared one after another in my imagination. I thought I saw celestial figures—angels streaming with light—surrounding my bed and that I heard divine concerts of harmonious voices from afar. I saw heaven half opened and God, seated on a resplendent throne, calling to me and reaching out his arms to me. I felt that he was truly watching over me and that his paternal hand was about to break my chains.

All of a sudden, I awake with a start and think I hear someone knocking at the turning-box. I listen and hear more knocking.... My heart begins to pound. But oh, what surprise, what indescribable joy! I hear a voice—a new voice which is not that of my tyrant! It seems like the voice of an angel descended from heaven to set me free! Beside myself, overcome with emotion, I join my hands together in the most fervent gesture of the deepest gratitude.

'Oh, dear God, it's a liberator you have sent me. I joyfully accepted death, and you have given my life back to me! Life is a precious gift from you, and I will cherish it.' As I utter these words, I try to get up and move nearer the tower, but cannot. My strength fails me, and I fall back on the bed. At that moment, the door opens and I see light. Someone enters the room. I sit up and try to see, but cannot make out anything. Deprived of daylight for so long, my eyes cannot bear even the dim lamplight and close involuntarily. The stranger draws closer.

'Who are you!' I cry in a broken, halting voice. With these words, I force open my eyes which, although still dazzled by the light, catch sight of a man kneeling beside me. He puts his arm under my head to support it and offers me food and water. Consumed by an overwhelming hunger, I can think of nothing else but to satisfy that pressing need; all my other thoughts are suspended as I eagerly devour the food given to me. After awhile, feeling my strength return, I turn toward my liberator; his face is in the shadows, and I am unable to distinguish his features. 'Oh, speak to me!' I cry. 'Are you in league with my persecutor, or have you come to rescue me?'

Interrupting me, the stranger exclaims: 'Oh heavens! What voice am I hearing! ... My God, where am I!' At these words, he rises suddenly, seizes the lamp, and returns to me. Holding the lamp close to my face, he stares intently at me with an expression of tender emotion mixed with horror. I look closely for a moment at his face, on which the lamplight is shining; his hair seems to be standing up on end, and he is pale and trembling. Yet it is impossible not to recognize him.

I try to speak, but my tears silence me, and I can only utter his name: the Count of Belmire.[11]

It is indeed Belmire. He falls at my feet and bathes them with his tears. Stammering some confused words, he gazes at me and then thanks heaven and rails against it at the same time. The intensity of his emotion gives an air of madness and torment to his joy. We both speak at the same time, without hearing or answering each other. The dungeon echoes with our cries. All of a sudden, the count stands up and cries: 'Oh, most barbarous of men, execrable monster! Is there any punishment harsh enough to punish you for your crime?' Then, helping me sit up, he declares, 'And you, ill-fated victim of a merciless tiger's rage, come—you are free.'

Hearing these words, my first impulse was to rush toward the door; but then stopping myself, I told the count: 'You have rescued me; I owe you my life and freedom! But can the blessings you are restoring to me truly make me happy? Alas, dare I ask about my father and mother?'

'They are alive and well.'

'Thank heavens! ... And my daughter?'

'She is in Rome and will soon be in your arms.'

'Dear God!' I cried, prostrating myself, 'How can I ever repay the debt I owe you? This moment alone has already made up for all my sufferings! And you, my generous benefactor!' I continued, addressing the count, 'as your reward, know that I am innocent. But before I tell you the sad details of my story, allow me to ask one question: The duke is no doubt ill?'

Fig. 16: 'I look closely for a moment at his face, on which the lamplight is shining; his hair seems to be standing up on end, and he is pale and trembling. Yet it is impossible not to recognize him.' Engraving by Pégard from a drawing by Telory. Illustration from the sixth edition of *Adèle et Théodore* published in 1862 in Paris by Morizot. (BnF)

'Afflicted with a fatal illness, he is on the brink of death and is not expected to live more than two days. Come—leave this horrible dungeon so that, before he dies, the monster knows you have been freed.'

'No,' I replied. 'My parents are the ones who must free me from this prison; it is only with their help that I can leave it.' I then asked the count to quickly send a messenger to my father, and he promised he would. He gave me paper and pencil, and I immediately began writing the following note:

Dear father, dear mother, I am alive and I am innocent!
Come and by your presence restore me fully to life.
Come take me from a dreadful dungeon and help me
forget all the miseries I have endured.

This note was barely legible. It took me nearly a quarter of an hour to write it, because I no longer knew how to form letters and I had completely forgotten how to spell.[12] Seeing that I was firmly resolved to remain in my prison until my parents' arrival, the count gave me the keys to all the doors and, with the deepest regret, took his leave, after promising to dissemble with the duke if he was still alive and to see me again early the next evening.

When I found myself alone again, I was seized with a terror almost as strong as what I experienced at the beginning of my captivity. And yet I was no longer in the dark because the count had given me a lamp and a dim lantern. I had also asked him for a watch, so that I could keep track of the time, because I did not expect to be able to sleep at all. Rooted to the spot where the count had left me, I could scarcely breathe. I was afraid to lift my eyes, and yet I could not help casting furtive glances around me. Far from reassuring me, the light only increased my anxiety, for it revealed my sad and sinister dwelling. Finally, unable to bear the situation any longer, I rose, took my lantern, unlocked the first door, and entered a long corridor, where the turning-box was located. I already felt great relief to find myself in a new place that brought me closer to the outside door of my prison. I hurried through this passageway, unlocked the door at the other end, and found myself at the foot of the steps leading to the double door that opened onto the garden. I shut the passageway door behind me, as if to separate myself from my dreadful dungeon. Then, after quickly climbing the stairs, I sat down on the top step and finally was able to breathe more easily.

Fig. 17: Illustration by H. Brevière-Rouery from *Camille, ou Le Souterrain,* plagiarized version of Genlis's novella published in Rouen in 1816 by Lecrêne-Labbey without the author's name. (BnF)

After such a happy and unexpected turn of events, I should have felt the purest and most intense joy, but I had suffered too long and been too miserable for my heart to dare give way to the seductive charm of such sweet hopes. It is true that I was overjoyed to know that all those I loved were still alive. Yet when I reflected on the inexpressible bliss I would feel to find myself once again in my mother's arms and to embrace my father and daughter, I could not believe that such happiness could ever be my lot. A thousand dreadful forebodings began to trouble me and darken my imagination and, in this state of dejection and melancholy, I mistook for premonitions all these far-fetched fears.

That memorable day when the Count of Belmire entered my prison was June 3, 17**.[13] He left me at midnight and, until six in the morning, I remained in the situation I have just described. Suddenly, I thought I heard some faint sounds. I pressed my ear to the door of my prison and listened with rapt attention. Despite the thickness of the door and that of the rock concealing it, I could distinctly hear the warbling of the birds awakened by the break of day. The elation I experienced at that instant is impossible to describe or to imagine. My sadness completely vanished, my heart opened up once again to happiness and hope, and tears of gratitude flowed from my eyes. However, my thoughts were still extremely confused, and I was so engrossed by the desire to hear what was happening in the garden that I was incapable of reflecting on the unexpected change in my situation. With my ear pressed against the door and holding my breath, I listened with an attention from which no other thought could divert me. I heard dogs barking, men walking about, and even snatches of conversation. All these different sounds filled me with inexpressible pleasure.

Yet by the end of the afternoon, I was anxiously awaiting nightfall so that I could see the Count of Belmire again. I longed to ask him a thousand questions that were running through my mind one after another as my thoughts became less jumbled. For example, I wondered how long I had been confined in my prison. Before the count's arrival, I imagined that I must be nearly fifty years old; his youthful aspect convinced me that grief and tedium make it difficult to measure the passage of time, but I still could not guess my age within four or five years.

The count returned at midnight. I could easily see from his pale countenance and from his expression of compassion and distress how deeply affected he was by the event that had changed my fate. Out of respect for my situation that obliged me to receive him alone in the middle of the night, as well as for the fatal knot about to be broken but that bound me still, he did not speak of the feelings I had dared to acknowledge in happier times, nor of those he still felt for me. After he told me that he had sent a letter to my father along with my note and that the duke remained very near death, I begged him to explain why his uncle had entrusted him with such an important secret. To satisfy my curiosity, the count related the following story:

'I had been traveling for a year when I received the news of your death. At the same time, I learned that the duke was inconsolable, and this circumstance greatly lessened the antipathy I naturally felt toward him. After traveling for two more years, I returned to Italy, recalled by my affairs. Obliged to see the duke, I had to come to this castle, since he very seldom left it, except occasionally to spend two or three days in Naples. I saw your tomb here and your portrait placed in almost every room. I became very attached to this place and even to the inhuman monster who had made you his victim. He displayed such intense grief, so deep a melancholy, that I soon preferred his company to all others and chose to spend five or six months every year with him in this castle.'

'A year ago, the duke developed an incurable illness; but refusing to acknowledge its seriousness, he continued to make occasional trips to Naples. This winter, he stopped going to Court altogether and wrote to me in Rome asking me to come see him. I arrived here toward the end of January and found him deathly ill, although he did not keep to his bed and continued to walk about. At times, it seemed that he was not entirely in his right mind. Over the previous nine years, his life had become an unbearable burden to him, consumed as he was by remorse, and yet he could not envision his death without horror. After growing progressively weaker every day, he suddenly was seized with convulsions that forced him to stay in bed. He remained in this condition for three days, at the end of which one of his valets came at nine o'clock in the evening to tell me he wished to speak with me. The servant added that, both that night and the preceding one, the duke had sent away his servants and had tried to get up without assistance; but too weak to stand, he had rung for them, and they had found him out of bed, half dressed.

'I went immediately to the duke's bedchamber. After sending his physician and attendants away, he told me that he was going to entrust me with an important secret and made me swear not to reveal it. Then, with a wild and troubled look on his face, he said: "Family reasons have obliged me to imprison in this castle a guilty woman who deserved to die for her crimes. She no doubt needs food and water; go take her some. Knock at the turning-box that serves this purpose. If she does not answer you, go into her prison and help her. But I must warn you that this woman is not in her right mind. Pay no attention to what she says and return here as soon as you have given her some nourishment. I promise one day to tell you her name and story." The duke then revealed to me the existence of the secret dungeon beneath his castle. After taking a set of keys from under his pillow, he gave them to me and urged me to carry out his request without delay. Believing I had never seen you, the monster thought that he could not choose a better person in whom to confide his secret and thus placed in my hands both your destiny and mine.'

When Belmire finished this account, he begged me to tell him my story. But since I could not relate it without speaking of the feelings I once had for him, I declared that I could only do so in the presence of my mother and father.

Based on the count's calculation, I expected my father to arrive within two days. Less agitated and more capable of reflection, I enjoyed twenty-four hours of joyful expectation. But, as the hour of my deliverance approached, my impatience increased; soon it knew no bounds and became an unbearable torment. I never felt anything that can compare to the intense emotions I experienced the night preceding the happiest day of my life. Staring intently at my watch, I became increasingly frustrated by the slow progress of the dials. Shuddering every time I thought I heard a noise, I felt my heart beat violently and my blood course through my veins. My agitation intensified when the singing of the birds announced the dawn of day, that happy day when I would be born again and recover my place as daughter and mother, with all its precious and sacred rights.

That moment destined to make up for an age of misery, that moment so passionately desired approaches ... and comes at last! Repeated cries and tumultuous voices are heard. Soon I can make out the muffled sound of carriages, horses, and armed men. The clamor increases and draws near. I tremble and shiver. Then, oh heavens! What voice reaches my ear and penetrates my very soul? It's my mother, and she's calling her daughter! My heart leaps at the sound! 'Lord, you who gave me the strength to bear my misfortunes,' I murmur, 'do not let this excess of joy overwhelm me! I feel faint; am I to die at my mother's feet?' As I utter these words, the door opens, and I dash outside. Despite the bright glare of day that dazzles and hurts my eyes, I catch sight of my mother and father, recognize them, and let out a piercing cry. I fling myself into their arms and fall in a faint.

Oh, who can describe the joy, the ecstasy I felt when I recovered my senses! I found myself wrapped in my dearest mother's arms, my head resting on her breast and my face bathed with her tears. My father was on his knees before me, clasping both my hands in his. To see the day, to feel the sunlight again, and to know that I soon would be reunited with my daughter—that instant fulfilled all my fondest hopes and heart's desires. It's impossible to describe my thoughts during these first moments. I felt too overwhelmed to be able to think or to express the intensity of my joy except through my sobs and tears.

Finally, my father lifted me up in his arms and said, 'Come, my dear daughter, come let us leave this dreadful place where crime has been the oppressor of innocence for so long.' At these words, I stood up and looked around me. I was surprised to see that we were surrounded by a large troop of armed men, among whom I recognized many relatives and some old friends of my father. He explained that he had called them together before he left Rome and brought them with him to Naples. Once arrived there, he had thrown himself at the king's feet, shown him my note, and had received not only his permission to rescue me by force, should force be necessary, but also troops to assist him. 'When I arrived here,' continued my father, 'I was informed that your vile persecutor had just died.[14] And so this happy day delivers you from a despicable tyrant, restores you to all those who love you, and secures your complete freedom.'

153

Fig. 18: 'I dash outside [...]. I catch sight of my mother and father, recognize them, and let out a piercing cry. I fling myself into their arms and fall in a faint.' Copper engraving by Luigi Schiavonetti drawn from an oil painting titled *The Duchess of C. coming out of the Cavern* by John Francis Rigaud (1742-1810). ©Trustees of the British Museum.

The only answer I could give my father was to embrace him and weep. Although I was overjoyed and had nothing more to fear, I could not help feeling deeply sorry for the Duke of C***. 'Alas!' I said to myself. 'Had I loved him, he would not have sullied his life with such criminal acts of rage; he would be alive and happy!' This thought filled my heart with compassion, but also with an aching sense of regret and sadness that, for a short time, poisoned my happiness. We set out at last. The following day, my delight as a daughter was increased by my joy as a mother when I was reunited with my deeply beloved child. I clasped her in my arms, saw her tears flow, and heard her call me mother!

The two first days after my arrival in Rome, I was in a kind of dazed state of intoxication, stunned by the noise, astonished at everything, and enjoying nothing fully, except for the happiness of seeing my daughter again and being with my mother and father. Once my heart was fully satisfied, I began to appreciate all the blessings that had been restored to me. The most ordinary things in life brought me new pleasure; everything was a source of wonder and enjoyment for me. The first time I walked in the moonlight, I experienced an indescribable feeling of admiration and awe in beholding once again that pure, gentle light and the star-studded sky. I could not walk in the country or a garden without stopping at every step to examine everything in detail. I never tired of gazing at the flowers, fruits, trees, and the luxuriant greenness of the fields, nor at the clouds, sunset, and rising sun—that sublime and enchanting sight. 'Dear God,' I cried, 'what wonders your good-ness has wrought, what treasures it lavishes upon us! Yet, some people are so ungrateful that they disdain all the blessings they enjoy and consider themselves unhappy!'

In this way, my heart ecstatically indulged in the happiness of which it had been deprived for so long. I felt intense pleasure to find myself once again in the palace where I was born and where I had spent the happy years of my childhood. But I confess that I could not help feeling somewhat distressed to see the Marquise of Venuzi, that former friend who was the initial cause of all my misfortunes.

The Count of Belmire soon followed me to Rome. In the presence of my mother and father, the Marquise of Venuzi, and some relatives, I told him my story. Scarcely had I finished, when, throwing himself at my feet, he expressed, in the most passionate terms, his deep gratitude and tender feelings.

'What!' he cried. 'By naming me, you might have escaped that terrible fate! It was I who plunged you into that abyss; and while you suffered there, I went on living and seeing the light of day that you were deprived of for me! Dare I hope that love can make up for all the miseries it has caused you? Could that heart so noble and tender, be otherwise than faithful? Have your misfortunes led you to renounce those feelings, without which I cannot live?'

At these words, my father affectionately embraced the Count of Belmire and, by this action, let me know that he approved his feelings. But, having given up even the thought of a passion that had once held such sway over my heart, I could not conceive how anyone could yield to it and, still less, how I could be the focus of such feelings. After a moment's silence, I addressed the count and described the state of my heart to him in such a sincere and candid manner that he instantly lost all hope of marrying me. He left Rome for a time; but the feelings that had caused him to flee soon brought him back; and, consoled by the friendship I showed him, he chose to settle there definitively.

In the meantime, far from taking for granted the happiness I enjoyed, each passing day made me treasure it even more. How delightful were my first thoughts every morning when I awoke! Looking around me, I felt the purest joy to see my daughter's bed next to mine and to find myself again in my father's house. I could no longer comprehend how I had been able to bear being deprived of these joys or even of the pleasures and conveniences that I was becoming accustomed to view as absolute necessities. These thoughts filled me with the most tender compassion for all those less fortunate than I. For nine years, I had slept on a bed of straw and suffered from hunger, thirst, and the cold. At least my misfortunes had the saving grace of inspiring these feelings that bring us closest to God. I no longer listened absentmindedly to cries for help from the poor; their fate reminded me of my own. I saw them as my fellow creatures and found the purest satisfaction in comforting them and in relieving their suffering. It was no longer enough to welcome them into my home; I went looking for them. For who deserves our help more than the suffering poor, who are often too timid or proud to ask for the modest aid that would save their lives? This desire to find the needy in order to change their fate was hardly a virtue on my part; it was my heart's most urgent need and my greatest pleasure.

But the more accustomed I became to the comfortable life restored to me, the more the memory of my captivity haunted me. Soon I could no longer speak of my past misfortunes or even listen calmly to other people talking about them or recounting experiences that could remind me of my own.[14] This limitation was only the first of many others. I could not bear darkness or complete solitude, even for a moment. I recall that, one night, my light went out. When I opened my eyes and found myself in utter darkness, I felt a terror that reason could neither conquer nor diminish. I let out a piercing scream; my servants came running and found me pale and almost unconscious, with a contorted expression on my face and agitated by the most frightful convulsions. These irrational fears and involuntary weaknesses—unfortunate results of my captivity—were not the hardest of my troubles to bear; the most distressing effect was that I found myself utterly incapable of directing my daughter's education. I had to learn to read, write, and count all over again. But what's both strange and remarkable is that I had forgotten almost nothing from all I had read in my youth. Having had no kind of distraction for nine years, I had often sought diversion in the past by recalling in detail what I had learned from books and conversations. As a result, all these memories remained engraved in my mind, perhaps more deeply than if I had never left society.

When I came out of my captivity, I was twenty-seven and my daughter was ten. For five years, I devoted myself entirely to her. Completely withdrawn from society, I confined myself to my private suite, where I saw only my father, mother, daughter, and occasionally the Count of Belmire. When my daughter turned fifteen, she became the most desirable match in all of Italy and her hand in marriage was sought after by the most distinguished suitors in Rome. But my choice had long been made deep in my heart. I consulted my daughter, and she confided that her feelings were the same as mine. My father and mother approved my plan, and I hastened its realization. Still young and charmingly handsome, the Count of Belmire was as virtuous as he was amiable. Although he possessed a considerable fortune, he had repeatedly refused the most splendid and advantageous matches. It was to this all too faithful suitor, this dearest friend, my liberator, that I offered my daughter's hand.

'I'm giving her to you,' I told him; 'she loves you, and she's yours. She's fifteen years old—the age I was when I saw you for the first time. Through her appearance and feelings, she brings to mind all that I was then. Today, fate is giving back to you what it robbed you of in the past; and as I was not destined to bring you happiness, I can be consoled only by seeing you made happy by my daughter.'

At these words, the Count of Belmire seized one of my hands and bathed it with his tears. And when I urged him to reply, he said at last: 'Ah! haven't you the right to decide my destiny!' That very night, the wedding contract was signed, and eight days later, the count married my daughter.

I remained in Rome for another year. Then, seeing my daughter settled and perfectly happy, I now thought only of withdrawing to a solitary life, in accordance with the vow I had made during my imprisonment. Moreover, since the air of Rome was very detrimental to my health, my doctors had urged me to go breathe the healthier air of Nice for a time. So I set out for Nice, traveling along the coastal road that the French call la Corniche.[15] When I reached Albenga, I was so delighted by its charming location that I decided to settle there. I had a simple, but comfortable house built where, upon my return from Nice, I took up residence for good.

I've been living in Albenga now for four years in the sweetest tranquillity, and my health is fully restored. It is here that I had the courage to write this story, which I intend for my granddaughters when they are old enough to benefit from my experiences. In withdrawing from society, I have not renounced those who are dear to me. Since taking up residence in Albenga, I have already made two trips to Rome to see my mother and father; and, every year, my daughter and son-in-law come to spend three months in my retreat. In short, I am as completely happy as one can possibly be. Every day, I praise God for the blessings I enjoy and even for the miseries I have suffered, since they have atoned for my faults, purified my heart, and taught me the full value of the happiness that has been restored to me.

Fig. 19: 'I'm giving her to you; she loves you, and she's yours [...]. Today, fate is giving back to you what it robbed you of in the past.' Copper engraving by Gaetano Testolini (1700-1795) from the oil painting titled *The Dutchess of C. Giving Her Daughter to Count Belmire* by John Francis Rigaud (1742-1810). ©Trustees of the British Museum.

Continuation of the baroness's journal

From Pietra, Sunday

When you have read the story of the Duchess of C***, you will easily imagine how difficult it was for us to leave Albenga. It was not until this afternoon that we were able to tear ourselves away. We traveled much of the way on foot, and as we walked the conversation focused continually on the beautiful and touching Duchess of C***. We observed that all her misfortunes arose solely from her lack of confidence in her mother; and that, without her faith, her dungeon would have been her tomb, or else she would have left it in a state of stupor or madness. After reading her story, Adele and Theodore now have a clearer view of religion. In Lagaraye, they saw its beneficent and heroic effects;[16] here in Albenga they have just seen that there are no setbacks or misfortunes that religious faith cannot help us bear with courage and resignation. They will never forget that religion is as consoling as it is sublime, that it infuses our hearts with virtues that we cannot derive from nature, and that it inspires us with a courage that reason alone cannot give us.[17]

NOTES TO THE TRANSLATION

[1] Albenga is an ancient coastal town in northwestern Italy on the Italian Riviera midway between Monaco and Genoa. In the notes to her edition of *Adèle et Théodore*, Isabelle Brouard-Arends points out that the itinerary followed by the d'Almanes was identical to that followed by Genlis on her trip to Italy with the Duchess of Chartres in the spring of 1776 and that the descriptions in the novel of the various places visited there, including Albenga, were taken directly from Genlis's travel journal. See *Adèle et Théodore, ou Lettres sur l'éducation,* ed. Isabelle Brouard-Arends (Rennes: Presses universitaires de Rennes, 2006), p. 652, n. 35. However, as Genlis explains in her memoirs, she did not actually visit the Duchess of Girifalco in Albenga, but instead saw her in Rome for only fifteen minutes during a dinner party hosted by the duchess's father, the Prince of Palestrina. See Appendix C for the references to the Duchess of Girifalco found in Genlis's memoirs.

[2] In his travel journal *Une année à Florence* (1851), Alexandre Dumas père recalls an afternoon he spent in Albenga and mentions Genlis's tale of the duchess: 'We stopped for lunch in Albenga, a town with a sweet-sounding name, but to which crumbling ramparts and dilapidated towers give a most sinister appearance. It is there, according to Madame de Genlis, that the Duchess of Cerifalco was kept prisoner for nine years by her husband in an underground dungeon.' [*Œuvres complètes d'Alexandre Dumas,* 17 vols (Paris: Au bureau du Siècle, 1850-57), VIII: *Impressions de voyage* (1851), p. 354.] This last sentence is incorrect, since the duchess was not imprisoned by her husband in Albenga, but (according to nineteenth-century historians Litta, Coppi, and Ademollo) in the castle of Girifalco in southern Italy. (See their accounts in Appendix G.) In Genlis's version of the duchess's story, the duke imprisons his wife in a castle near Naples, far from both Girifalco and Albenga.

[3] Genlis occasionally uses italics to indicate quotes within a quote. In this passage, Mme d'Almane is quoting the Viscountess de Limours, the friend to whom she is writing.

[4] *Genlis's note*: This description is not at all exaggerated; it is taken from the author's travel journal written at Albenga and is completely true.

[5] La Corniche (or la Route des Corniches) is the name given to the narrow coastal road that crosses the Esterel mountain range (le Massif de l'Estérel) along the French Riviera from Saint-Rafael to the Italian border and then continues eastward along the Italian Riviera to the Gulf of Genoa, where Albenga is located. The road, much of which still exists today, offers dramatic views of the Mediterranean and of the rugged, reddish mountain cliffs overlooking the sea.

[6] *Genlis's note*: 'The basic facts of this story are entirely true: the nine

162

years of captivity in a dungeon impenetrable to the light of day, the duchess's presumed death, the way she lived and was fed, and her rescue; all these details are completely accurate. The only fictional parts of the story concern the love plot and the characters of the lover and the female friend. In 17**, the author saw the Duchess of C*** in Rome and dined every day with this intriguing woman's father.'

In the fourth edition published in 1804 by Maradan in Paris, we find a shorter, but more informative version of this footnote: 'The basic facts of this story are entirely true. In 1776, the author saw the Duchess of Cerifalco in Rome and dined every day with the Prince of Palestrina, this intriguing woman's father.' The discrepancy between the two versions of this footnote is discussed in the section titled 'About the Text and Translation,' pp. 25-27.

[7] Contrary to Genlis's claim, the duchess was not the only child born to the Princess of Palestrina. Married at twelve in 1728, Cornelia Barberini bore seven children in the first nine years of marriage and two or three more children after that. Olimpia was her second daughter and eldest surviving child. See Caroline Castiglione, *Patrons and Adversaries: Nobles and Villagers in Italian Politics, 1640-1760* (New York: Oxford University Press, 2005), pp. 108, 181. See the family tree on p. 181 that gives birth and death dates for Olimpia and her parents.

[8] The French here reads 'à douze lieues de Naples' [about twelve leagues from Naples]. According to *Le Petit Robert, une lieue* is roughly equivalent to 4 kilometers, so 12 *lieues* would have been about 48 km or 30 miles. Other sources give different equivalents, ranging from 3.98 to 4.4 km per *lieue*; this discrepancy is hardly surprising given that units of measure varied from region to region until the metric system was adopted. As for traveling times in the eighteenth century, Henri Sée remarks that 'sur les routes, les diligences ne font que deux lieues par heure, les carrosses huit à dix lieues par jour' [by the main roads, stagecoaches travel only two *lieues* per hour, carriages eight to ten *lieues* per day]. Given the difficulties of travel on the mountain roads around Naples (which Genlis describes in her novel), the journey by horse-drawn carriage from Naples to the duke's castle would probably have taken a full day. Henri Sée, *La France économique et sociale au XVIIIe siècle* (Paris: Armand Colin, 1967), p. 111.

[9] A turning-box (*un tour*) was a device traditionally found in convents. It consisted of a round cupboard embedded in the wall by which nuns received provisions from the outside without seeing or being seen. Inside the cupboard was a rotating circular shelf on which provisions and parcels were placed outside the wall and then moved to the inside compartment as the shelf was manually rotated. A similar device was used in the conclave

of the cardinals in the Vatican. In French convents, the keeper of the turning-box was called *la tourière*.

[10] *Genlis's note*: In this same manner, the unhappy Duchess of C*** received undergarments, bedlinens, and clothes when she needed them.

[11] In her memoirs, Genlis claims that the imprisoned duchess was discovered by a valet who recognized her and released her from captivity. (Genlis, *Mémoires inédits,* III, p. 49.) Nineteenth-century chroniclers offer quite different versions of the duchess's rescue. Litta claims that two Capuchin monks passing by the castle one night heard her cries and sent for help. Coppi and Ademollo both dismiss this story as apocryphal and maintain that the duchess was able to get word of her plight to her father through her confessor, whom her husband allowed her to see during her captivity. See Appendix C for this and other passages in Genlis's memoirs concerning the duchess and Appendix G for nineteenth-century Italian accounts of her story.

[12] In her memoirs, Genlis describes the profound impression this note made on her when the duchess's father showed it to her during her stay in Rome: 'The prince had carefully preserved his daughter's note, which he treasured. I begged him to show it to me, and he agreed. I gazed for a long time at this little scrap of paper. The handwriting, the expressions, the words (from which nearly all the last syllables were missing)—everything about that note was precious to me. A curious observation—which, as far as I know, has never been made before—is that, in cases where memory has been lost without any change in mental capacity, it is always the last syllables of words that are forgotten. Such was the case with Alexander Selkirk, an English sailor who was rescued after spending twenty-five years on a desert island. He still spoke English very well, except for the last syllable of each word, which he had forgotten. I observed the same phenomenon in a young woman who had been blind for fourteen years and who recovered the ability to write with my help—an experience I relate later in my memoirs.' (Genlis, *Mémoires inédits,* III, p. 50.) See Appendix C for additional commentary on this passage.

[13] In a letter written to her friend Mrs. Stokes on 9 August 1786, Anna Seward recalls the story her brother-in-law told her in 1764 about the duchess, who (he claimed) had recently been released from captivity: 'But what an interesting story is that of the imprisoned duchess! [...] When, in 1764, Mr Porter came over from Italy to marry my lovely sister, he told us that singular and almost incredible circumstance of a woman of fashion, in that country, having then been just discovered and rescued from a nine years confinement in a subterraneous dungeon.' [*Letters of Anna Seward: Written between the Years 1784 and 1807,* 6 vols (Edinburgh, Scotland: Archibald Constable, 1811), I, p. 399.] However, the dates given by Genlis in her memoirs and in her version of the duchess's story suggest

that the duchess was released from captivity in 1759. Regarding the chronology of the duchess's story, see Appendix A.

[14] According to Luigi Russo, the Duke of Girifalco died on August 15, 1766, several years after his wife was rescued from captivity. (Russo, 'I Catasti Onciari di Orta e Casapuzzano,' in *Note e documenti per la storia di Orta di Atella*, ed. Franco Pezzella (Frattamaggiore: Istituto di Studi Atellani, 2006), pp. xlviii-lxi (p. lvi).

[15] We find this same detail in Pompeo Litta's account of the duchess's story: 'She never said a word about what had happened, nor did she ever permit anyone to speak to her about it.' [Pompeo Litta, *Famiglie celebri italiane*, 13 vols (Milan: Presso P. E. Giusti, 1819-1852), II (1838), folio 20 verso.] See Appendix G for the full Italian text and translation.

[16] See note 5 above.

[17] Genlis is referrring here to an episode earlier in the novel (recounted in vol I, letter 63, and vol II, letter 2, of the 1782 edition) regarding the Lagarayes, whom the d'Almanes had visited before returning from Paris to their country estate in Languedoc. After losing their only child, the Lagarayes had renounced their comfortable society life to study medicine in Montpellier. They had then returned to Languedoc, where they transformed their ancestral château of Lagaraye into a hospital and hospice that served the poor and provided jobs to the local population. In a footnote, Genlis explains that this episode is based on a true story. The parallels between the experiences of the Lagarayes and the Duchess of C*** are clear, as Genlis herself points out: Both stories serve to illustrate the power of religious faith to overcome misfortune and to inspire a desire to help others less fortunate than oneself.

[18] An additional paragraph is found at the end of a translation of the duchess's story published in 1798 in Manchester by George Nicholson under the title *Moral tale. The Dutchess of C—:* 'How unfortunate has been this amiable, this virtuous, this affecting woman! How severe her sufferings! Ah, may we guard our hearts against the fatal impressions of love! May a passion never be known that can produce such misery and guilt! And let us not fail to deduce from the narrative of the Duchess of C*** two important truths: the first, that an indulgence of the passions may plunge us into the deepest abyss of human woe; and the second, that there is no calamity that religion cannot help us bear.' This passage does not appear in the original French text of the novella published in 1783, nor is it found at the end of the duchess's narrative in *Adèle et Théodore*. It appears to have been drawn from a passage in *Adèle et Théodore* preceding the duchess's story in which she speaks privately with Mme d'Almane. See the discussion of this passage at the end of the introductory section titled 'About the Text and the Translation.'

Appendix A

Chronology of the Duchess of Girifalco's Story

The following chronology of the Duchess of Girifalco's life is based on the dates Genlis gives in her memoirs and in her versions of the duchess's story, but also takes into account the sometimes conflicting information provided by nineteenth-century historians Litta, Coppi, and Ademollo.

1731 (November 1): Birth of Olimpia Barberini Colonna, Princess of Palestrina and future Duchess of Girifalco, in Rome.

1748 (January 29): Marriage at 16 to Gennaro Caracciolo, Duke of Girifalco.

1749: Birth of the duchess's daughter in Genlis's tale. (No mention of the birth of any children is found in the carefully researched family tree provided by Litta.)

1750: Imprisonment of the duchess by her husband in a castle dungeon shortly after weaning their daughter. (This castle is near Naples in Genlis's tale; but Litta, Coppi, and Ademollo all maintain that she was imprisoned in the castle of Girifalco in southern Italy.)

1759: The duchess's release from captivity (in Genlis's account); the actual year of her rescue is uncertain.

1765: Move to Albenga one year after her daughter's marriage. (Litta, Coppi, and Ademollo all maintain that, following her rescue, the duchess retired to a convent in Rome, where she died in 1800.)

1766 (August 15): Death of Gennaro Caracciolo, Duke of Girifalco, at the age of 46.

1770: Fictional meeting in Albenga of the d'Almanes with the duchess.

1776 (spring): Genlis's meeting in Rome with the duchess, who was 44 at the time.

1782: Publication of *Adèle et Théodore*, in which Genlis's version of the duchess's story first appeared.

1783: Publication by Genlis of a separate edition of the duchess's story, titled *Histoire intéressante de madame la duchesse de C****.

1800 (December 22): Death of the Duchess of Girifalco at a convent in Rome.[1]

1825-26: Publication of Genlis's 10-volume memoirs in which she recalls her meeting with the duchess and her friendship with her parents, the Prince and Princess of Palestrina.

Appendix B

Preface to the 1783 Edition of
*Histoire intéressante de la duchesse de C****

L'Histoire de la duchesse de C*** a charmé tous les lecteurs d'*Adèle*; mais plusieurs l'ont trouvée déplacée dans un ouvrage destiné à la jeunesse et à ceux que le vice et la frivolité n'ont point dépouillé du tendre intérêt qu'elle inspire. Ce morceau monté sur le plus haut ton du genre romanesque leur a paru peu d'accord avec l'harmonie de tout l'ouvrage; c'est ce qui nous engage à le détacher et à le présenter séparément au public.

On l'a déjà dit, le vrai n'est pas toujours vraisemblable; il arrive au physique et au moral des accidents qui embarrassent et étonnent le spectateur faible et ignorant; ces accidents rendus ensuite par le poète ou par le peintre ne lui arrachent point son incrédulité. *On ne voit rien de nouveau sous le soleil* est une phrase vulgaire qu'inventa l'ignorance et que répète la paresse. Quoi! il n'y a pas dans la nature deux êtres entièrement semblables, deux caractères parfaitement les mêmes, et il n'y aurait rien de nouveau! Tous les jours un spectateur attentif peut voir quelque scène nouvelle, et la curiosité seule devrait attacher à la vie celui qui sait observer. *L'Histoire de la duchesse de C**** confirme cette vérité; elle est singulière sans doute, et cependant le fond en est vrai, à quelques changements près, qui en augmentent l'intérêt. Cette dame vit encore dans une ville d'Italie.

L'Histoire de la duchesse de C***, infiniment intéressante par les caractères, par les événements, et par les détails vrais et piquants des sentiments qu'éprouva cette infortunée, écrite d'ailleurs avec agrément, a encore un point de vue très moral. On ne sait, après en avoir fait la lecture, qui l'on doit plaindre davantage, de la victime ou du tyran. La victime a du moins les consolations de l'innocence et d'un grand sacrifice, mais son tyran n'en peut avoir aucune. Son orgueil blessé, son cœur flétri, sa conscience déchirée par les remords, nous offrent un grand et utile exemple. O vous, dont le cœur est sensible et délicat, frémissez à la vue de ce tableau; ne cessez point de combattre votre plus dangereux ennemi, cette jalousie rongeante ou furieuse qui entraîne aux plus grands excès les cœurs les plus tendres. Si vos efforts sont vains, vos combats impuissants, si vous sentez toujours son ascendant cruel, fuyez, sachez souffrir seul.... Et ne vous vengez jamais.

—Genlis, 'Préface des Editeurs.' *L'Histoire intéressante de madame la duchesse de C***. Ecrite par elle-même. Traduite de l'italien.*[2] Lausanne: Henri & Luc Vincent, 1783, pp. iii-vi.

* * *

The duchess's story charmed all the readers of *Adèle et Théodore*. However, some found it out of place in a novel intended for young readers and for those whose affectionate concern for young people had not been dissipated by frivolity and vice. In their view, the story's highly dramatic style and tone seemed to disrupt the novel's harmony, and this is why we chose to publish it in a separate edition.

It has already been said before that what is true is not always believable. People at times undergo extraordinary emotional or physical experiences that perplex or surprise the dull witted spectator, whose incredulity is not in the least diminished when these events are depicted by a poet or painter. *There's nothing new under the sun* is a commonplace devised by ignorant people and repeated by indolent ones. What! There's never anything new when in nature no two beings are completely similar, no two characters exactly the same! Every day brings some new scene, and curiosity alone should lead an attentive observer to cherish life. The *Story of the Duchess of C**** confirms this truth; the tale is no doubt most unusual, and yet it is essentially true, except for a few changes that enhance its appeal. This lady is still alive and resides in a town in Italy.

The *Story of the Duchess of C**** is extremely interesting because of the characters it depicts, the events it recounts, and its realistic and engaging descriptions of the feelings experienced by its unfortunate heroine. It offers not only a most pleasing style, but also a highly moral point of view. After reading it, one does not know whom to pity more—the victim or the tyrant. The victim at least has the consolation of her innocence and of the great sacrifice she has made, whereas the tyrant can find no consolation whatsoever. His wounded pride, his withered and corrupted heart, his conscience racked with remorse provide us with an example that is both powerful and constructive. Oh, you whose heart is sensitive and delicate, shudder at the sight of this portrait; never stop fighting your most dangerous enemy, that furious and self-destructive jealousy that leads the most tender hearts to such violent extremes. If your efforts are in vain, your inner struggles fruitless, if you are unable to overcome its cruel influence, then flee and learn to suffer alone.... And never seek revenge.

APPENDIX C

REFERENCES TO THE DUCHESS OF GIRIFALCO IN GENLIS'S *MÉMOIRES*

The following references to the Duchess of Cerifalco (Girifalco) are found in Genlis's memoirs, *Mémoires inédits de madame la comtesse de Genlis, sur le dix-huitième siècle et la révolution française, depuis 1756 jusqu'à nos jours*. 10 vols (Paris: Ladvocat, 1825), III, pp. 48-50 and 176-78.[3]

[pp. 48-50]

Ce prince de Palestrine[4] était père de la duchesse de Cerifalco, qui passa neuf ans dans un souterrain, et dont j'ai conté l'étonnante histoire dans *Adèle et Théodore*. Le prince donna une fête à madame la duchesse de Chartres: la duchesse y vint par respect pour une princesse de la maison de Bourbon, car elle vivait dans la plus grande retraite, étant sujette, depuis ses malheurs, à tomber du haut mal; elle ne resta qu'un quart d'heure à cette fête; j'allai m'asseoir à côté d'elle pour la contempler à mon aise. Quoiqu'elle n'eût que quarante-six ans,[5] elle paraissait en avoir soixante-dix; elle n'avait plus de traces de beauté; son maintien me frappa, et je l'ai dépeinte d'après nature; elle avait la tête et les yeux baissés, et de temps en temps de petits tressaillements. Le prince me conta toute son histoire, dont j'ai mis beaucoup de détails dans mon épisode.

Cette malheureuse personne était d'une douceur et d'une piété d'ange. Elle a toujours ignoré, et l'on n'a jamais su, pourquoi son barbare époux l'avait enfermée dans ce souterrain.[6] La religion, utile à tout, lui sauva la vie, car ce monstre, qui en avait conservé quelques sentiments, n'osa pas l'empoisonner; et lorsqu'il fut lui-même à l'article de la mort, il confia à un valet de chambre que y pour des raisons de famille, il avait enfermé dans un souterrain une femme coupable et folle. Il ne dit point que ce fût la sienne que l'on croyait morte depuis neuf ans.

Le valet de chambre, qui reçut une clef du souterrain pour

secourir l'infortunée, qui depuis deux jours manquait de nourriture, frappa inutilement au tour; elle ne vint point recevoir son pain et son eau, elle était évanouie. Le valet de chambre entra, la secourut, la reconnut, lui donna dé la nourriture pour plusieurs jours, lui laissa la clef du souterrain, et, obligé de rester auprès du duc, envoya à Rome un courrier au prince de Palestrine, avec un billet de la duchesse, qui, dans quatre lignes et demie, lui apprenait son existence et l'appelait à son secours.[7] Le prince, suivi de tous les hommes de sa famille, alla se jeter aux pieds du roi de Naples et lui conter cette histoire. Le roi lui donna un régiment pour l'escorter au château du duc, dans le cas où la force serait nécessaire. Quand le prince de Palestrine y arriva, le duc vivait encore. On lui apprit, de la part du prince, que son crime était connu et qu'on allait délivrer sa victime. Le duc expira peu d'heures après.[8]

Le prince avait précieusement conservé le billet de sa fille; à mon instante prière, il me le montra; je ne pouvais me lasser de contempler ce petit morceau de papier; l'écriture, les paroles y les mots auxquels il manquait presque toutes les dernières syllabes, tout en était précieux à mes yeux.

Une remarque singulière, et qu'à ma connaissance on n'a point faite, c'est que dans des pertes de mémoire sans altération de la raison, ce sont toujours les dernières syllabes des mots qu'on oublie. Ce fut ainsi que John Selkirk, matelot anglais, retrouvé au bout de vingt-cinq ans dans une île déserte,[9] parlait toujours fort bien anglais, à l'exception des dernières syllabes de chaque mot, qu'il avait oubliées. J'ai observé le même phénomène dans une personne jeune encore, mais aveugle depuis quatorze ans, à laquelle, comme je le dirai par la suite, je rendis la faculté d'écrire.

[p. 176-78]

En revenant d'Italie, je me trouvai à un souper chez madame de Meulan, placée à table entre M. de Champfort, le bel-esprit, et M. de Rulhières. Je leur contai l'histoire de la duchesse de Cerifalco, et j'ajoutai que ce sujet formerait un beau roman. Ils me répondirent qu'ils avaient vu mille fois, dans les romans, des femmes enfermées dans des souterrains et que cette histoire fort singulière formerait un roman très commun. Je répliquai qu'on rendrait le sujet tout neuf en s'attachant à décrire les idées et les sentiments que l'on peut successivement éprouver pendant neuf ans dans un souterrain. Ils prétendirent qu'il n'était pas possible de s'identifier à une telle situation. Lorsque l'ouvrage parut, l'épisode de la duchesse eut un succès universel.[10] Je rappelai à M. de Rulhières ce qu'il m'avait dit sur ce sujet chez madame de Meulan: 'Il est vrai, madame,' répondit-il, 'mais je ne savais pas alors que vous aviez passé neuf ans dans un souterrain.' C'est le plus charmant éloge que j'aie reçu sur cette histoire.

* * *

[pp. 48-50]

The Prince of Palestrina[11] was the father of the Duchess of Cerifalco, who spent nine years in an underground dungeon and whose remarkable story I recounted in *Adèle et Théodore*. The prince gave a party for the Duchess of Chartres. Out of respect for this princess of the house of Bourbon, the Duchess of Cerifalco attended the party. But she usually lived completely withdrawn from society, for since her imprisonment, she suffered from severe bouts of malaise and disorientation. She stayed at the party for only a quarter of an hour. I sat down next to her in order to have time to study her carefully. Although she was only 46 years old at the time,[12] she looked as if she were 70. All traces of her former beauty had vanished. I was very struck by her bearing, which I have described exactly as it was. She kept her head bowed and eyes downcast, and from time to time, she shuddered slightly, as if startled. The prince told me her whole story, from which I drew a number of details for my episode about her.

This unfortunate woman had the sweetness and piety of an angel. She never knew, nor could any one ever discover, why her barbarous husband had imprisoned her in that dungeon.[13] Religion, which can help us in so many ways, saved her life; for that monster, who still had some religious feelings, dared not poison her. And when he himself was on his deathbed, he confided to his manservant that, for family reasons, he had imprisoned in a underground dungeon a madwoman guilty of serious crimes. He did not acknowledge that this woman was his own wife, who was believed to have been dead for nine years.

After receiving the key to the dungeon, the valet went to assist the unfortunate prisoner, who for two days had been without food and water. He knocked in vain at the turning-wheel; she did not come for her bread and water, for she had fainted. The servant entered, gave her the necessary assistance, recognized her, gave her food and water for several days, and left her the key to the dungeon. As he was obliged to remain with the duke, he sent an urgent message to the Prince of Palestrina in Rome, along with a note from the duchess, who in four and a half lines told him she was alive and asked him to come rescue her.[14] The prince, followed by all his male relatives, went to the king of Naples, told him the whole story, and pleaded for his help. The king gave him a regiment of solidiers to escort him to the duke's castle, in case force became necessary. When the Prince of Palestrina arrived, the duke was still alive. The prince's messenger told him that his crime had been discovered and that his victim was about to be freed. The duke died a few hours later.[15]

The prince had carefully preserved his daughter's note, which he treasured. I begged him to show it to me, and he agreed. I gazed for a long time at this little piece of paper. The handwriting, the expressions, the words—from which nearly all the last syllables were missing—everything about that note was precious to me.

A curious fact—which, as far as I know, has never been noted before—is that, in cases where memory has been lost without any change in mental capacity, it is always the last syllables of words that are forgotten. Such was the case with Alexander Selkirk, an English sailor who was rescued after spending twenty-five years on a desert island.[16] He still spoke English very well, except for the last syllable of each word, which he had forgotten. I observed the same phenomenon in a young woman who had been blind for fourteen years and who recovered the ability to write with my help—an experience I relate later in my memoirs.

[pp. 176-78]

When I returned from Italy, I attended a dinner at the home of Mme de Meulan. Seated between witty M. de Champfort and M. de Rulhières, I told them the Duchess of Cerifalco's story and added that it would make a fine novel. They replied that tales of women imprisoned in dungeons could be found in a thousand works of fiction, and that this story, unusual as it was, would make a most ordinary novel. I insisted that the subject could be made fresh and original by describing step by step the ideas and feelings one might experience in the course of nine years spent in a dungeon. They claimed that it was impossible to imagine oneself in a situation of that kind. When my novel was published, the episode concerning the duchess was the object of universal acclaim.[17] I reminded M. de Rulhières what he had said to me about the duchess's tale at Mme de Meulan's home. 'It's true, madame,' he replied, 'but I didn't know then that you had spent nine years in a dungeon.' These were the most charming words of praise I received for this story.

APPENDIX D

SUBSEQUENT REFERENCES TO THE DUCHESS AND HER FAMILY IN *ADÈLE ET THÉODORE*

The volume and letter numbers refer to the original edition of *Adèle et Théodore* published by Lambert and Baudoin in Paris in 1782. Some later editions of the novel are divided into two or four volumes (instead of three) and consequently use a different numbering system for the letters.

Tome 2, Lettre 39

La baronne à la victomtesse. De Gènes.

Nous sommes arrivés à Gènes avant-hier matin, ma chère amie; j'ai trouvé aujourd'hui une voie sûre dont j'ai profité pour vous envoyer mon petit journal de la Corniche et l'histoire de la duchesse de C***. [...]

Tome 2, Lettre 42

De la vicomtesse à la baronne. De Paris.

Croirez-vous, ma chère amie, que je n'ai reçu qu'avant-hier, c'est-à-dire, à quatre mois de date, votre journal de la Corniche et l'histoire de la duchesse de C***? L'homme que vous aviez chargé de ce paquet a été malade en route, et n'est arrivé à Paris que jeudi dernier.

Je me suis enfermée avec Madame d'Ostalis et le chevalier d'Herbain dans ce petit cabinet que vous connaissez; et là, nous avons lu avec un plaisir inexprimable cette terrible et touchante histoire. Le chevalier d'Herbain prétend que le duc de C*** ressemble beaucoup à la barbe-bleue; mais malgré cette moquerie, le chevalier a pleuré tout autant que nous. Il a trouvé que la duchesse de C*** peignait avec une vérité très-attachante les différents mouvements qu'elle a éprouvés dans des situations si extraordinaires. Oh, quel monstre affreux que ce mari! Plaignons-nous des nôtres à présent! Osons nous plaindre aussi des petites contrariétés qui nous surviennent, après un tel exemple de patience, de résignation et de courage! ... Je me sens humiliée en songeant combien je suis loin de ce degré de perfection humaine. Oh, sûrement je serais devenue folle dans le souterrain; j'y serais morte, ou, pour mieux dire, je n'y serais point entrée, car j'aurais tout dit, tout déclaré, du moins j'en ai bien peur. Je ne suis pas trop contente du comte de Belmire; je comprends bien que la duchesse, en sortant de sa caverne, ne pouvait plus l'aimer. Neuf ans d'une semblable captivité doivent en effet refroidir la tête; mais son amant devait toujours l'adorer, lui qui n'avait ni jeûné ni couché sur de la paille! Il a tort de n'être plus amoureux d'elle. Se trouver tout-à-coup le gendre de sa maîtresse est une étrange chose;[18] cependant je pourrai l'excuser si la comtesse de Belmire ressemble parfaitement à sa mère. Vous me manderez cela quand vous serez à Rome, et, je vous en prie, avec détail. [...]

Tome 2, Lettre 47

La baronne à la vicomtesse. De Rome!

Vous qui supposiez que je datais avec tant d'orgueil de Venise, j'imagine que vous me croyez bien plus fière de pouvoir écrire de Rome; mais heureux ceux qui, comme vous, ma chère amie, datent toujours d'Auteuil et de Pantin. Vous n'imaginez pas à quel point on aime son pays, lorsqu'on en est à la distance où je suis du mien. Je ne rencontre pas un Français qui ne me paraisse aimable; j'en voyais deux à Venise dont la société m'était devenue nécessaire, et qui vraisemblablement m'ennuyeraient beaucoup à Paris. Enfin, tout ce qui peut me rappeler la France est véritablement intéressant pour moi.

Mais revenons à Rome, puisque j'y suis arrivée hier au soir. Vous jugez bien que mon premier soin a été d'envoyer chez la fille de la duchesse de C***, cette comtesse de Belmire que j'avais tant d'envie de connaître. Prévenue par sa mère, elle est arrivée chez moi, le soir même avec son mari, et j'ai retrouvé en elle toute la politesse et toutes les grâces de la duchesse de C***. Elle lui ressemble d'ailleurs autant que vous pouvez le desirer, quoiqu'elle ne soit pas aussi régulièrement belle. Je suis fâchée de vous dire que le comte de Belmire paraît l'aimer de manière à faire craindre que le souvenir d'Albenga ne soit pas toujours bien présent à sa pensée. Cependant il a l'air mélancolique, et quand on parle de la duchesse de C***, il soupire et devient rêveur. Au reste, j'étais si excédée de lassitude que je n'ai pu l'observer et l'examiner avec l'attention nécessaire pour pouvoir vous en rendre un compte bien détaillé. Mais je dîne aujourd'hui chez lui, et dans ma première lettre je satisferai pleinement votre curiosité.[...][19]

Tome 3, Lettre 11

La baronne à la vicomtesse. De Rome

Nous partons demain pour Florence, ma chère amie; il m'est impossible de regretter l'Italie quand je retourne en France; cependant je ne quitterai pas Rome sans attendrissement. Vous connaissez mon attachement pour M le C de ***; je ne puis m'accoutumer à l'idée que vraisemblablement je ne le reverrai jamais. [...]

Je laisse encore à Rome deux personnes (le comte et la comtesse de Belmire) dont je conserverai toujours le souvenir. Adèle aime véritablement la comtesse, elle pleure depuis hier; Miss Bridget[20] la gronde d'une sensibilité qu'elle ne peut concevoir, car elle brûle de retourner en France; et nous, malgré nos regrets, nous faisons nos paquets de bon coeur, et nous tressaillons de joie en pensant que nous serons à B*** dans trois mois au plus tard.[21]

* * *

Volume 2, Letter 39

The baroness to the viscountess. From Genoa

My dear friend, we arrived in Genoa the day before yesterday in the morning. Today, I took advantage of a sure means I found to send you the story of the Duchess of C*** and my journal describing our trip to the Corniche. [...]

Volume 2, Letter 42

The viscountess to the baroness. From Paris

Would you believe, my dear friend, that I did not receive the Duchess of C***'s story and the journal describing your trip to the Corniche until the day before yesterday, four months after they were sent? The man to whom you entrusted the package fell ill on his way to Paris and only arrived here last Thursday.

I withdrew with Madame d'Ostalis and the Chevalier d'Herbain to the little study you're familiar with; and there, with inexpressible pleasure, we read that terrible and touching story. The Chevalier d'Herbain maintains that the Duke of C*** greatly resembles Bluebeard; but despite his mocking tone, he shed as many tears as we did. He felt that the Duchess of C*** described with moving realism the different feelings she experienced in those truly extraordinary situations. Oh, what a monstrous husband! After such an example of patience, resignation, and courage, dare we now complain about our husbands or about the little vexations that come our way? ... I feel humiliated when I think how far I am from that degree of human perfection. Oh, surely I would have gone mad in that dungeon; I would have died there or, to be more precise, I would never have entered it; for I would have admitted everything, at least I am afraid I would have. I am not too pleased with the Count of Belmire; I understand very well why the duchess was no longer in love with him by the time she left her prison. Nine years in such harsh captivity would necessarily dampen one's feelings; but her sweetheart should have adored her forever—he who never had to sleep on a bed of straw or go without food! He was wrong to no longer be in love with her. To suddenly become son-in-law to the woman one loves is odd indeed,[22] yet I could excuse him if the Countess of Belmire fully resembles her mother. I am counting on you to send me a detailed account when you meet her in Rome. [...]

Volume 2, Letter 47

The baroness to the viscountess. From Rome!

You who supposed me so proud to write to you from Venice, you no doubt believe me even prouder to be able to write from Rome; but happy are those who, like you, my dear friend, still write from Auteuil and Pantin. You cannot imagine how much we love our country when we are as far away as I am from mine. Every French person I meet seems charming to me; I became acquainted with two in Venice whose company became absolutely necessary to me, but who probably would bore me terribly in Paris. In short, anything that can remind me of France is of great interest to me.

But let us return to Rome, where I arrived yesterday evening. As you can imagine, my first thought was to send a message to the

Duchess of C***'s daughter, the Countess of Belmire, whom I was so eager to meet. Informed of my trip to Rome by her mother, the countess arrived at my lodging that very evening with her husband, and I recognized in her all the duchess's courtesy and grace. What's more, she resembles her as much as once could wish, although she is not as strikingly beautiful as her mother. I am sorry to say that the Count of Belmire seems to be so in love with her that the memory of Albenga may not always be very present in his thoughts. Yet he has a melancholy air about him, and when anyone mentions the Duchess of C***, he sighs and appears lost in thought. However, I was so overwhelmed with fatigue that I was unable to observe him with the attention needed in order to give you a very detailed account. But I am dining at his house today and will fully satisfy your curiosity in my next letter.[...][23]

Volume 3, Letter 11

The baroness to the viscountess. From Rome

We set out tomorrow for Florence, my dear friend. It's impossible for me to regret leaving Italy when I'm returning to France; yet I will not leave Rome without feeling my heart soften. You know my affection for the Count of ***; I cannot get used to the idea that I probably will never see him again. [...]

There are two other people I'm leaving behind in Rome whom I will always remember: the Count and Countess of Belmire. Adele truly loves the countess and, since yesterday, she has been crying at the thought of leaving her. Miss Bridget[24] has gently chided her for this sensibility she cannot comprehend, given her own eagerness to return to France. As for the rest of us, despite our regrets at leaving our friends, we are packing willingly and rejoice at the thought of being back in B*** in three months' time.[25]

APPENDIX E

REFERENCES TO THE DUCHESS OF GIRIFALCO
IN ANNA SEWARD'S LETTERS

In a letter written to her friend Mrs. Stokes on 9 August 1786, the English poet Anna Seward recalls the story about the Duchess of Girifalco recounted by her brother-in-law Mr. Porter in a letter he sent her from Italy, where he was living when the duchess was rescued.

Lichfield, August 9, 1786.

[...] As for Madam Genlis on education, I like not the experiments she is perpetually making on the minds and dispositions of her pupils, at the expense of truth. Truth ought never to be violated with children, much less should its violation form part of a system. [...] But what an interesting story is that of the imprisoned Duchess! I am in possession of some original letters from Dr Johnson to Miss Boothby, for whom he had a platonic passion. One of them begins thus: 'It is midnight; I am alone, and in no disposition to slumber. How shall I employ this waste hour of darkness and vacuity?'

Alas! for the story is true; how did that unhappy woman employ nine waste years of darkness and vacuity? When, in 1764, Mr. Porter came over from Italy to marry my lovely sister, he told us that singular and almost incredible circumstance of a woman of fashion in that country having then been just discovered and rescued[26] from a nine years' confinement in a subterraneous dungeon into which no ray of light had, in the long interval, ever penetrated. But he did not, like Madam Genlis, represent her innocent, though with great horror and compassion, he instanced that dire revenge as a consequence of Italian jealousy which had not reconciled itself to the *cicesbeo* privileges.[27]

— Letter from Anna Seward to Mrs. Stokes of 9 August 1786, in *Letters of Anna Seward: Written between the Years 1784 and 1807* 6 vols (Edinburgh, Scotland: Archibald Constable, 1811), I, letter 35, pp. 169-70.

181

APPENDIX F

THE ROLE OF THE *CICISBEO* IN EIGHTEENTH-CENTURY ITALY

In eighteenth- and early nineteenth-century Italy, the *cicisbeo* (or *cavalier servente*) was the publicly acknowledged gallant (and often lover) of a married woman who attended her at social events, in church, and on other occasions and who had privileged access to her. This arrangement, called the *cicisbeatura* or *cicisbeismo*, was widely practiced in Italy during this period, especially among the nobility of the major Italian cities of the period, including Naples.

Some scholars see the practice as a sign of the increasing emancipation of aristocratic women. Typically, husbands tolerated or even welcomed the arrangement, as Smollet remarks in a letter from Nice dated 2 July 1764: '[Y]ou must understand, this Italian fashion prevails at Nice among all ranks of people; and there is not such a passion as jealousy known. The husband and the *cicisbeo* live together as sworn brothers; and the wife and the mistress embrace each other with marks of the warmest affection.' In a subsequent letter from Nice dated 28 January 1765, Smollett notes that attempts by the husband to ward off prospective *cicisbei,* or disapproval of the practice in general, was likely to be met with ridicule and scorn: '[E]very married lady in this country has her *cicisbeo*, or *servente*, who attends her everywhere and on all occasions and upon whose privileges the husband dares not encroach, without incurring the censure and ridicule of the whole community.'

Cicisbei played by set rules, generally avoiding public displays of affection. At public entertainments, they typically stood behind their seated mistress. Customs of the time did not permit them to engage in relationships with any other women during their free time, making the arrangement rather demanding. Either party could decide to end the relationship at any time.

In a letter written to her friend Mrs. Stokes on 9 August 1786, Anna Seward maintains—contrary to Genlis's claim—that the duchess was *not* innocent and that her husband's jealousy appears to have been provoked by an adulterous liaison. (See the excerpt from Seward's letter in Appendix E.) Seward's claim was based on a letter she had received decades earlier from her brother-in-law Mr. Porter, who was living in Italy at the time of the duchess's rescue. She adds that the duke's Italian contemporaries considered his jealousy both unjustified and monstrous in its consequences, given the widespread tolerance of extra-conjugal affairs, particularly among the Italian aristocracy.

Genlis herself describes the role of the *cicisbeo* (or what the French call *sigisbée*) in a letter that Mme d'Almane sends to Mme de Limours immediately following the letter relating the duchess's story, but without drawing any connection to her experience: '[T]out ce qu'on raconte des sigisbées est exactement vrai; il faut absolument en avoir un au bout d'un an de mariage; c'est le mari et les parents qui le choisissent; ainsi, vous jugez bien qu'on ne s'en tient pas toujours à celui-là: il doit suivre en tous lieux sa *sigisbea*, jouer avec elle aux assemblées, être à côté de sa chaise à porteurs, l'ouvrir, la refermer, porter le manteau, l'éventail, etc.' (*Adèle et Théodore*, I, letter 39). [Everything people say about *cicisbeos* is entirely true; it is absolutely essential for a woman to have one by the end of the first year of marriage, chosen by her husband and parents. You understand, of course, that a woman does not necessarily content herself with their choice, since the *cicisbeo* must follow his *cicisbea* everywhere, accompany her to gaming tables at social gatherings, walk alongside her sedan-chair, open and close it for her, carry her cloak, her fan, etc.]

APPENDIX G

Genlis's novella is based on the experiences of Olimpia Barberini Colonna (1731-1800), daughter of Giulio Cesare Colonna di Sciarra, Prince of Carbognano (1708-1787), and Cornelia Constanza Barberini, Princess of Palestrina (1716-1797). Olimpia was the eldest surviving child of nine or ten children born to the couple.

In 1747, at the age of sixteen, Olimpia was married to Gennaro Caracciolo, Duke of Girifalco (1720-1766). Genlis gives the duke's name as 'Cerifalco,' a mispelling of 'Girifalco,' the name of his duchy centered in a town of that name in the province of Catanzaro, in the region of Calabria in southern Italy. There is no record of any children born to the couple.

The Duchess of Girifalco's story was widely known in eighteenth-century Italy and was chronicled by several nineteenth-century Italian historians. Perhaps the best known of these accounts is that of Pompeo Litta in his *Famiglie celebri italiane:*

OLIMPIA.

Nata nel 1731, 1 novembre. m 1748 Gennaro Caracciolo Duca di Girifalco.

Sorpresa dal marito con un giovine in ginocchio a' di lei piedi, e che s' involò nel momento, in cui egli entrava nella camera, ove accadeva il fatto, fu rinchiusa in un sotterraneo del castello di Girifalco. Costante Olimpia nel rifiutarsi a palesare il nome di chi poteva esser sagrificato da un uomo brutale, visse parecchi anni nella condizione più lagrimevole. Il duca la fece credere morta e ne celebrò i funerali. Due Cappuccini passando di notte tempo presso il castello udirono de' lamenti. Cercarono di investigare il luogo preciso donde provenivano, ed essendosi assicurati che una donna era rinchiusa in un sotterraneo, sollecitamente avvisarono il guardiano del convento. Venne a' Cappuccini dubbio, che la morte della duchessa fosse supposta. Presero essi allora deliberazione di spedire secretamente a Roma un loro collega ai parenti della prigioniera per dar parte de'loro sospetti. Ne fu subito da Roma informata la Corte di Napoli, che spedì ordine al marchese di Campredon, preside della provincia di Calabria, di assicurarsi del fatto. Fu investito il castello dal preside che si fece accompagnare dalle milizie, onde superare con sollecitudine le difficoltà che poteva opporre un uomo inumano e prepotente qual era il duca. Le porte del sotterraneo furono abbattute, e la prigioniera liberata.

Olimpia volle ritornare in Roma, ove morì nel 1800, 22 dicembre nel monastero dell' Incarnazione del Verbo Divino, detto delle Barberine, patronato di sua casa, senz' aver mai proferito parola intorno alle passate vicende, nè permesso che alcuno di quelle le parlasse. Questo fatto diede occasione a molte rappresentazioni teatrali in Italia col titolo di *Sepolta Viva,* prestò argomento a madama de Genlis di formare una novella e ad una folla di romanzi. Che Olimpia cercasse rifugio presso i proprj parenti per sottrarsi alle stravaganze ed agli strapazzi del marito, è cosa infallibile; ma che tutte le narrate circostanze abbiano accompagnato il fatto non ne son certo. Tale ad un dipresso però è il racconto che ne fanno universalmente in Napoli.

– Pompeo Litta, *Famiglie celebri italiane.* 13 vols (Milan: Presso P. E. Giusti, 1819-1852), II (1838), folio 20 verso.[28]

* * *

OLIMPIA

Born November 1, 1731. Married in 1748 to Gennaro Caracciolo, Duke of Girifalco.

She was caught by her husband with a young man kneeling at her feet who fled at the moment the duke entered the room, and then she was locked in one of the underground dungeons of the Castle of Girifalco. Olimpia was constant in her refusal to disclose the name of the young man, who might have been murdered by her brutal husband, and thus she lived for several years in the most piteous condition. The duke made everyone believe she was dead and celebrated her funeral. Two Capuchin monks, passing by the castle during the night, heard some cries. After determining the exact place the sounds were coming from and, having learned that a woman had been confined to an underground cell, they quickly advised the head of the monastery. The monks began to wonder if the death of the duchess had been faked. They decided, then, to send someone to Rome in secret to speak with the relatives of the prisoner about their suspicions. A dispatch was immediately sent from Rome to the Court of Naples, and orders were given to the Marquis of Campredon, head of the province of Calabria, to check on the matter. The castle was attacked by the governor of the province, who was accompanied by troops in order to overcome as quickly as possible the difficulties that a man as inhuman and overbearing as the duke might pose. The doors of the dungeon were forced open, and the prisoner was liberated.

Olimpia returned to Rome, where she died on December 22, 1800, at the Convent of the Incarnation of the Divine Word (also known as the convent of the Barberini nuns), that was patronized by her family. She never said a word about what had happened, nor did she ever permit anyone to speak to her about it. This event inspired many theatrical pieces in Italy with the title *Sepolta Viva* ['Buried Alive'] and also provided material to Madame de Genlis for a novella and for a host of novels. That Olimpia sought refuge among her own relatives because of the outbursts of her husband is certain, but I am not sure that all the events narrated here actually took place. However, the story they tell all over Naples is just about the same as this one.

— Translated by Courtney Quaintance

A shorter, perhaps more historically accurate account of the duchess's story is also found in Antonio Coppi's history of the Colonna family: *Memorie colonnesi* (Rome, 1855), 405-6.[29]

OLIMPIA DI GIRIFALCO

1731-1800.

I. Fra le figlie del Principe Giulio Cesare e Cornelia Barberini vi fu Olimpia, nata al primo novembre 1731.

II. Nell' anno 1748 fu maritata a Gennaro Caracciolo Duca di Girifalco.

III. Viveva questi in quel suo Castello nella Calabria ulteriore, e colà maltrattando la Consorte la tenne chiusa in modo che non la lasciava parlare con altri che col suo confessore. Per di lui mezzo l'infelice Principessa informò di tutto il proprio genitore, il quale andò subito a Napoli, ed ottenne di liberarla, e condurla seco a Roma. Quivi essa ritirossi nel Monastero Teresiano detto delle Barberino, e vi morì nel 1800.

IV. Si raccontò poi che quel Barone per semplici sospetti avesse fatto rinchiudere la consorte in un carcere sotterraneo del Castello e l'avesse tenuta per vari anni, annunziando pubblicamente che fosse morta, e facendone eziandio celebrare solenni funerali. Intesi finalmente i gemiti dell'infelice da due Cappuccini che passavano di notte presso il Castello, fosse stata liberata dal Preside della provincia.

V. Le sventure di questa Principessa, accresciute dalla fama e dalla malignità, somministrarono materia a romanzi ed a produzioni teatrali in prosa col titolo di *Sepolta viva*, ed in musica ad un dramma di Paër intitolato la *Camilla*.

* * *

OLIMPIA OF GIRIFALCO

1731-1800

I. Among the daughters of Prince Giulio Cesare and Cornelia Barberini was Olimpia, born on the first of November in 1731.

II. In 1748, she was married to Gennaro Caracciolo, the Duke of Girifalco.

III. The duke lived in a castle in southern Calabria. Mistreating his wife, he kept her under lock and key and let her speak with no one but her confessor. With the help of this man, the unhappy princess informed her father of all that had happened, and he went immediately to Naples, where he obtained permission to free her and take her with him to Rome. There, she retired to the Teresian Monastery, known as the convent of the Barberini nuns, where she died in 1800.

IV. Later, it was said that this powerful nobleman, on the basis of mere suspicions, had his wife locked up in one of the dungeons of the castle and that he kept her there for several years, announcing to the public that she was dead and even commemorating her death with solemn funeral rites. Supposedly, her moans were eventually heard by two Capuchin monks passing by the castle one night, and she was freed by the governor of the province.

V. The misfortunes of this princess, increased by fame and malevolence, provided material for novels and for theater pieces in prose with the title *Sepolta viva* (Buried alive) and in music for a drama by Paër entitled *Camilla*.

— Translated by Courtney Quaintance

An account of the duchess's life, very similar to Coppi's, is also found in the notes to Alessandro Ademollo's book about prominent Italian families of the seventeenth and eighteenth centuries, including the Colonna family:

Figlia del principe Giulio Cesare Colonna e di Cornelia Barberini fu anche quell'Olimpia (nata al 1 novembre 1731) che, maritata nel 1748 a Gennaro Caracciolo Duca di Girifalco, ebbe in sua vita vicende molto strane.

Viveva il duca nel suo castello nella Calabria ulteriore, e colà maltrattando la consorte la tenne chiusa in modo che non la lasciava parlare con altri che col suo confessore. Per di lui mezzo l'infelice principessa, informò di tutto il proprio genitore, il quale andò subito a Napoli ed ottenne di liberarla, e condurla seco a Roma. Quivi essa ritirossi nel monastero Teresiano detto delle Barberino, e vi morì nel 1800.

Si raccontò poi che quel barone per semplici sospetti avesse fatto rinchiudere la consorte in un carcere sotterraneo del Castello e l'avesse tenuta per vari anni, annunziando pubblicamente che fosse morta, e facendone eziandio celebrare solenni funerali; e che intesi finalmente i gemiti dell'infelice da due Cappuccini che passavano di notte presso il castello, fosse stata liberata dal preside della provincia. Le sventure di questa principessa, molto misteriose nella loro causa, somministrarono materia a romanzi ed a produzioni teatrali in prosa col titolo di *Sepolta viva,* ed in musica ad un dramma di Paër intitolato la *Camilla.*

—Alessandro Ademollo, *Il Matrimonio di suor Maria Pulcheria al secolo Livia Cesarini. Memorie particolari riguardanti le famiglie Colonna, Orsini, Altieri, Cesarini, Sforza, e Sforza-Cesarini nei secoli decimosettimo et decimottavo.* Rome: A. Sommaruga, 1883, p. 163, n. 20.[30]

* * *

Olimpia, born on November 1, 1731, daughter of Giulio Cesar Colonna and Cornelia Barberini, was married in 1748 to Gennaro Caracciolo, Duke of Girifalco, and had many strange experiences in her life.

The duke lived in a castle in southern Calabria, where he mistreated his wife by restricting her freedom to such an extent that he allowed her to speak to no one, save her confessor. Through him, the unhappy princess informed her father of her plight. Her father went immediately to the Court of Naples to obtain her freedom and then to take her to Rome. There, she withdrew to the Teresian monastery, known as the convent of the Barberini nuns, and died there in 1800.

It was said that, on the basis of mere suspicions, this powerful man had his wife imprisoned in a dungeon beneath his castle and held her there for a number of years. He announced publicly that she had died and had funeral rites celebrated. Supposedly, her groans were finally heard by two Capuchin monks passing by the castle one night, and she was then liberated by the governor of the province. The princess's misadventures, which resulted from mysterious causes, supplied material for novels, for theatrical productions in prose titled *Buried Alive*, and for an opera by Paër entitled *Camilla.*

—Alessandro Ademollo, *The Marriage of Livia Cesarini, also known as Sister Maria Pulcheria. Stories of the Orsini, Altieri, Cesarini, Sforza, and Sforza-Cesarini Families in the Seventeenth and Eighteenth Centuries.*

— Translated by Jonathan Druker

NOTES TO THE APPENDICES

[1] Coppi, Litta, and Ademollo all maintain that the duchess died in 1800 at the Convent of the Incarnation of the Divine Word (also known as the convent of the Barberini nuns), that was patronized by her family. (See their accounts of the duchess's story in Appendix G.) This does not necessarily mean that she became a nun. It was common practice among aristocratic women in the seventeenth and eighteenth centuries to take up residence in convents (temporarily or permanently) after their husband's death or following some sort of traumatic event or scandal.

[2] In posing as the text's translator and editor, Genlis was following a well-established tradition among eighteenth-century novelists, from Montesquieu to Rousseau to Laclos. In some cases, as in Montesquieu's *Lettres persanes*, this ploy was used to veil the author's identity in an effort to elude censorship. But in most cases, including Genlis's tale of the duchess, this device served to heighten a text's air of authenticity and dramatic impact.

[3] The full text of Genlis's memoirs is available on-line on the Bibliothèque Nationale of France's Gallica website: http://gallica.bnf.fr/Search? ArianeWireIndex=index&q=genlis%2C+ memoires&p=1&lang=en

[4] The duchess's father was not born Prince of Palestrina, but acquired the title through his marriage in 1728 to Cornelia Barberini, Princess of Palestrina, daughter of the last male Barberini. Among his contemporaries, he was better known by his hereditary title Giulio Cesare Colonna di Sciarra, Prince of Carbognano.

[5] When Genlis met her in the spring of 1776, the duchess (born in November, 1731) was actually 44 years old.

[6] In a letter written to her friend Mrs. Stokes on 9 August 1786, Anna Seward maintains—contrary to Genlis's claim—that the duchess was *not* blameless and that her husband's jealousy appears to have been provoked by an adulterous liaison. Seward's claim was based on a letter she had received decades earlier from her brother-in-law Mr. Porter, who was living in Italy at the time of the duchess's rescue. (See the excerpt from Seward's letter in Appendix E.) She adds that the duke's Italian contemporaries considered his jealousy both unjustified and monstrous in its consequences, given the widespread tolerance of extraconjugal affairs, particularly among the Italian aristocracy of the period. (Regarding the practice of *cicisbeismo* in eighteenth-century Italy, see Appendix F.) Rumors of a love affair involving the duchess circulated widely in

eighteenth-century Italy and are echoed in nineteenth-century chronicles cited in Appendix G.

[7] Nineteenth-century Italian chroniclers offer quite different versions of the duchess's rescue. Litta claims that two Capuchin monks passing by the castle one night heard her cries and sent for help. Coppi and Ademollo both dismiss this story as apocryphal and maintain that the duchess was able to get word of her plight to her father through her confessor, whom her husband allowed her to see during her captivity. See Appendix G for these accounts of her rescue.

[8] According to Luigi Russo, the Duke of Girifalco died on August 15, 1766, several years after his wife was rescued from captivity. (Russo, 'I Catasti Onciari di Orta e Casapuzzano,' in *Note e documenti per la storia di Orta di Atella*, ed. Franco Pezzella (Frattamaggiore: Istituto di Studi Atellani, 2006), pp. xlviii-lxi (p. lvi).

[9] Alexander Selkirk was the prototype for Robinson Crusoe, hero of the novel published by Daniel Defoe in 1719.

[10] *Genlis's note*: 'Et l'on prit dès lors ce sujet pour le mettre au théâtre sous le titre de *Camille, ou Le Souterrain*, opéra en trois actes.' [This story was soon adapted for the theater under the title *Camille, ou Le Souterrain*, opera in three acts.]

[11] See note 4 above.

[12] See note 5 above.

[13] See note 6 above.

[14] See note 7 above.

[15] See note 8 above.

[16] See note 9 above.

[17] See note 10 above.

[18] See the introduction, p. 15, for a discussion of this aspect of the novel.

[19] Mme d'Almane never follows through on her promise to recount her dinner with the Belmires or to describe the couple in greater detail, nor does she offer any explanation for this. However, in the letter immediately following (vol III, letter 1), the Baron d'Almane explains to M. de Limours that they had to leave Rome soon after their arrival due to an epidemic, which may have caused them to postpone their dinner with the Belmires. There is only one further reference to the couple in the novel, found in a letter to Mme de Limours some two months later (vol III, letter 11) that focuses on the d'Almane's impending departure for France. (See the text of this letter in Appendix D.) In this letter, Mme d'Almane

mentions that Adele had grown very attached to the Countess of Belmire, which suggests that the d'Almanes had become well acquainted with her; however, Genlis provides no account of other visits to the Belmires.

[20] Miss Bridget is Adele's British governess. Her principal function is to teach her English, since Mme d'Almane gives her daughter most of her other lessons.

[21] B*** refers to the d'Almanes' estate in Languedoc, which they had chosen as their principal residence after leaving Paris to devote themselves to their children's education.

[22] See note 18 above.

[23] See note 19 above.

[24] See note 20 above.

[25] See note 21 above.

[26] The dates given by Genlis in her memoirs and in her novella suggest that the duchess was released from captivity in 1759 (not 1764). However, the actual year of her rescue is uncertain. Regarding the chronology of the duchess's story, see Appendix A.

[27] Regarding the role of the *cicisbeo* in eighteenth-century Italy, see Appendix F.

[28] Litta's account of the duchess's story is quoted almost in its entirety in a quarterly journal titled *Biblioteca italiana, o sia giornale di letteratura, scienze ed arti* 93 (January-March, 1839), 310-11.

[29] The full text of Antonio Coppi's history of the Colonna family, *Memorie colonnesi* (Rome, 1855) is available from Google Books.

[30] The full text of Alessandro Ademollo's *Memorie particolari* (Rome, 1883) is available from Google Books.

BIBLIOGRAPHY

SELECTED WORKS BY GENLIS

Genlis, Caroline-Stéphanie-Félicité Du Crest, comtesse de. *Adèle et Théodore, ou Lettres sur l'éducation contenant tous les principes relatifs aux trois différens plans d'éducation des princes & des jeunes personnes de l'un & de l'autre sexe.* 2nd edn, 3 vols (Paris: Michel Lambert and F. J. Baudoin, 1782).

_____ . *Adèle et Théodore, ou Lettres sur l'éducation*, ed. Isabelle Brouard-Arends (Rennes: Presses universitaires de Rennes, 2006).

_____ . *Adelaide and Theodore; or Letters on Education.* Translated from the French of Madame la Comtesse de Genlis, 3 vols (London: C. Bathurst & T. Cadell, 1783).

_____ . *De l'Influence des femmes sur la littérature française comme protectrices des lettres et comme auteurs; ou Précis de l'histoire des femmes françaises les plus célèbres* (Paris: Maradan, 1811).

_____ . *Histoire intéressante de madame la duchesse de C***.* Lausanne: H. and L. Vincent, 1783. Reprinted in *Mademoiselle de Clermont; suivie de L'Histoire intéressante de la duchesse de C****, ed. Alix S. Deguise (Geneva: Slatkine, 1982).

_____ . *Mémoires inédits de madame la comtesse de Genlis, sur le dix-huitième siècle et la Révolution Française, depuis 1756 jusqu'à nos jours.* 10 vols (Paris: Lavocat, 1825-28); trans. *Memoirs of the Countess of Genlis, Illustrative of the Eighteenth and Nineteenth Centuries. Written by Herself* (London: Henry Colburn, 1825).

_____ . *Œuvres de Genlis* (Paris: Lecointe et Durey, 1825-1826).

_____ . *La Religion considérée comme l'unique base de bonheur et de la véritable philosophie* (Paris, 1787).

_____ . *Les Veillées du château, ou Cours de morale à l'usage des enfants* (Paris: Michel Lambert and F. J. Baudouin, 1784).

Bessire, François and Martine Reid, eds. *Madame de Genlis: Littérature et éducation*. Mont-Saint-Aignan: Publications des universités de Rouen et du Havre, 2008.

Birkett, Jennifer. 'Madame de Genlis: The New Men and the Old Eve.' *French Studies* 12 (1988), 150-64.

_____ . 'Madame de Genlis et l'éducation des filles. Pédagogie et romance.' In *L'Education des femmes en Europe et en Amérique du Nord, de la Renaissance à 1848. Réalités et représentations*, ed. Guyonne Leduc (Paris: Harmattan, 1997), pp. 433-41.

Broglie, Gabriel de. *Madame de Genlis* (Paris: Librairie Académique Perrin, 1985).

Brouard-Arends, Isabelle. 'Madame de Genlis: De la mondanité à la retraite.' Introduction to *Adèle et Théodore, ou Lettres sur l'éducation*, ed. Brouard-Arends (Rennes: Presses universitaires de Rennes, 2006), pp. 7-39.

_____ . 'Soumission et indépendance: La dynamique intertextuelle à l'égard de l'*Émile* dans *Adèle et Théodore* de madame de Genlis.' In *Emile et l'éducation*, ed. Tanguy L'Aminot. Special edition *Études Jean-Jacques Rousseau*, 9 (1997), 140-50.

Brown, Penny. '"Candidates for My Friendship," or How Madame de Genlis and Mary Wollstonecraft Sought to Regulate the Affections and Form the Mind to Truth and Goodness.' *New Comparison* 20 (1995): 46-60.

Cook, Malcolm, '*Adèle et Théodore* ou Les Liaisons dangereuses.' *Studies on Voltaire and the Eighteenth Century*, 284 (1991), 371-83.

Dalayrac, Nicolas and Benoît-Joseph Marsollier des Vivetières. *Camille, ou Le Souterrain* (Paris: Brunet, 1791). Libretto by Marsollier; music by Dalayrac. [Opera based on Genlis's novella.]

Decottignies, Jean. 'A l'occasion du deuxième centenaire de la naissance d'Anne Radcliffe. Un Domaine "maudit" dans les lettres françaises aux environs de 1800.' *Revue des sciences humaines,* 16 (1964), 447-75.

Deguise, Alix S. 'Présentation.' Introduction to *Mademoiselle de Clermont; suivie de L'Histoire intéressante de la duchesse de C**** (Geneva: Slatkine, 1982), pp. i-xiii.

DeLamotte, Eugenia C. *Perils of the Night: A Feminist Study of the Nineteenth-Century Gothic* (Oxford University Press, 1990).

Diaconoff, Suellen. 'Feminized Virtue: Politics and Poetics of a New Pedagogy for Women.' In *L'Education des filles sous l'Ancien Régime. De Christine de Pizan à Fénelon,* ed. Colette H. Winn. Special edition of *Papers on French seventeenth-century literature* 24 (1997), 121-36.

_____. 'The Romance as Transformative Reading: Félicité de Genlis.' In *Through the Reading Glass: Women, Books, and Sex in the French Enlightenment.* Albany: State University of New York Press, 2005, pp. 77-100.

Dow, Gillian. 'The British Reception of Madame de Genlis's Writings for Children: Tales and Plays of Instruction and Delight.' *British Journal for Eighteenth-Century Studies*, 29 (2006), 367-81.

_____. '"The Good sense of British readers has encouraged the translation of the whole": Les traductions anglaises des œuvres de Mme de Genlis dans les années 1780.' In *La Traduction des genres non romanesques au XVIIIᵉ siècle*, ed. Annie Cointre and Annie Rivara (Metz: Centre d'études de la traduction, 2003), pp. 285-97.

_____. 'Introduction.' *Adelaide and Theodore; or Letters on education*, ed. Gillian Dow (London: Pickering & Chatto, 2007), pp. ix-xx.

Ellis, Kate Ferguson. *The Contested Castle: Gothic Novels and the Subversion of Domestic Ideology* (Urbana: University of Illinois Press, 1989).

Goldin, Jeanne. 'De Félicité de Genlis à George Sand.' In *L'Education des filles au temps de George Sand*, ed. Michèle Hecquet (Arras: Artois presses université, 1998), pp. 163-77.

Grosperrin, Bernard. 'Un manuel d'éducation noble: *Adèle et Théodore* de Madame de Genlis.' *Cahiers d'histoire* 19 (1974), 343-52.

Harmand, Jean. *Madame de Genlis, sa vie intime et politique* (Paris: Perrin, 1912); trans. *A Keeper of Royal Secrets: The Private and Political Life of Madame de Genlis* (London: Nash, 1912).

Kerby, William Mosely. *The Educational Ideas and Activities of Madame la Comtesse de Genlis, with Special Reference to Her Work 'Adèle et Théodore'* (Paris: Presses universitaires de France, 1926).

Laborde, Alice. *L'Œuvre de Madame de Genlis* (Paris: Nizet, 1966).

Le Brun, Annie. *Les châteaux de la subversion. De la naissance du roman noir en France, 1760-1800* (Paris: Pauvert, 1986).

Massé, Michelle. *In the Name of Love: Women, Masochism, and the Gothic* (Ithaca: Cornell University Press, 1992).

Masseau, Didier. 'La hantise éducative dans *Adèle et Théodore* de Madame de Genlis.' In *Roman de formation, roman d'éducation dans la littérature française et dans les littératures étrangères*, ed. Philippe Chardin (Paris: Kimé, 2007), pp. 121-34.

Mayo, Robert D. *The English Novel in the Magazines, 1740-1815* (London: Oxford University Press, 1962).

Moers, Ellen. *Literary Women*. London: W. Allen, 1977.

Plagnol-Diéval, Marie-Emmanuelle. *Madame de Genlis* (Paris, Rome: Memini, 1996).

Robb, Bonnie Arden. *Félicité de Genlis: Motherhood in the Margins* (Newark: University of Delaware Press, 2009).

Schaneman, Judith Clark. 'Rewriting *Adèle et Théodore*: Intertextual Connections between Madame de Genlis and Ann Radcliffe,' *Comparative Literature Studies* 38 (2001), 31-45.

Schlick, Yaël, 'Beyond the Boundaries: Staël, Genlis, and the Impossible *Femme Célèbre*.' *Symposium,* 50 (1996), 50-64.

Schroder, Anne L. 'Going Public against the Academy in 1784: Mme de Genlis Speaks Out on Gender Bias,' *Eighteenth-Century Studies,* 32 (1999), 376-82.

Sedgwick, Eve Kosofsky. *The Coherence of Gothic Conventions* (New York: Arno Press, 1980).

Stewart, Joan Hinde. *Gynographs: French Novels by Women of the Late Eighteenth Century* (Lincoln: University of Nebraska Press, 1993).

Trouille, Mary. 'Buried Alive: Genlis's Gothic Tale of Marital Violence in *Histoire de la duchesse de C***.*' In Trouille, *Wife-Abuse in Eighteenth-Century France* (Oxford, UK: Voltaire Foundation, 2009), pp. 243-71.

_____ . 'The Influence of Class and Politics on Women's Response to Rousseau: Stéphanie de Genlis and Olympe de Gouges.' In Trouille, *Sexual Politics in the Enlightenment: Women Writers Read Rousseau* (Albany: State University of New York Press, 1997), pp. 237–91.

_____ . 'Toward a New Appreciation of Mme de Genlis: The Influence of *Les Battuécas* on George Sand's Political and Social Thought,' *The French Review*, 71 (1998), 565-76.

Van Dijk, Suzan. ''Gender' et traduction: Madame de Genlis traduite par une romancière hollandaise, Elisabeth Bekker.' In *La Traduction des genres non romanesques au XVIIIe siècle,* ed. Annie Cointre and Annie Rivara (Metz: Centre d'études de la traduction, 2003), pp. 299-314.

Wahba, Magdi. 'Madame de Genlis in England,' *Comparative Literature,* 13 (1961), 221-38.

Walker, Lesley H. 'The Good Mother, or The Sex Born to Suffer.' In *A Mother's Love: Crafting Feminine Virtue in Enlightenment France* (Lewisburg, PA: Bucknell University Press, 2008), pp. 134-63.

_____ . 'Producing Feminine Virtue: Strategies of Terror in Writings by Madame de Genlis,' *Tulsa Studies in Women's Literature,* 23 (2004), 213-36.

Williams, Anne. *Art of Darkness. A Poetics of Gothic* (Chicago: University of Chicago Press, 1995).

Wyndham, Violet. *Madame de Genlis: A Biography* (London: André Deutsch, 1958).

Yim, Denise, ed. *The Unpublished Correspondence of Mme de Genlis and Margaret Chinnery and Related Documents in the Chinnery Family Papers*, *SVEC* 2 (2003), xviii-184.

Ademollo, Alessandro. *Il Matrimonio di suor Maria Pulcheria al secolo Livia Cesarini. Memorie particolari riguardanti le famiglie Colonna, Orsini, Altieri, Cesarini, Sforza, e Sforza-Cesarini nei secoli decimosettimo et decimottavo* (Rome: A. Sommaruga, 1883), p. 163, n. 20.

Barberini, Maria Giulia. 'La galleria dei ritratti nel mezzanino di palazzo Barberini. Una strategia di famiglia.' In *I Barberini e la cultura europea del seicento*, ed. Lorenza Mochi Onori et al. (Rome, 2007), pp. 605-18.

Castiglione, Caroline. *Patrons and Adversaries: Nobles and Villagers in Italian Politics, 1640-1760* (Oxford & New York: Oxford University Press, 2005), pp. 108 and 181.

Coppi, Antonio. *Memorie colonnesi* (Rome, 1855), pp. 405-6.

Litta, Pompeo. *Famiglie celebri italiane*, 13 vols (Milan: P. E. Giusti, 1819-1852), II (1838), folio 20 verso.

> Litta's account of the duchess's story is quoted almost in its entirety in a quarterly journal entitled *Biblioteca italiana, o sia giornale di letteratura, scienze ed arti*, 93 (January-March, 1839), pp. 310-11.

Russo, Luigi. 'I Catasti Onciari di Orta e Casapuzzano.' In *Note e documenti per la storia di Orta di Atella*, ed. Franco Pezzella (Frattamaggiore: Istituto di Studi Atellani, 2006), pp. xlviii-lxi

Williams, George L. *Papal Genealogy: The Families and Descendants of the Popes* (Jefferson, NC: McFarland, 1998), pp. 128 and 213.

MHRA Critical Texts

This series aims to provide affordable critical editions of lesser-known literary texts that are not in print or are difficult to obtain. The texts will be taken from the following languages: English, French, German, Italian, Portuguese, Russian, and Spanish. Titles will be selected by members of the distinguished Editorial Board and edited by leading academics. The aim is to produce scholarly editions rather than teaching texts, but the potential for crossover to undergraduate reading lists is recognized. The books will appeal both to academic libraries and individual scholars.

Malcolm Cook
Chairman, Editorial Board

Editorial Board
Professor Catherine Maxwell (English)
Professor Malcolm Cook (French) (*Chairman*)
Professor Ritchie Robertson (Germanic)
Professor Derek Flitter (Spanish)
Professor Brian Richardson (Italian)
Dr Stephen Parkinson (Portuguese)
Professor David Gillespie (Slavonic)

Published titles
1. *Odilon Redon, 'Écrits'* (edited by Claire Moran, 2005)
2. *Les Paraboles Maistre Alain en Françoys* (edited by Tony Hunt, 2005)
3. *Letzte Chancen: Vier Einakter von Marie von Ebner-Eschenbach* (edited by Susanne Kord, 2005)
4. *Macht des Weibes: Zwei historische Tragödien von Marie von Ebner-Eschenbach* (edited by Susanne Kord, 2005)
5. *A Critical Edition of 'La tribu indienne; ou, Édouard et Stellina' by Lucien Bonaparte* (edited by Cecilia Feilla, 2006)
6. *Dante Alighieri, 'Four Political Letters'* (translated and with a commentary by Claire E. Honess, 2007)
7. *'La Disme de Penitanche' by Jehan de Journi* (edited by Glynn Hesketh, 2006)
8. *'François II, roi de France' by Charles-Jean-François Hénault* (edited by Thomas Wynn, 2006)
9. *Istoire de la Chastelaine du Vergier et de Tristan le Chevalier* (edited by Jean-François Kosta-Théfaine, 2009)

Forthcoming titles

For details of how to order please visit our website at
www.criticaltexts.mhra.org.uk